Zakharov tre

The video feeds came as a confused jumble on the tac table in front of him, as if he had broken an expensive vase and now stared helplessly at the shattered pieces. "What has she done? Genetic warfare!"

Daniel simply stood by quietly as the death stats rolled in. The virus had taken the entire base in the space of an evening, choking the hospitals. Talents were whisked in past drones and hapless Ordinaries into the back rooms of the one nanohospital, where nanosurgeons worked furiously to rebuild shattered respiratory systems. Several riots broke out, with dying, bleeding citizens storming into hospitals and tearing the masks from top surgeons.

Daniel conferred with Zakharov. "Shall we airlift people to the next base?"

Zakharov shook his head. "By the time we get sufficient help there, this virus will have run its course. Do what you can, but we'll maintain strict quarantine. No one enters or leaves that base."

A priority link came in, and Daniel took it. "A transport left Academy Park this morning, within the incubation period of the virus."

Time seemed to stop for Zakharov. He felt his mortality again, closing in on him, his death closer than ever. He swallowed.

"Where was it going?"

"Here," said Daniel, and it looked as if his body would fall, like a sack without support. "It arrived one hour ago."

SID MEIER'S
ALPHA
CENTAURI™

BOOK III of III

Twilight of the Mind

MICHAEL ELY

POCKET BOOKS
New York   London   Toronto   Sydney   Singapore

This book is a work of fiction. Names, characters, places and incidents are products of the author's imagination or are used fictitiously. Any resemblance to actual events or locales or persons, living or dead, is entirely coincidental.

An *Original* Publication of POCKET BOOKS

 POCKET BOOKS, a division of Simon & Schuster, Inc.
1230 Avenue of the Americas, New York, NY 10020

ISBN: 0-671-04079-0

First Pocket Books printing February 2002

10 9 8 7 6 5 4 3 2 1

POCKET and colophon are registered trademarks of Simon & Schuster, Inc.

For information regarding special discounts for bulk purchases, please contact Simon & Schuster Special Sales at 1-800-456-6798 or business@simonandschuster.com

Printed in the U.S.A.

To Mom and Dad

Author's Note

For those of you just joining the series, here is a little background. This series of three books is based on the best-selling game *Sid Meier's Alpha Centauri*, published by Firaxis Games in 1999. *Alpha Centauri* is a sprawling future-history strategy game, in which the player takes control of one of seven factions and tries to build an empire on an alien planet.

The background of the game sets the stage for the three books. In the not-too-distant future, Earth is torn by violent war and environmental tragedies. The United Nations manages to send a starship named *Unity* to Chiron, the only habitable planet orbiting Alpha Centauri's primary star. But on the way there is a malfunction, and the captain is assassinated during the mutiny that results. Seven landing pods rocket down to Chiron, but instead of landing together they land apart, each one led by a different ship's officer. Each pod must survive on its own until communication can be re-established, and each officer has a different vision for the future of this new world.

There is Corazon Santiago, the militant survivalist, and Deirdre Skye, the environmentalist. There is Prokhor Zakharov, the scientific visionary, and

Miriam Godwinson who believes her faith will support her in this strange world. There is Nwabudike Morgan, the economic wizard, and Sheng-ji Yang who believes that a controlled life in underground cities will ensure his longevity. And there is Pravin Lal, the peacekeeper and idealist, who most believes in the United Nations' original mission of peace.

Each faction sets out to build a new civilization. On Chiron there are barren red hills, and strange crimson xenofungus that seems to "sing" to the human visitors. There are mindworms and other forms of native life that boil forth from the fungus and attack the psyches of nearby humans, eventually devouring them. But in spite of these perils the humans manage to rediscover the lost knowledge of Earth, and even form a planetary government known as the Planetary Council.

Book One, *Centauri Dawn,* and Book Two, *Dragon Sun,* chronicle the first two hundred thirty years of human life on Chiron. As *Twilight of the Mind* opens, the original leaders are still in power, kept alive by sophisticated genetic technologies. They live together in an uneasy peace, thousands of citizens living under each of them. But conflicts of vision are inevitable, and so the future of Chiron resembles the past of Earth, marked by times of war and times of peace, and seven visions competing to define the future of humanity.

This is the final chapter of that story.

"I loved my chosen. How then to face the day when she left me? So I took from her body a single cell, perhaps to love her again."

—COMMISSIONER PRAVIN LAL,
Time of Bereavement

Historian's Note

This story is set one hundred forty years after the events of *Dragon Sun*.

chapter one

TWO SUNS.

Miriam stood on a hilltop, the hot red sand staining the hem of her white robes. A heavy cowl covered her head, and the very sand seemed to thrash around her, kicking high in the grip of random gusts of wind, stinging her face and eyes.

Two suns. They both hung in a sky that seemed heated from pale blue to an almost white heat, Centauri A burning like Sol in the desert, Centauri B hanging below that, an angry orange haze of light.

And beneath those suns, the low buzz, a hum that seemed woven into the fabric of the world.

Another cloud of red dust kicked up and she turned away, blinking. Behind her four of her Templars stood, the Holy knights who were assigned to guard her and the church that was an extension of her faith, uncomplaining in their heavy white and red armor.

"Kola." She nodded to her head Templar, who walked over to her. He was a stocky man, also dressed in red and white armor, a flaming sword emblazoned beneath the silver cross on his chest. "How long will it be, now?"

"Seven days," he said. "Then it will be perihelion, when Centauri B is at its closest point to this world."

"So it's going to get hotter?"

He smiled, since the temperature had been rising steadily for several years. "A little. But we've been through this before."

"Something feels different this time." She turned and walked back toward the edge of the high, sandy hill, feeling the heat beating her back.

"The Almighty is testing us, for sure," said Kola. "Little food left, and a thousand more seekers come every day."

"We have our faith," said Miriam, but something shook inside of her. Her faith, the prayer that sustained her every day, seemed distant, like a small animal that had crawled away before the blazing eyes of the two suns.

She reached the edge of the hill. New Jerusalem lay at the foot of the hill below them, a jumble of metal buildings crowding narrow streets, the weak flickering of a stolen tach field surrounding it. In the center rose the church, her pride and joy, and she let her eyes rest on it for a moment. Made of synthmetal and crafted stone, it towered above the base, with clean, sweeping lines. The stained synth-glass windows gleamed like jewels, lit from within, and the flying buttresses curved like wings around the high towers.

Then she looked around the periphery of the base, outside the tach field. Hundreds of tents spotted the sand, and thousands more people, many in plain brown robes, sat in the red sand or walked in prayer circles or huddled under tents, sheltering themselves from the burning sky. The sound of hymns drifted up to her even at this height.

"Something's going to break," she said. "It will be in the settlements, or in the world itself." She glanced back at the suns, which burned down onto a body that had become thin and stiff with time. "Let's go back down to the city."

"Ahmin."

They approached the gate to New Jerusalem. As they came down from the slopes and to the wide valley that held the base, Miriam could see groups of people, ragged and hungry, gathered outside of the tach field. They clustered around stained bubbletents and huddled into simple robes as the desert night began to cool, the day's heat escaping into the sky. As Miriam passed eyes turned to follow her, and voices whispered back and forth in the darkness.

"Is there enough food for these?"

Kola nodded once. "We're holding out. Didn't the Earth Jesus feed the masses with one loaf of bread?" He glanced at her, but she didn't answer.

Several among the huddled groups craned their necks, trying to get a better look at her. She could see fat, fleshy men and women who were clearly Morganites, and even the simple robes they wore for their pilgrimage looked somehow extravagant, as if the tiny tears in the cloth had been placed by a master tailor. She could see tall, brittle-looking University citizens, and legions of drones from who knew which base. Even a few Gaians, their tan bodies shifting beneath their dull brown robes, like butterflies ready to burst forth from their woven shells.

Miriam lifted one thin hand to them, and more of the pilgrims hopped to their feet. Scattered cheers broke out and a few people started in her direction.

"Let's go inside," said Miriam. "Make sure these get fed."

Two Templars came forward from the gate in thick white and red armor, fingering their weapons quietly. One discreetly turned her head and spoke through a tiny voicelink, and then the tachyon field deactivated between two metal posts. Miriam passed through, and the tachyon field flickered back into existence.

The streets of New Jerusalem were paved with stones, the low-slung metal buildings set close. Thin metal lampposts lined the streets, too far apart to give an even wash of light, so that shadows crept into the streets and collected on the sides of buildings. Dark figures sat along the streets, hugging the shadows, and the whispering of the New Lord's Prayer slipped back and forth among the hunched figures.

As Miriam and the Templars neared the center of the base, two priests approached. The moment they saw Miriam they fell to their knees, supplicating themselves before her. She gripped their hot fingers and enjoyed the connection for a moment.

Behind them the church rose, its tall spires piercing the sky. Miriam looked up and the sight lifted her, as it always did, and then the great metal doors swung open. The booming sound of the New Lord's

Prayer, chanted by a thousand deep voices, struck her like hammer blows from inside, followed by a hymn that lifted her spirit up to Heaven.

On a range of gray stone mountains, on the eastern edges of the core settlements, a cluster of metal towers topped with smooth golden domes dotted the sides of craggy slopes. The domes were not for aesthetics, but for function; in each one resided sensitive monitoring equipment, the eyes of the University, watching sea and sky and stars. This was University Base, the crown jewel of Prokhor Zakharov's University faction, with its observatories and labs, its centers of culture and wide streets bathed in cool mountain air.

And as night fell across the base, Zakharov himself paced the observation deck located outside of the vast Starscope that protruded from the tallest dome. He could hear the servo motors hum as the scope turned this way and that at precise intervals, driven by the astronomers on the observatory floor inside.

There was a tiny flash far in the sky and an orange streak, followed by several more, like falling fireworks in the distance to the east. He stopped and watched them, then took a sip of Planet brandy from the glass in his hand. His fingers were tight on the glass, the only visible sign of his nervousness.

There was a clattering as heavy footsteps came up the metal stairs and onto the mesh surface of the deck. No need to turn around . . . the heavy breathing gave the man away. "Watching the drop troops, are you?" said a low, gravelly voice, the words coming at a pace that was just slow enough to be soothing.

Zakharov turned around. "Yes, Isaac."

"You've got the base in quite a stir." Isaac walked over to a pair of metal chairs and sank into one. "Would you tell me why?"

Zakharov took another sip of the Planet brandy, waiting for the warm liquid to soothe his jangled nerves. Unfortunately, as his life had extended indefinitely, his reactions to stimuli had slowly died, such that he only felt the most extreme pleasures and pains now. It would take three more of these brandies to stoke even the smallest fire in his belly. "Something's been stolen, and we need to get it back."

"Stolen?" Isaac shifted in his chair, changing the quality of shadow around him. "I thought you were searching for a person." Zakharov looked at him, and Isaac smiled. "I still hear things. You may have demoted me to your library project, but I have ears."

"You weren't demoted."

The Star Scope turned, moonlight glinting off its great metal carapace. Below his feet, in the heart of the base, Zakharov's systems hummed, knowledge building on knowledge, the true mind of Chiron. "You're right," Zakharov continued. "It's a person we seek. He vanished from a secret lab in Academy Park, and we lost him there. I have reason to believe that he may try to go to New Jerusalem."

"Oh? A top scientist, joining the lost and estranged that head for the Holy lands?" Isaac thought for a moment, his breath idling softly. "That's odd. Did he take something important?"

"Not exactly."

"Then what?" Isaac produced a translucent flask

from somewhere and took a sip of the pale glowing drink inside. He closed his eyes and smiled, the smile lingering on puffy lips. "You might as well tell me. It will go into the historical record, you know. Besides, you look wrung out. Unburden yourself, Academician."

Zakharov tipped back his head and let the rest of the brandy sluice into his throat. He blinked as the stars quivered for a moment. "All right, Isaac. Come with me."

Zakharov led Isaac down through a series of security checkpoints, and finally to a lab complex with pale gray walls and a deep blue floor covering. A few strategically placed potted plants and some framed holo-art on the walls gave the area a kind of hushed, homey feel, like a freshly cleaned room.

Isaac had produced a white handkerchief and wiped his heavy brow, which was damp with sweat. Zakharov remembered that he was born during a time when genetic tweaking was still more art than science; his brain was powerful, but his body a faulty hormonal soup.

And the man loved to eat.

"So who is this marvelous person that you're so worried about?" asked Isaac. "It must be someone important, with all the secrecy."

"You'll see." Zakharov checked something on his quicklink and walked down a side hallway, stopping at a metal door. He touched a DNA lock mechanism and the door clicked open.

The room they entered was a small, but clean, cafeteria room. Long metal tables with rubbery padded benches marched in neat rows down one side, and a series of white vending machines covered a section of the far wall. The place was fairly empty, but a scattering of people sat at the tables, one group laughing quietly over some shared joke. One man sat alone at a far table, spooning a dark soup to his lips.

"Look there," said Zakharov. "Closely."

Isaac studied the man eating the soup. He was tall and broad-shouldered, but with a tight, narrow waist. His skin was fair and pale under the cool wash of light in the room, and his hair was a striking silvery blond. He glanced up, and Isaac could see that his eyes were deep brown, like wells. They started walking toward him.

"Is that the head scientist? He seems a bit stiff."

The man lifted another spoonful of soup to his lips. His face seemed frozen in time, held in an expression of utter calm and self-possession.

"That's what I've brought you to see," said Zakharov. "We call him the Ideal. A perfect Perfect, suited in every way to thrive in this world. A genetic masterpiece." He cleared his throat and said, in a whisper no louder than a soft breath, "Please lift your left hand."

The man did, his expression never changing.

"Amazing," said Isaac, transfixed. The man nodded and smiled, blinking once.

His eyes were now a bluish silver.

They left the room after talking to the man, whom Isaac was amused to learn was named Gene. As they walked slowly back toward the lab entrance, Isaac ruminated.

"He seemed a normal enough fellow. A bit distant. And his hand felt cool, like a piece of metal left out in the night air."

"If so, it was his choice. He has conscious control over skin temperature. He can constrict the blood, making his hands cold, or he can heat them to a significant degree."

Zakharov continued with his list of traits. "He has broad range hearing, an order of magnitude beyond a human. Eyes that can see in several spectrums, and can adjust to see in the dark or in extreme sunlight. Great strength in relatively compact limbs, which gives him phenomenal muscle speed. Skin that doesn't sunburn, a digestive system that needs half the food intake of you or I, hypersensitive touch."

"He seems a little dull, though. It's an impression I can't shake." Isaac sipped from his flask.

Zakharov nodded. "The impression is mistaken. His mind is wide open, the folds of cerebellum deeper than any human on Chiron. In fact, some of the Ideals are working in our most secret labs, generating new technologies for us. But you're right, they do have a certain blank aspect. Their minds must be trained to deal with a flood of sensory input greater than you or I could imagine. With their hypersensitive touch, and hearing, and sight, they have to adapt, by putting a kind of wall between themselves and the world. It's the only way they can survive."

"They? There are others?"

Zakharov nodded. "The man you saw is the second Ideal. There are about a hundred more. But it's the first one, the very first one, that has vanished."

Isaac's broad, soft hand touched Zakharov's arm. "Is this the man you're looking for? One of those?"

Zakharov nodded. "As I said, he's flawed. We didn't know how to train him to adjust to the power of his own mind. He was working in Academy Park when he became unstable, killed a security guard, and vanished."

"You can't locate him?"

"He's smart. And we think he's staying in the fringes, which aren't well patrolled. But my greatest fear is that he's gone to the Believers. Before he left he downlinked several of Sister Miriam's writings. All of them, in fact."

They stepped into a cool gray elevator that whisked them back to the upper levels of the tower. Isaac leaned against the wall, deep in thought. Finally he nodded. "Why the drop troops, Zakharov? Why the air search? It's just one man."

Zakharov stared at the elevator indicator panel as the lights winked softly there, measuring distance. "He was privy to a lot of our secrets. But that's not all."

He turned to face Isaac, dark emotions shadowing his ancient face. "Not one part of his genetic code remains untouched."

"The Xynan-Dylan Protocol?"

"Yes. We've compared their genetic profile to the Protocol. The average settlement human has no more than one standard deviation. Some Talents, and children who have been tweaked by their parents in various ways, may have three deviations, which is the limit allowed by the Protocol."

"And what do your Ideals have?"

Zakharov let out a short breath, as if pushing a

heavy weight away. "Six deviations. By the Council genetic protocols, they aren't even human."

The next morning, Miriam Godwinson awakened in a room with cool slate walls. The room was spacious but sparsely decorated; the wooden crosses carved into the top of her four bedposts the only decorations. On the other side of the room was a stone basin filled with water to wash her face and hands, and a hard wooden bench if she chose not to perform her morning prayers in the small chapel located nearby.

She blinked at the featureless ceiling. Her body was thin, her hair snowy white and her skin nearly translucent. Such were the effects of the genetic treatments on the seven Council leaders, who had now been alive for almost three hundred years. Like the other leaders she felt very little in the way of pain or pleasure anymore. But unlike the others she had her faith to sustain her, and it showed in radiant green eyes that captivated her followers.

She swung her thin legs out of bed, then wrapped herself in a gray blanket and crossed to the stone basin. Already she was rehearsing her morning prayers, seeking strength in that ritual. Hot dreams from the night before left traces in her consciousness, dreams of dark forces stirring in the world.

And she felt it . . . the sliver of doubt that had lodged in her, like an infection. As more and more lost citizens swarmed her bases, the doubt grew, slipping into the soft places of her body.

She lifted a double handful of cool water from the basin and splashed her face. The cold shock of it cleared her head a little.

The world is out of control.

She imagined the forces ranged against her, in the glittering settlement lands to her west. Spartan warriors with muscles packed thick on their torso, looking more like dolls than people. Director Morgan's lost population of fad freaks, Datajacks and Datajills, SexClones, people with abnormal physical traits, manipulated by their parents into living fads, for a price.

And what she sensed from them, from the crowded lands to the west, was a deep fatigue, and a growing hunger.

She shook her head. There was no mirror in the room, but she could use the calm surface of the water to stare at her reflection. God had crafted this face, and these hands, and this will, as she had done for the rest of the settlement leaders. Why had they turned on the Almighty?

She lifted another handful of water from the basin. The water was Holy, pure and blessed. And every time the chill water hit her face, it pushed the dark visions that much farther from her consciousness.

A soft tapping at the door, and then a small-boned woman wearing a gray habit entered. The habit swept up and covered the woman's head, so that Miriam's overall impression was of a short pillar of cloth from which a pale, earnest face stared.

"How are you, Sister Miriam?" the woman asked. She carried Miriam's elaborate white and gold robes over her arms as if they were gossamer.

"Good, Leta." Miriam let her blanket fall to the floor and waited as Leta helped her into the robes.

As Leta bustled around her, adjusting buckles and sashes, Miriam considered the agenda of the day.

As Kola had said, the refugees were flowing into her settlements at the rate of a thousand per day. Although most were drones and Ordinaries, the flotsam and jetsam of the settlements, at that pace it was bound to be a thorn in the settlement leaders' sides. She anticipated repercussions.

Still, it was their own policies that caused it. She accepted anyone, from anywhere on Chiron, with one condition . . . no genetic tweaking. And for that, the drones and Ordinaries considered her a hero, because she didn't play God.

When Leta was finished they left the room, passing through a tall arched door and into the cool hallways beyond. She would pray for two hours, ignoring the ache in her back and knees, and in her prayers she would ask the Almighty to guide her through the day.

After her prayer, Miriam walked the streets of New Jerusalem. Everywhere she looked she saw devotion, and that made her own doubt tremble inside her. She finally found herself by a Church-controlled building near the front edge of the base. On a whim she went inside, finding herself in a training and barracks room, basically a series of stalls around a center area. Each stall contained minimal furnishings and a silver cross above the bed. In the center area a group of men and women trained, swinging abnormally heavy cudgels in time to a sung rhythm.

Miriam watched for a moment, pleased that none of the warriors had broken their rhythm when she entered. After a moment she crossed to a wooden staircase in one corner of the room, and climbed up to a balcony level, where she could look down on the training hall from above.

The warriors began sparring. They were mostly tall and rangy, and all of them were lean, many to the point where she could see their ribs and the hollows where their bellies should be. Their hair was almost uniformly long and matted, and they wore simple brown pants or even loincloths, dirty with sweat and dust.

A door clicked open on the balcony level and someone approached her. It was Sister Kathryn in her clean white and green robes, one of her top advisors and a former Gaian Empath. She always looked chaste, very well put together, and insisted that her robes be laundered daily. But an exaggerated hip sway beneath those crisp white robes served to test many of the younger faithful in her charge. Miriam remembered a former Morganite seeker who had been found with a holo of Sister Kathryn in a revealing robe, the words *Lead Me Not Into Temptation* splashed above her.

Miriam had actually found the holo amusing, though the man still required some time in the Penitence Square.

Kathryn walked up next to her, smiling. "Light, Miriam."

"Light, Kathryn." The two lapsed into a silence, watching the training progress to a series of strength drills, until Kathryn made a clucking sound with her tongue. "Such a waste."

"That they're hungry, or that they spend time fighting rather than praying?"

"That they waste away before us. So strong . . ." She considered a tall rangy blonde with hair tied back behind his head, swinging an ancient penetrator rifle at a sand dummy. A silver cross on a chain swung around the man's neck, thumping on his chest.

"You could do without the temptation, Sister."

She smiled. "Temptation is just a test of faith, Sister Miriam. And fighting is a form of prayer, I suppose."

Miriam considered that and nodded. "Good thoughts, Kathryn." She paused. "I know these men and women are ready . . . they're steeped from birth in our way. But what of the newcomers?"

"Ah. You can see some from the roof of this building. Would you like to take a look?"

"Please show me."

Kathryn led her through a thin metal door and up a series of steep steps, until finally they exited through another door and onto the hot, square roof of the building. The two suns hung in the sky, baking the rooftop in oppressive heat. Miriam already felt a thin film of sweat on her body, and she blinked against the reflection of sun from the pale stone roof.

"This way." They walked to one edge of the roof, where the wall extended an extra meter or so, topped with a pitted metal railing. "There are the new faithful," Kathryn said, motioning toward the tach field surrounding the city, where another line of people gathered at the gates, their clothes and boots scuffed with fine red dust.

"And don't you think they would fight for our cause?"

"They'll fight for it. But will they die for it?" She shrugged. "They certainly haven't been steeped in the Way from birth. Besides, these aren't the most genetically fit in the settlements."

Miriam's brow wrinkled. "Let the settlements keep their canisters."

"Canisters?"

"Empty, brittle containers. Shiny on the outside, processed junk on the inside."

"Full of beans?"

Miriam smiled. "That's right. They live privileged lives, but when they're tested, when they're forced to reach deep, there will be nothing there. Mark my words." Still, looking at Kathryn's smooth skin and bright smile, Miriam sometimes wondered if she had somehow cheated the genetic tests the Templars administered.

"And what if there are spies there, or saboteurs?"

"Do you remember when you came to the Holy Lands?"

Kathryn remained still for a moment, recalling the scenes in her Empath way, including the emotional resonances. She nodded. "I do."

"The refugees can't bring any weapons in, since they're searched. They can't steal any secrets, since our faith can't be taken. And if they lack true belief, they won't survive the first difficult encounter."

"Ah." Kathryn let one slender hand rest on the hot railing. "And has your faith been tested lately, Sister?"

Miriam stared at her, a shock rolling through her body and settling around her heart. *Has she seen my doubt? Has it taken root in my face?*

Kathryn smiled at her. "I mean that it's been twenty years since our last raids on the settlements.

And our food supplies are low. The faithful go hungry for you."

"The Council frowns on such raids, Sister," Miriam whispered.

Kathryn started to speak again when the door behind them banged open. Leta stood there, clutching her gray habit about her throat. "Sister, something has come to Kola's attention. He says that one of the refugees has news you might want to hear for yourself."

"Thank you, Leta." Miriam nodded to Kathryn. "We'll continue this talk later, Sister."

"Ahmin."

Miriam walked with Leta back to the church and from there down a series of winding stone staircases, passing down through the hot upper floors and into the cooler levels beneath the ground. Leta pointed the way to a peaked wooden door off a stone hallway, and Miriam entered.

She found herself in a plain room with a wooden table and three chairs in the center. On one wall hung a large silver cross, and the light from a single glowlamp mounted on the ceiling caused shadows to pool under the table.

Kola paced the room in his thick armor. In a chair sat a young man, dressed in a simple brown robe, his fingers rubbing the cloth of the sleeves, which were a little too long for him. He sat stiffly, and a slight widening of his eyes betrayed his nervousness. One eye was covered with a bruise, like the shadowy side of a mountain.

"This young man comes to us from the University," said Kola. "He has some interesting news."

Miriam nodded to him and pulled out a chair to sit opposite him. She fixed him with her green eyes, and he flushed slightly. "Are you comfortable?"

He nodded.

"Please tell me what you know."

The young man swallowed, then spoke. "I work in gamma lab at the Academy Park."

"I thought all University labs were identified by number," said Kola from behind Miriam.

The young man shook his head. "Not these labs. I had to pass several security clearances to even start working there. First I was just a gopher, running simple experiments, getting the lay of things. It didn't take me long to see what the experiments were . . . they all dealt with genetics."

Miriam settled back a little in her chair, and the mood in the room shifted imperceptibly.

"Over time I proved my discretion, and was hired on as a full time junior sci-tech. They told me it was a top secret position, and it would remain my workplace for life. The whole operation was run by a Talent named Jason Strang, who worked at both University Base and Academy Park. Apparently he himself was tweaked, the folds of his cerebellum three times deeper than the average human."

Miriam smiled. "And yet, not three times smarter, or more worthy."

The young man shrugged. "He was a strange guy. I think being tweaked made his ego big enough to guarantee his success. Not that he wasn't smart, because he was, as far as I could tell."

"Completion?" Kola again. Miriam continued to hold the young man's gaze.

"Actually, the experiment is ongoing, but the first

success happened twenty-three years ago at University Base. I was just a cog in the wheel, so I didn't know. I ate next to him almost every day."

"Him?" Miriam felt an electricity gather at the back of her spine. "What do you mean, him?"

The young man touched the bruise on his face and started talking faster. "This was a radical experiment. The idea was to stop just tweaking the genes of ordinary people, and instead to start from scratch, with *no preconceptions*. To make the most perfect human, capable of thriving in the environment of Chiron. This thing . . ." He swallowed again. "It looks human, but every gene is tweaked. Every single one."

"Almighty." Kola had frozen against the back wall, a part of the stone. "And you saw him?"

"He ate in the food banks. He never stood out much . . . it was only later I realized that things changed about him. His eyes, his voice. And it was about that time I found out I had been genejacked for loyalty. My parents let the prenatal docs do something called Flattening, adjusting the biochemical makeup of my mind so that the concept of betrayal wouldn't enter my consciousness. It's ninety-six percent effective." He shrugged. "I'm the other four percent. When I found out I flew into a rage. Attacked my father with a concussion hammer."

From his position by the wall, Kola rustled, and without looking Miriam could tell that he smiled.

The young man dropped his hands to the table again and stared at them. "They went looking for me. Academy Park is self-aware, and even the streets know where you are by code chips in your boots. I had to take them off, run barefoot into the drone quarters. From there they took me in."

"Who?" asked Miriam.

"You. The J-freaks and J-drones. The ones who understand. They hid me, and smuggled me out of the city, and from there I came to you. But before I left I heard rumors from the lab."

"What sort of rumors?"

"That he's coming. The first Ideal. He's vanished from the University, and they say he's coming this way."

Miriam stepped out into the quiet hallway, Kola right behind. They stood near the wall, waiting for a pair of worshippers to whisper past in their brown robes and bare feet. Miriam smiled at them as they passed, then turned to Kola.

"If what he says is true, Zakharov is in violation of the Xynan-Dylan Protocol limiting human genetic experimentation."

"If that thing the kid described can even be called a human," said Kola.

Miriam nodded, her hands loose at her sides. "When word of this spreads, our people will be restless. This contradicts every tenet we believe in."

"There have already been riots, demonstrations in other bases. But the people are ready."

She stared at him. A kind of unshakable fury blazed from his eyes, the kind of blind faith she had possessed many years before.

"I'll put the word out to the faithful in all settlement bases," she said. "We must find this creature."

"Ahmin."

chapter two

PRAVIN LAL TRACED THE BONES OF THE WOMAN'S HAND with his fingers. The hand was delicate, smooth and brown under the soft light in the room. Beyond her hand a slender wrist extended from the sleeve of her pale blue dress, and an elegant silver bracelet glimmered there.

He glanced up at her face, then away for a moment. He stretched the muscles in his back, which felt tight and firm, a welcome sensation. He had just emerged from the Gene Baths, Zakharov's latest and greatest, buying himself another dozen years of life. His body felt young and supple, his skin clear and bright, like he was thirty years old again.

In fact, he felt around the same age as the woman opposite him, though his eyes still held the complexities of a long life in their depths, creating an odd juxtaposition with his smooth face.

He was young again. This was his window, before the gravity of time pulled on his body, rendering it stiff and dry once again.

His heart started racing just a bit. The two of

them sat at a small white table in his apartment, tall windows to his left, tinted dark against the blazing suns outside. To his right the apartment sprawled on, plush spaces under high ceilings.

Back to her face ... eyes still closed, but even closed they gave the impression of mystery. The softest brush of glittering violet set off the skin there. Her brows arched, two fine lines, and her dark, lush hair framed her face and spilled down to her shoulders. She swayed a little, having fallen asleep in her chair, and he wondered what kept her up last night, and if she resented coming here today.

He shifted in his chair and stood up slowly. His heart rate increased, and he moved carefully around the table toward her.

Her face. It was just like *her,* down to every detail. He reached out ...

His quicklink beeped at that moment, a soft beep but he still jumped, his heart surging into his throat. He stepped back from her, cutting off the sound with a quick motion. She tipped a little, righted herself automatically, murmured something to someone he couldn't see.

He quietly padded through an archway into a small, immaculately clean kitchen area. He looked down at the quicklink, the small wrist-mounted messenger that kept him connected to every vital person and system in the territory.

"Yes, Webster?"

The clean-cut young man in the crisp-looking uniform of the diplomatic corps nodded to him. "Pardon the intrusion, Governor. The meeting will begin in five minutes, and I didn't want you to be late."

"Thank you."

"No problem, Governor. See you soon."

Pravin walked back to the table and picked up his uniform jacket, heavy with the golden braids and ribbons of his station. He looked at the woman again and reached out to brush her hair, once, softly. It was as light as air, yet a part of it clung to his hand, some soft essence.

He debated waking her, but instead turned away and quietly left the room, heading for his front entrance. As he left the room, the woman's eyes opened. She looked after him, and then looked down at her hand, still resting on the table.

The buzz of the world always struck him after he left his quiet apartment. The hurried gaits, the loud voices of the Perfects (now called the more politically correct Talents, ever since the holobook manifesto *You're Ordinary, You're Special* had swept the settlements some fifty years ago), the hum of commlinks and game boxes and the soft beeps of a thousand devices, blending individual minds into a soup of technology and culture.

Why even have a face-to-face meeting anymore? came the old rhetorical question.

Because faces still matter!

Indeed, as he entered the meeting, Webster had his new FaceBoy out, a small oblong device with a rounded top that projected holographic heads of various speakers. He was laughing as Pravin's own face stared at him and gave him a firm admonition.

Pravin cleared his throat. Webster looked up, dismayed, and even the tiny cartoonish Pravin head swiveled and looked up in horror. Pravin couldn't help but laugh. "At ease, both of you."

"Yes, Governor." Webster's face suddenly broke into an irrepressible grin. "I was just listening to you tell me the importance of arriving at meetings on time."

"I'm here now." He released a breath and looked around the meeting space, located at the top of the tallest tower in his United Nations Headquarters base, called UNHQ for short. His top advisors sat in plush, high-backed chairs. The room was an elegant blending of clean white lines and huge windows showing the sweep of Chiron and UNHQ, which had been remodeled now into a base worthy of the center of settlement government.

In the distance, past tall, sleek buildings surrounded by tended lawns and parks, Pravin could see the reassuring crackle of a Mark V tachyon field. The sight gratified him, lifting him above the memories of a time when this very base had been thrown into terrible war, and his beloved wife, son, and grandson were killed in one shattering day.

Never again had become his mantra. And if that meant hard-nosed realism had replaced wistful idealism, so be it.

"Let's begin," he said, glancing around at the others. "What news from the settlements?"

"I'll activate the map." That was Blanca, her voice soft but with a commanding edge. She was the oldest of Pravin's diplomatic corps, and the most experienced. Her face was tanned from frequent trips to the shores.

A holo of the settlement territories appeared in the center of the table. There were three continents, shorthanded as Hive, Central and Eastern. The Cen-

tral Continent was the location of the main settlement territories, where Pravin Lal's Peacekeepers
found themselves in the center of four other territories: the Gaians to the northwest, the Morganites to
the northeast, the Spartans to the southwest, and
the University to the southeast. It was as if the
Peacekeepers were the center of a big X, and main-
taining their position, and their power, had tested
and hardened Pravin over the years.

Beyond Zakharov's territories to the east lay
Miriam Godwinson's territory in the Great Dunes.
The heart of the recent troubles, if Zakharov was to
be believed. Beyond the eastern shore lay the Great
Marine Rift, and then the Eastern Continent. This
narrow continent was unremarkable in most ways
except for a vast expanse of xenofungus that
swathed the northern tip. Morgan, Skye and Zakharov had all placed small bases on this continent,
along with Sister Miriam.

Back to the west of the Central Continent, across
the Chiron Sea, lay the Hive Continent, so-called
because until recently that continent was the exclu-
sive domain of the Human Hive, whose restrained
citizens lived in vast underground complexes. But
not long ago Morgan had struck a treaty with the
Human Hive, allowing him to build a base on the
north end of that continent, a most unusual devel-
opment. From the south of the Human Hive, Santiago pushed in, hungry for more land.

The holomap reflected the current political situation, extrapolated from Zakharov's most recent
satellite feeds. The bases of the various territories
glimmered across the map like multicolored jewels.

"We know what the current crisis is," said Blanca.

"Zakharov is turning over the settlements, looking for some traitor."

"His drop troops are searching all the way to the borders." That was Arthur, a man with bad teeth and thinning hair. He was generally regarded as the smartest of Pravin's diplomats, but he maintained a generalized bitterness because his parents had refused to give him even the most basic genetic tweaks. And it showed: he was damn ugly. "He seems to be concentrating the search on his eastern borders."

"Near the Great Dunes," said Pravin. "Why there?"

"Maybe he figures this person has sought sanctuary with Miriam."

"Sanctuary?" That was Beth, the youngest of Pravin's diplomats. She was clearly a Perfect, her skin smooth and flawless, her hair a rich golden blond. She wore cleanly pressed blue pants and a sleeveless white vest that exposed her arms. Along one arm ran a series of scars, like red blisters snaking their way from her elbow to her shoulder.

"An ancient concept," said Arthur, not looking at her. "Criminals could seek sanctuary in a church. The church was obligated to take them in, and the police were obligated to stay away. It wasn't socially permissible for armed representatives of the state to barge into a house of worship."

"I know what it means. I just doubt that Zakharov will honor it."

Pravin set his jaw, deep in thought. "I return to the same question as always . . . does this threaten the balance of power in the settlements?"

Blanca glanced at the map. "Morgan and Zakharov are ready to burst out of their territories. Morgan in particular seems to be trying to suck up every last energy credit on Chiron. This alliance he made with the Hive concerns me."

"I was training with Santiago's people," said Beth, touching the scars on her arm. "She wants the land on the Hive Continent."

Pravin nodded. "We'll keep an eye on that. As for Miriam, we're losing citizens to her as well. She has a growing power base among the disenfranchised, right here in our own bases. If we wait too long, that power base will overwhelm us."

Blanca shook her head. "Everything's getting too crowded. I can feel it. We're on the verge of a firestorm. We need to contact Zakharov and find out what he's up to."

Pravin stared at the map, where the colored indicators had taken on the air of tiny spirits, trapped and pushing at invisible cages. When he looked back at Beth she was rubbing her arm, where the scars bloomed like angry red flowers on her skin.

"You see, Isaac, it has begun." Zakharov sank into his thick, low chair and stared into space. "Governor Lal is asking about our drop troop activity, and our roundup of citizens on the fringes is causing unrest."

They sat in a dimly lit holobar on the recreation commons. Thick, low chairs were scattered everywhere, and a holo projection made a thousand stars glimmer above the long, sleek bar. A young man in a clean white tunic brought them two drinks, a simple brandy for Zakharov and a complex, shimmering chem-X concoction for Isaac. Isaac leaned forward the instant the glasses clinked on the smoked glass table between them.

"Next to the vapors, my favorite companion," he said. He lifted the drink in Zakharov's direction and then sipped from the blue glass, carefully, as if drawing off only the top layer of the beverage. He blinked and his thick belly shuddered with pleasure before he turned to Zakharov. "So you're afraid that Miriam will get the Ideal and lay your secrets bare to the world?"

"Of course." Zakharov took a sip of brandy, his face heavy in the dim lights of the bar. "She's always one for melodrama. She won't try to settle this privately, through some kind of arrangement that might benefit her."

"Really?" He set down his glass on the table, although his eyes never left it. "Is this personal, Prokhor? Is it her speeches about our lost humanity that really bother you?"

"Nonsense."

"You don't have the benefit of an impending death, Prokhor. You have access to the most expensive and powerful genetic treatments on Chiron. But the rest of us, who will die, often turn to philosophy to prepare ourselves for the inevitable. Miriam isn't completely wrong in reminding us of our humanity."

"Our *flawed* humanity." Zakharov took another drink and stared at the stars projected on the ceiling. "You're wrong about one thing, Isaac. I do know I'm going to die. I feel it more than ever, my body stiffening by degrees. But I built this place, this fortress of the mind, against such as Miriam who seek to overthrow knowledge and truth with their ephemeral belief systems. University Base, and all of its collected knowledge, will be my legacy. This is the mind of Chiron that must be preserved."

Isaac stared at him, then smiled. "I didn't know you had it in you, old friend. But you may have a problem. If Gene and his like violate the Xynan-Dylan Protocol, the Council will step in, if for no other reason than people like Santiago feel threatened."

"What if I didn't classify them as citizens? That would put them outside the Protocol."

Isaac chuckled in his drink. "So what are they? Chimpanzees?"

"Citizenship is purely a paper distinction. The Ideals exist, they have self-awareness, and that's all that matters."

"Academy Park is self-aware, and it's not a citizen."

"Exactly! It's a base. And the Ideals are simply . . . structures. Bases of flesh!" He smiled.

"The Ideals are humans, Zakharov. Or they look like humans." Isaac shifted his bulk, the mirrorlike surface of his drink sloshing up toward the rim of his glass. "For Chiron's sake, old friend, don't you worry what people will think of these Ideals? You already have ten percent of your population heading for the exits as fast as their bare feet can take them."

Zakharov shook his head and took a deep breath. The white-tunicked waiter appeared from the shadows, set down a second brandy, took the first with a practiced motion and faded away. The two men sat in silence for a while, letting the tension drain from their conversation.

"You've done great things, Prokhor. I don't doubt that."

"This is the greatest, Isaac. It's as if my mind has created another mind, a greater mind, and a greater body. It's more like art than science."

Isaac laughed. "Now *you* sound like Miriam."

The light shifted in the bar as a new holo program began. Great green leaves pushed from the shadows behind the tables, and behind the bar a waterfall glimmered. Zakharov looked over at it, still deep in thought. "Besides, you know what Governor Lal himself has done."

"Something you might want to remind him of, before the next Council." Isaac lifted his glass in a toast, then stared around the quiet bar. There were only three other people present, all of them older academics carrying on restrained conversations. He sighed.

"You know, say what you will about the fringes, but that's where the action is."

Academy Park, the fringes

The streets of Academy Park were silent after midnight, even though a kind of bristling awareness permeated the streets. To the citizens who slept in their secure metal hab dorms, or those who worked late in the lab complexes that dotted the heart of the city, the silence meant nothing. Anyone who journeyed home or out to the quiet rec commons would do so in utter safety, every part of their journey monitored by the hidden mind of the city core.

But for those who sought action, or who lived in the shadows of the University, there were the fringes—ramshackle rows of blank gray buildings clustered away from the core base. For those who lived on the fringes, the J-freaks and X-hoppers, the downtrodden and those who sought dangerous pleasures, the eyes of the colony were one step removed, the sly, narrow scanners of the flybots less ubiquitous.

On this moonless evening, as night slipped into the dead chill of the early morning, a man stepped through a gray metal door, allowing the heavy thump of Planet-Trance music to tumble into the street before the door banged shut behind him. The scent of sweat and vapors and a mix of Morganite colognes clung to his pale white clothing; almost without thinking his olfactory centers parsed each odor and then screened it from his consciousness. He glanced up and down the streets, which were dark and glistening from the night "rain," a fine mist triggered inside the pressure domes to wash the buildings and streets.

The door opened and another man, named Oliver, tumbled into the street, his thinning hair sticking out in odd directions. His clothing was in disarray, and he stumbled into the first man, who, without thinking, registered the exact weight and momentum of the man and nudged him back to his feet. Oliver swayed, blinking at the misty buildings, and then leaned back against the door. He took a small silver tin from the wide sash belt he wore and popped a tiny white pill.

A moment passed, and then he laughed. "That's clearing it, then." He pointed to the first man's feet, which were bare, boot chips unreadable by the smart streets of the base. "You like your privacy?"

"Something like that."

Oliver shrugged, his balance returning by degrees. "It's not uncommon. You're an odd one, but it was a pleasure drinking with you." As the clarity pill took effect, banishing the fog of the vapors, Oliver began sizing up his companion with a new cunning. "You know, we vaped all night, but I don't remember you pulling out your chit card."

"You're mistaken. But that's all right." He thrust out his hand. Oliver looked at the jutting jaw, odd puffy cheeks, the blue eyes. Finally he reached out and took his hand.

"Why don't you walk with me? The tram stops at this end of the street."

Behind them a door banged open, and a sonorous chanting echoed from farther away. A small cloud of something like burnt paper swirled down the barren street, tiny pieces of ash clinging to the slick surface. Oliver looked away, and when he looked back his companion was several meters away, and walking at a fast clip. "Hey!" he shouted.

"Go home," said the first man, whose given name was Adam. "Rest."

Oliver looked after him, then the other way. Three shadowy figures had come from a nearby alley, and he heard the sung harmonies of dedicated J-freaks, their hymns echoing on the gray streets. He shook his head, getting a sudden chill. Pulling a thermal hat from his coat pocket, he rolled it down over his head and set off toward home.

Walking away, Adam released his face muscles, his jaw relaxing and cheeks shifting in subtle ways, altering his appearance. His eyes were brown now.

He would discard his coat at the first opportunity, but if he threw it in the streets a garbot would pick it up, and they might brush it for DNA material. You couldn't be too careful.

The chems and vapors consumed by Adam had very little effect on him. He wondered what it felt like, to be washed free from your own consciousness, an experience that Oliver and many others seemed to enjoy. He would never know.

Only fifteen steps later he felt the subtle tension in his bladder as the buildup of waste in his body urged him to vacate. He turned into a narrow alley, the side of some five-floor building by the look of it, with only a few windows, high up and screened from prying eyes. He walked two steps down the alley and pissed, the stream arcing out into the low gutter at his feet. He took the opportunity to look around, examining the plain, bare walls of the alley.

About five meters farther down, scrawled on the wall with an etch gun, were the words "We Must Dissent."

He stopped the flow of his urine instantly. He opened up his mind, allowing sensory input that he had screened out to flood in, scanning it quickly for relevant information.

Academy Park was self-aware, but he was in the fringes. Still, any such graffiti would be eliminated within three hours or so, which meant this was recent. The saying itself was one trumpeted by followers of Miriam Godwinson and her Believers, and he had been warned that the Believers and their ilk wouldn't take kindly to his existence. An odd thing to think about.

From the mouth of the alley a low, thrumming

voice sounded, and another joined it. Two figures appeared there, silhouetted against the dull amber wash of light. He adjusted his vision quickly, examining their odd visages, their tattered clothes and their matted hair. They appeared to be fringe dwellers, but there was a tension in their stance.

"What do you want?" he asked.

"We saw you." One of them spoke while the odd chant continued. It grew louder, but he could parse the voices . . . three more outside the alley, making five in total. "We knew you when you walked in."

"What do you mean by that?"

The lead two were shuffling forward, swaying slightly. Now he caught the sound of a scuffle behind him, deeper in the alley. He turned, just slightly, and the speaker's voice cracked out again.

"You hear that, monkey?"

Monkey?

He could smell the odors coming off these people, sweat and grime and the tang of adrenaline. They seemed utterly fearless.

He took a step toward the mass at the head of the alley, intending to push right past them. He flexed his hands, and carefully monitored the adrenaline his body was squeezing into his bloodstream. His heart rate increased.

They ran at him suddenly, all five of them, the stink preceding them like a wave. From behind him he heard more scuffling . . . two more. He also heard the click of a weapon being cocked back there.

It wouldn't be standard issue . . . weapons are outlawed in the base. Must be a homemade job, which means a wide field of fire, and no accuracy . . .

He leapt up, hit the wall and pushed off sideways.
A booming crack echoed in the alley, and he saw a
flash illuminate the mass of flesh below him. Shot
peppered the wall where he had stood, and one of
the attackers collapsed, a victim of friendly fire.

No one shouted. Good discipline, but the shot
alone would alert the flybots. He wanted no part of
that.

He landed near one of the attackers in the alley
mouth and lashed out. The man fell, shinbone
splintering, and he turned to the next, only to feel
the first one sinking teeth into his calf.

He grunted, a mix of surprise and pain, before
shutting off all sensation to that leg. He kicked out
again and again, feeling teeth and jaw crack from the
blows. Another fell on him and tangled his arm, and
that one he stabbed in the eye with his left thumb.

But she didn't let go!

He felt a second rush of adrenaline and threw off
the thick bodies around him. He saw the weapon
now, a makeshift shotgun. He grabbed the first
man, the speaker, and held him close, bending the
man's arm hard and using him as a human shield.

"If you fire, this man will die."

But the attacker still fired. There was a wide spray
of shot; he felt his hostage's head snap back as the
man's face filled with bloody fragments. Both of
them fell back from the force of the blow, and he
felt a warm peppering in his side.

He directed his capillaries to squeeze shut, con-
stricting the flow. Two more fell on top of him, and
another shot rang out. He saw an arm blown off,
but felt another peppering of shot around his chest
where that arm had held him.

Unreal.

A high-pitched wail sounded from above them, and a clean white light flooded the entire alley. He looked up to see a flybot whirring over their heads, its paste guns swiveling into position already.

Two more shots rang out, one of them clipping the flybot's rear stabilizer. It suddenly veered away and clanged into one wall. He used the chance to lash out, forcing himself through the press of bodies.

He felt something cold and metal and he grabbed at it, then he pushed away, through bleeding, stinking flesh, and out of the alley, as the whir of a second and third flybot grew louder.

Twenty minutes later, Adam sat on the magtrain, feeling the generator hum through his bare feet on the floor. There were windows, though he wasn't sure why, since the only thing visible was the side of the magtube, darkness laced with bands of orange light that flashed by once a second.

And his face. He could see his face, reflected in the window, the orange bands slicing by behind it. He blinked, his eyes deep brown, penetrating the shadows outside. He could see more there than anyone else on the train, things that they would never imagine existed. He could hear tiny skittering in the walls, he could see imperfections in the steel even though the train moved at 200 km an hour. He could smell the mustiness of his stolen coat, and feel the blood soak his shirt underneath.

Monkey.

He couldn't fathom exactly why the J-freaks had set on him with such fury. He doubted there was anything about his appearance that would tip off a casual observer, although he supposed he might have looked too steady for a man just leaving a vape-house. Still, why attack him?

He looked down inside his coat. His clothes were sticky with blood, but he had constricted those capillaries, stanching the blood flow. He was all right for now.

He looked up again and his breath fogged the window. He could feel himself getting suddenly icy. He blinked, and his eyes were silver-gray. He blinked again, and they were brown.

Freak.

"Are you all right?"

Someone stood above him. It was a man, his hair shaggy and falling about his shoulders, wearing the heavy overcoat of a construction tech. "You don't look well, friend. I heard you muttering to yourself."

"I'm all right."

"Here." The man slid in next to him, extending a flask in a gloved hand. "Have some. It'll steady you."

Adam could smell his overcoat and glove, which held some faint chemical residue, and as the man leaned closer the odor intensified. Adam parsed it, analyzed it, and let it go. He was tired, and he welcomed the coming darkness.

The chemical smell grew thick in his throat, but he stopped fighting it. He leaned against the window and slept.

"Academician." The man, Daniel, gave him a bow of respect from the touchscreen beside Zakharov's bed. Daniel was one of his top advisors, a young but brilliant scientist with all of the healthy, strong look of the newly Chiron-born. He also managed to remain very tan, in spite of their relatively cloistered lives.

"What is it?" Zakharov blinked at him from an angry sleep.

"Something happened in the fringes last night. We've found traces of the Ideal."

"Traces? Be clear, Daniel."

"He was attacked, Academician. On the fringes of Academy Park. We found his blood."

Zakharov and Daniel convened in a small meeting room near Zakharov's chambers. A University security officer was waiting for them, an Officer Bayliss, with heavy-lidded eyes and a gruff voice.

"Who are they?" asked Zakharov.

"Fringe dwellers. Seven of them. Three dead, and three more committed suicide when we caught them. The last won't talk. I assure you we've used every means of persuasion."

"They're J-freaks."

"It appears so." Bayliss set a touchscreen on the table and called up a vidfeed from a damaged flybot. The alley was bathed in light, showing Adam, with his pale blue clothing and silvery hair, whirling in the center of a mass of attackers. As Zakharov and Daniel watched, he went down. The image froze.

"He fought like a banshee, but they cut him," said Bayliss. A quick zoom into the frozen image revealed the flash of a knife. "He still got away. He evaded the flybot, but we think we have him going into a magtube station a ways up the street."

"Where was it bound?"

Bayliss gave him a tight smile. "You tell me. It's a gold line. Hooks right into the planetary transit system. We're working with the other factions to try and track him, but he could be almost anywhere."

"Could he be in Believer lands?" asked Zakharov, anger edging his voice.

Bayliss shrugged. "I suppose he could. Yes. He could have gotten off at Baikonur, and crossed from there into the desert."

Zakharov stood up and pointed at Bayliss. "Check there first. This man is a high-ranking University official, and I want him back. You sweep the entire colony, you send scanners out onto the roads, everything."

"He's not in the University ID banks," said Bayliss, clicking his mouth shut.

"You have his blood and his picture. Find him. And round up all of the freaks, the drones, everyone on the fringes. Round them all up now."

"Yes, Academician." Bayliss gathered up his touchscreen and exited. Zakharov shook his head and paced the narrow room. Daniel cleared his throat.

"Who is this man, Academician?"

"He's the first of the Ideals, Daniel. He's the man we're searching for."

"But surely he wouldn't betray secrets to the Believers, Academician."

Zakharov expelled a deep breath, letting his emotions settle into thought. A chess match. Think two steps ahead, four steps ahead, watch the possibilities branch into infinity, and play them to your advantage.

"His blood will betray him, Daniel. His blood is all they need."

And while University security forces combed the settlements, a stolen rover crossed the desert, grinding its way across the hot sands as the two suns floated toward their apex. Baikonur lay far behind, and ahead lay New Jerusalem, the towers of the great church rising up in its midst.

One hour later, a sharp knock at the door brought Miriam out of a reverie. She shifted, pulling herself up to her feet, and turned to the door of her small chapel as Kola opened it. He bowed to her.

"We have him, Sister. A Believer in Academy Park found him and brought him through Peacekeeper lands to us."

Miriam felt her breath leave her, her doubt retreating for a moment. "Very good, Kola."

"Would you like to see him?"

She adjusted her elaborate robes. She looked at the great cross on the wall, and then back to Kola. "Yes. Let's go talk to this superhuman."

Kola smiled. "He's down in interrogation."

She sat opposite him, at the long wooden table. He looked like a human, but in his face there was something alien, something cool, like dry ice on a metal table. His eyes were a pale silver blue, and his skin and hair had an odd silvery cast, even though he had been in the blazing suns.

He shifted slightly, and behind her Kola shifted as well, on edge. The Ideal had thick metal restraints that held his arms behind his back and his legs were attached to the metal chair. His clothes were soaked with blood in several places, and

Miriam could smell its tang. Still, he seemed utterly calm.

Inhuman.

Miriam studied his face in silence, then reached out to him, extending her hand across the table. "What's your name?" she asked. He didn't answer. "You can tell me that. It will make it much easier to talk."

He considered that and nodded. "My name is Adam." She paused for a moment, surprised. "And I do know who he is. In your Bible."

"Do you? And do you know who I am?"

"You're Sister Miriam Godwinson of the Believers." He smiled at her. She looked back to Kola.

"Are the restraints really necessary?"

"Yes, Sister. He's already broken out three times. I don't want to show you what happened to those Templars."

"And yet here he sits," said Miriam. She stood up and walked around the table toward him. "He's quite attractive. Yet something is missing." She leaned closer to him, reached out to touch his shoulder. "Adam, would you harm me if I freed you from these restraints?"

"Of course not."

"Why? Don't you want to return to the settlements?"

He shrugged. "I have no urge to return."

"Really?" She stared at him with her luminous green eyes. "That surprises me. As a child of Zakharov—"

"I'm not his child."

She felt a flush of pleasure at finding a sensitive spot. "But he created you. Not the Almighty."

"Random chance created you. Focused thought shaped me. But I'm my own being."

"And here you are. Did you really fall for such a simple trap? A common chlorovapor?" She studied his face at length. "I think you want to be here, to learn our ways."

He smiled once more, a smile that didn't reach his eyes. "Your ways wouldn't take."

Miriam shifted back. "They wouldn't *take?* What do you mean by that?"

He turned to look at her, his arms flexing in the restraints. Miriam saw a flash of turmoil cross his face. "I found my University files, Sister, and I read them. I saw Zakharov's plan for me. He considers the need for religion a flaw of human nature. And in me, and my kind, he made sure to eliminate it."

"What?"

"Religion is a weakness built into the human mind. My mind, my body, my training, all shape me to see reality exactly as it is." His muscles trembled. "Sister, I don't need your faith. It's as worthless to me as a tail."

He grinned at Miriam and blinked again. His eyes were now deep green, a perfect mirror of hers.

chapter three

MIRIAM KNEELED IN HER CHAPEL, THE COOL STONE WALLS rising around her. She felt old, her body like rotting vines, which scarcely bothered her. What bothered her was the darkness inside of her, the cold, empty space where the eyes of Adam now lived.

He had shaken her. Her way of life depended on faith, on a bedrock human spirituality that lay beneath all of the intellectual trappings of the modern world. But here was a product of that world, canceling out everything she believed in.

She bowed her head and continued her prayer. She reached deep inside of her, and released everything, every shred of doubt or preconception. But still those green eyes blinked at her, soulless.

And from outside, somewhere, that low humming grated on her nerves, echoing across the face of the world.

A soft voice behind her interrupted her prayers. She looked back to see the pale face of Leta, eyes downcast. "Forgive the interruption, Sister. Someone wants to contact you in the NuSpace."

"Who is it?"

"It's Academician Zakharov. He said it regards 'the return of settlement citizens held against their will.' "

"Ah." She rose slowly, gathering the skirts of her robes. "Very well. I'll go to the connector room."

"Is it all ready, Daniel?" asked Zakharov.

"Yes, Academician. All it needs is your mind." Daniel gestured to the small connector booth in the center of the room. The rest of the room was bare, except for a single chair and a touchpanel used to monitor the person in the booth.

"Is the rescue team on standby?"

"Yes, Academician. The drop troops are in the needlejets, and positioned at Baikonur right where we verified that the Ideal crossed into Believer lands. If diplomacy fails, we'll send them in."

"Good."

Zakharov turned sideways and slid into the booth. A curve of soft plastic served as a chair, holding him steady while the connector mechanism descended around his head like a crown. He glanced up to see the metal ring with the tiny sensors ranged around it like glowing barbs. He could already feel a kind of haziness in his brain as the sensors homed in on the various thought centers there.

As always, his stomach turned over in nervousness. As usual, he wondered if that were a side effect of the scanners, or if it was genuine fear or anticipation.

"Ready, Academician?" That was Daniel's voice from the monitor panel, although Zakharov could no longer see him.

"Ready. Jack me in." He set his jaw, preparing for the transfer.

The world rippled, and then tore open, to reveal a new world behind it.

NuSpace was an invention of Zakharov's that seemed to have no limit to its functionality or value. It was really an extension of the virtual world that Zakharov had experienced long ago in the Human Hive; since that time he had become obsessed with replicating the experience, creating a multisensory space that allowed anyone to jack into his network nodes and share information, symbols, language, even touch and smell if they so desired. It was the ultimate chat room, and he had installed one in every base of the settlements. On this secure diplomatic channel he could instantly meet with and talk to Governor Lal or any of the other settlement leaders.

In this case, he decided to go straight to the source of his problems. Miriam Godwinson.

Miriam had chosen a Chapel program to run for their meeting space, naturally. It was a high, sweeping space, and light glowed in the elaborate stained glass windows overhead. As he looked up he saw that the scenes in the windows were shifting . . . saintlike men and women with halos carried food and water to the starving; two dogs with a thousand eyes guarded the foot of a massive throne lost in a haze of golden light.

He shook his head. A ripple of light brightened the walls even further, and then Miriam appeared, her projection simple, lined by a rim of silver haze. Like many who used the NuSpace she floated slightly above the ground; it took mental discipline to adhere to the physics of the real world in Nu-Space, an ability Zakharov prided himself on. His projection was a perfect mirror of his real self.

"Greetings, Prokhor. Doing some soul searching?"

"You know what I'm looking for, Miriam. One of my citizens has vanished into your lands, and I want him back."

"Thousands of your citizens have come to me, Prokhor. What makes this one so special?" The light around her seemed to pulse, reflecting a tension she tried to mask.

"You know who it is. An individual who worked in my labs became unbalanced, and fled to New Jerusalem."

"Unbalanced? To your thinking anyone who embraces my way of faith is unbalanced. How would I know this person?"

"He was injured. Shot in the side. By your people, I might add."

"Anyone in your base is your people, Prokhor, whether they wear a silver cross or not. Settlement citizens are free to think as they wish. You should know that better than anyone." She nodded in satisfaction.

"They're free to think, but not when they come under the mind control techniques of a witch like you."

The light in the room dimmed. Zakharov glanced up to see the stained glass windows shifting to dire scenes of heavenly soldiers casting tortured souls down into fiery pits.

"Many come to me, Prokhor. Every one of them gets screened by a genetic scope and matched to the citizens' records in the planetary datalinks. So who is this person you seek? What's his ID code?"

"He's not in the citizens' records, Miriam."

She nodded. "One might think you have something to hide, Prokhor. If the Council learns that you've created something that violates every tenet of the Xynan-Dylan Protocol, the genetic inspectors are going to make your life very difficult. And they should. What you made would not even be human."

"You mean he has no soul?" Zakharov smiled, a smile that spread like an oil slick on water. "Then return my property if that's how you want it. But I have motions of my own before the Council. Every settlement leader has seen citizens vanish into your blasted desert. The techniques you use to lure and control our citizens include sophisticated mind control, and virtually amount to probe-team actions. If you don't return my citizen, I'll have Council psyche teams showing up at your gates to screen every member of your flock, and bring back those who have fallen under your spell."

She stared at him. "They come willingly to me, Prokhor."

"Then you won't mind the psyche screening, Miriam. You have nothing to be afraid of. But remember that you have few friends on Council."

"Do what you will, but I know nothing of this creature you're looking for."

She vanished. Prokhor took one last look at the stained glass windows, where a thousand different Miriams now stared down at him. He smiled and vanished from the NuSpace.

* * *

"So what now?" Kola stared at Miriam as she lifted an orange from a crystal bowl. She could still feel anger twisting at her from the meeting. She calmed herself by looking at the fruit, at its texture, at the way it seemed to steal the light from the room.

"It's going to get difficult. Zakharov has a vendetta against us, and he, and the rest of the Council, are going to try and get their people back. But I won't allow University soldiers or Council inspection teams to enter New Jerusalem."

"We aren't weak, and we aren't afraid to die, but prayer alone won't be enough."

"The way things are going I'll be suspended from the Planetary Council." She searched deep inside of herself for the answers, for the Almighty's voice to show her the way, but she ended up again at the roadblock of Adam's infernal eyes.

"Sister? What is your plan?"

She set down the orange and looked at Kola. "I don't know. But in the meantime let's have a fellowship meeting tonight, for all of the faithful. We must cleanse ourselves for what is soon to come."

That night

Two moons hung in the cloudy sky, casting a soft, reflected light down over the sandy hills north of New Jerusalem, touching the tops of the rolling dunes. The tachyon field winked off, leaving the base open, and thousands of the faithful walked slowly from the cramped buildings, leaving their rigorous worship. Into a soft valley, like two hands cupping a fragile light, streams of dark figures flowed.

They walked in groups, their robes wrapped about them, singing hymns in practiced harmony. They flowed into the valley like dark, slow water, filling it from the bottom, standing and spreading blankets to sit . . . men and women, adults and children, silver crosses gleaming. Fine particles of sand churned in the air, adding a haze that seemed to hold the moonlight in the valley.

More came, and more, until the streets of the city lay empty behind them, like a metal corpse drained of its life. But in the valley people stood and sat and kneeled, flesh touching each other in a massive pool of humanity. And then, atop the hill that rose over them and against the dark sky, something flickered into existence.

It was Sister Miriam, wearing her white and gold robes, the silver cross gleaming on her chest. The holo projection towered a hundred meters into the sky, slightly translucent so that they could see the clouds and stars through her, but even from that height her green eyes swept down across them. Those who were close enough to the hill could see the real Miriam, standing on a platform and looking down, moving in perfect tandem with her projection.

"People of the Light, I welcome you."

"Light," came the greeting, rolling across the gathered, who numbered now close to a million. On adjacent hills, and in adjacent valleys, and at other bases they gathered as well, watching transmissions of her holo towering above them all.

"We're here to reaffirm our faith in our basic human nature, and in the Almighty's love that comes down on us like a shower, unbidden and endless."

"Ahmin," the voices rumbled, becoming as one, and Miriam imagined a mountain shaking with that voice.

"Them." And here she, and her towering projection, extended a hand to the west, where the settlements lay. "Rather than choose to embrace the Almighty, they have chosen to become as gods themselves, and to play with the very substance of the sacred body. But we will not fault them for their misguided notions."

There were murmurs from the crowd. Miriam felt a twinge of uncertainty, as if the uneasiness of the masses was mirrored in her, rather than the masses mirroring her faith. She continued.

"It isn't their fault that they do not see the Way. It isn't their fault that they do not understand the precious spark that is our human soul, given to us by a power far greater than any they can imagine. It isn't for us to question their misguided ways."

"Ahmin," came a few voices.

"But we will not stand by and turn over the world of Chiron to those who aren't even human. To those who are more like machines than men, and seek to displace you, you who were created by God's hand alone. Do you agree?"

"Ahmin!" the shouted voices came.

"I want to show you something." Her projection froze, and a moment of empty silence slipped across the desert night. Something appeared next to Miriam, its projection smaller than hers. It was a man in thick shackles, clothes hanging tattered from his body, but he still looked through a mask of perfect calm. "This is the creature that has come to us from the settlements. This is what the false gods have created in their image. But this is not a man.

"He feels no pain. He has never suffered. His soul is as dry as the desert, as twisted as a mindworm, as empty as a borehole. But they would turn this creature, and his kind, against you. Will you stand for that?"

The resounding shout shook the high mountains.

"To be human isn't enough for them. So I ask of you, my brothers and sisters in the voice, to join hands and lift your voice to Heaven, and show this world what it means to be human. Show the world what they have forgotten, in their rush for creature comforts, in their questing for final knowledge, ever farther from the source of all life. Lift your hands and show them!"

From around her, at a distance of kilometers, each Believer lifted a tiny white glowlamp, until the entire hill was lit by a million bright stars. Miriam lifted a light of her own, and so did her projection, and that magnified light shone above her on the hilltop, like a heavenly star fallen to Earth.

She tilted her face up to the sky, and began to sing, in a voice surprisingly clear and bright, that cut the night and floated down over them.

The pool of humanity that surrounded her seemed to catch its breath at once, and then she looked down at them and the entire mass lifted their voice with hers, so that the hilltops echoed with their song, one hymn after another, and their eyes brightened with fellowship.

"Their tach field is down." That was Daniel addressing Zakharov, who sat in his lab playing with a new device sent by Director Morgan that involved two rings and a small white mouse.

"Be precise."

"New Jerusalem. We have an orbital scan on the tach field power source, and it shut down. They're wide open."

Zakharov held the white mouse and rubbed one hand along the edge of his desk as if rubbing out a mark. "Why did she lower the field?"

"They're gathered in some kind of religious meeting outside the base." Daniel passed him a scan, taken by a needlejet doing a flyover at a distance. Zakharov examined the scan, staring at the flicks of light pooled in the valley with the Miriam holo towering overhead. "As you can see, there's a lot of them."

"They're just Believers." Zakharov studied the scan. "Who's that with her? Who's the second holo projection?"

"It may be the Ideal," said Daniel. "We're eighty-nine percent certain. And the drop troops are ready. Still, there are hundreds of thousands of them—"

"Unarmed. Our drop troops are the envy of the world, and the Believers' tach field is down. Wait for the masses to disperse, and then go in and get him back," said Zakharov, his fingers tightening. "No deaths unless necessary, but hurt them. And hit the church if you can. Destroy it."

He shook his head and stared at the scan, and at the pool of humanity at Miriam's feet.

University soldier Colonel Mack watched the night sky outside, two moons hanging low to the horizon. Business as usual, but racing by like this, in their HALO needlejet, it took on a new charged excitement.

He shifted in his harness and looked at the others. Their uniforms were a pale orange, made of a material so tough and flexible it was like a second, impenetrable skin. The equipment they carried was the highest technology, light and compact, including weapons that would fit in the palm of their hands but could easily lay waste to the poorly armed Believers.

He adjusted his hoverchute and reviewed the image of the target. An odd-looking man, and it was strange that his eye color wasn't identified. Still, they would steal him right from under the Believers' noses.

He caught the eye of Sara, a young, exuberant woman who constantly looked around the cabin, wired from excitement. He gave her a fist-forward salute, and she returned it.

A mounted display beeped and then flickered on. All eyes turned to it.

"The satellite feeds have pinpointed our location, and they've been relayed to your hoverchutes." Mack checked; the hoverchute indicator on his equipment strap confirmed the downlink. "You're going to land in the semicircular formation that we discussed at briefing, right around the hill. There's a lot of them, so grab the target and then use your hover to jump out, down the backside of the hill. Be careful out there, but have some fun."

Fun. It was common knowledge that the genetic profile of the typical soldier was set pretty much from birth. It included diminished fear response, and a hair-trigger adrenaline reaction. He could feel

it wiring his body as they approached the drop site
(counted down in hundredths of a second on a display clock and on his quicklink), and he wouldn't
have it any other way. He could see it in the grins of
his fellow soldiers. Only Johnson, who was a soldier
by choice rather than birth, looked ill-at-ease, even
with his stocky build. He fingered the trigger of his
tiny Q-gun as if it were a scab that needed picking.

Soon it was one minute to go, and he checked his
equipment. Then it was ten seconds, and five, and a
series of tones counted it all down.

Then the bottom fell out of the jet, and the air
and the sky rushed past him as Chiron spun below.

The University drop technique allowed Zakharov's relatively small army to respond to changing situations in the settlements quickly, so that he
could avoid fielding an army as large as Santiago's.

This meant nothing right now to Colonel Mack,
who spun through the high atmosphere as the
wedge of three needlejets vanished into the high
distance. He could feel his hoverchute operate; it
actually accelerated his fall, while adjusting the
path whenever the high desert winds knocked him
off. In fact, the hoverchute's adjustments were far
from gentle, feeling like invisible kicks to his torso
as the electrostatic fields altered his trajectory.

But as he looked around and saw the string of
glinting lights that were his comrades, he took rel-
ish in the beautiful systematic elegance behind it
all. They would land in precise points, and could
even have their final positions adjusted in midair
by the controllers back at University Base.

Now he focused on the land below. From high up

it took the form of gently rolling hills of the reddish earth of Chiron, the fields of xenofungus spreading like nerve endings to the north and south. He could see the dark uneven shape in the center of it all that was the Believer worshipers, and the lights clustered there, slowly dispersing back to the base. As his fall continued he began to make out shapes . . . the tall rangy figures, the light glinting off the tall crosses that some of them carried, giving the whole mass the impression of a bristling animal.

He reached up to touch his small Q-gun, clipped on his equipment sash. His fall path made it look as if he were rocketing into the center of this chaotic mass, which spread out over the hills below and the nearby base.

Suddenly he could see some among the Believers pointing up and shouting, and an anger, a venom, spread through the mass as the word spread.

Here we go, then . . . His earlink blipped, and then he heard Johnson's voice. "I think they're getting pissed. Aren't they supposed to be praying?"

"No worries," said Mack, before a terse voice from command ordered them into radio silence.

But now he could look past his feet and see the anger, almost smell it. It was a mass fueled by rage instead of tactics, and he wondered just what they expected to do, carried by nothing but this deep wave of passion.

From the horde below he saw a few white-clad soldiers lifting their weapons, slightly old disruption rifles from the look of it. Technology had advanced, the weapons were smaller and deadlier, but when a thousand people lifted their long, barbed guns to the sky and opened fire, it had its impact. The sky filled with streaks of white fire, and Mack felt his hoverchute kick in, jerking him small amounts to the left and right to confound enemy fire.

He looked up to see his comrades falling into this upside-down rain of fire, the white streaks rising to meet them and the bright pale blue sky beyond that. He saw one of them jerk as a penetrator bolt struck, and then a second. A death tone sounded in his earlink.

"What the fuck!" shouted Johnson. "They're not supposed to be armed!"

"I see Godwinson. She's still on the hilltop. They're heading down in a rover."

"We're adjusting your flight path," said the cool voice from command. "Maintain calm."

"Just don't set us down in the middle of that—" shouted Johnson.

His voice was cut off, as suddenly as if a land line had been cut. Mack's hoverchute jerked him sideways, toward the downslope of the hill, where a small black rover churned the sand. The rover was open and he could see Miriam inside, and the remaining Believers parted, letting her through effortlessly.

And then one bolt cut into him, right through his personal defense field and into the bottom of his foot, filling his leg with white fire. He grunted, and a soothing voice, an automatic, prerecorded response, sounded in his ear.

"It's going to be OK. Remain calm." Harmonic tones designed to suppress his pain centers sounded in his ears, and his smart suit adjusted various pressures in his body.

But the bolt, inside his leg now, felt as if it were

still burning with that white fire, and *moving,* burrowing its way deeper into his leg. He could feel the waves of hot pain, as if someone dumped buckets of icy water one after the other down his torso. At the center of this pain was that bright worm of agony, squirming. He could hear the shouts of the Believers below them, a blend of blind faith and holy rage.

Two more deathtones sang. He thought he could see the limp bodies. But the others lived, over thirty total, and that would be enough.

His hoverchute decelerated, and he grunted. He hit the sand hard, and felt another bolt of pain shoot up his leg, and then a wave of endorphins filled his body and he felt as if he were mainlining synthmeth back home. His smart suit gave him an extra juice of M-88, the painkiller, and he grinned, ready to rock.

Several of his comrades landed nearby, everyone in perfect position. He pulled out his Q-gun and looked around. A hoversled touched down next to him and he hopped on and activated it.

"You all right to do that?" It was Sara, staring at him from behind her gray visor, and even though she was three meters away her voice came through the earlink.

"Better than. No worries!"

He kicked the sled into high gear, scooting it across the hill. The first armored Believer that challenged him was taken down by the intersection of no less than three quantum bolts. The big man fell, utterly and instantly dead, his white armor gleaming in the moonlight.

And the next moment, as Mack went past, the

body exploded with a burst, sending a shock wave into Mack that rocked his hoversled.

"They've rigged their own bodies!" That was Johnson, shouting over the open links. Over his earlink he heard Sara's breath hitching in a kind of drawn-out scream; she had probably opened the link to tell him something. He looked back to see her body, half burned from the explosion, which had been strong enough to penetrate her Personal Defense Field. He broke the link with her and turned back.

Down the other side of the mountain he could see the retreating Believers. Except now he saw that the ordinary brown-clad worshipers, rather than fleeing to the base and letting the soldiers take care of them, had turned back. He saw children with them, running back up the red sandy hill toward the attacking University troops. There were thousands of them.

"We have a problem here," he said. "They're turning back on us."

"Who?" That was the voice of command.

"All of them."

The horde of Believers flowed back up the hill like a dark stain. Mack saw Miriam's rover, which was now caught between the attacking University troops and the approaching Believers. From somewhere higher on the slope a perfectly placed disruption bolt hit the rover and destroyed its chassis. He saw the rover tumble over, pieces of its structure dropping into the sand, and the white figure of Miriam and the bound figure of their target roll into the red sand.

"I see the target. Back these off."

"If I fire a lot of them are going to die," said Morris' voice, refreshingly calm from his position at the top of the hill.

Mack weighed the alternatives of immediate retreat and taking out a few Believers. The target, hands bound and rolling on the hill, clinched it. "You may fire into the front of the crowd. They'll back off. Johnson, Thorton, lock on our target. Go get him when the disruption stops."

From higher up the mountain the disruption bolts flew, cutting into the crowd of Believers. Mack saw the brown-clad seekers fall, their bodies disintegrating into grayish clouds that settled into the sand. He heard their screams cut off as lungs vanished.

"They'll back off now," said Morris.

But they didn't. Mack, sledding forward, saw Miriam crouch behind a rock outcropping. He saw her turn and point up the hill, and he heard something, her voice, enhanced by a projection device, exhorting her people on. And then he saw them surge up the hill even faster, right into the teeth of the chaos guns.

For himself, skimming toward the target, he saw the dark mass of Believers coming up on his left side, and a sudden stabbing pain reminded him he was injured.

He took out his Q-gun and started firing. One Believer fell, and another, but they were swept away by the advancing tide, now only forty meters below him. He looked up the hill and saw his troops kicking disruption blasts into the teeth of the horde, but then he saw the armored Believers crossing fire into the chaos guns. And then another wave of Believers came over that hill, and his heart sank.

"There's more. Command, swing back with the needlejet."

He could no longer see the target. He fired at Godwinson, but she had shifted behind the rock, part of which disintegrated from his fire. He could see her moving around the rock and up the hill, too far away for a clean shot.

"Command, bring in the air power."

"What's your request, Colonel?"

He could smell the horde, their sweat and fury. He kicked his hoversled up the hill, away from them, in time to see the figure of Morris fall under several armored figures. "Missile strike on the hill. Back them off. Then meet us at the rendezvous."

What's left of us.

He sounded the retreat, the pain in his leg sending hot lead up his spine. From the moonlit sky he heard the low drone of a needlejet, and then suddenly a wave of fire washed the bottom of the hillside. A sick elation rose in him and he saw the Believer wave fall under fire, tumbling back down the hill, their robes and hair and flesh burning.

And then he saw them, still coming.

Silhouetted against the flaming bodies of their own people, more Believers rushed up the slopes at him.

The needlejet droned again on its second pass, and now he heard a missile. A fiery white streak rocketed straight down into the hillside, thumping into the ground. It detonated, sending red rock and sand into the air. Gray rocks buried in the sand shattered, the pieces tumbling down the mountain.

He grinned and swung his sled around. And then he saw the big man rushing at him, the man's thick hair and beard smoking and layers of flesh peeling off his hands and face. The man caught him with a wild swing and knocked him off the hoversled.

The first blow snapped Mack's head back, and at the second he heard a cracking sound. Lights exploded in his vision and a shooting pain crossed his body like lightning crossing from sky to earth, and then there was nothing. He understood, he supposed, that his neck had been broken.

The big man reached down and took Mack's Q-gun, his state-of-the-art weapon, and then left him in a crumpled heap. He heard a jumble of voices in his earlink, thought he heard his name. Was someone calling him? Did someone need him?

Then, the darkness came, and he realized at last that he didn't know what lay on the other side.

When the concussion missile hit, Miriam was scrambling back upslope, watching Kola pull the Ideal away from the wash of flame that engulfed the hillside.

"Get down!" shouted Kola, but his voice was lost in a wave of ash and heat. Then the missile thumped into the ground, and the explosion rocked the earth, throwing sand and rock down into the faithful.

The rocks above Miriam shattered. Kola stumbled back, taking the Ideal with him. Miriam started after them, but she was no longer running on flat ground, and a hail of grayish dust filled her eyes so that she couldn't see. She blinked once and saw the dark shapes tumbling down on her, and the doubt that clutched her rose up to swallow her whole.

The rocks buried her in a wash of jagged darkness.

The next morning

"Look here," said Kola. "She's gone. The Almighty has claimed her." Five Templars stood around him, their impassive faces turned toward the shattered face of the rockslide. The hot suns blazed down on the aftermath of the attack.

"We have to keep looking." That was Pastor Prana, a small man with hard features and piercing gray eyes. "Alive or dead, we can't leave her body there."

"We also have to prepare for another attack," said Kola. He glanced past the Templars, where a group of Believers had gathered downslope, a dark, shifting crowd. From one edge a small figure in gray detached itself and came toward them.

"Stand back!" said Kola, jabbing a finger at the approaching figure.

"I won't," the figure said, though she stopped between the Templars and the crowd. It was Leta. "Sister Miriam, the very voice of the Almighty, she who led all of us from damnation, lies under that rubble. Why aren't you digging?"

"Because there may be further aggression," said Kola. "She wouldn't want us to risk more lives to rescue her body, when her soul has already departed."

"You don't know that." Leta turned back toward the crowd so they could hear her. "You don't know that the Almighty has taken her. Only the Almighty knows that."

Kola stared at the crowd, hearing the murmurs ripple like a change in the wind. He looked from them to the pile of jagged stone, and finally he nodded. "If you want to dig, then dig. But we can't help you. We must prepare for another attack."

Several figures detached from the crowd, approaching the rubble. Quiet and solemn, they began to shift rocks.

"I'll send an engineer to direct this operation," said Kola. "May the Almighty watch over your souls."

He turned and strode away, down slopes covered with red dust and cracked stone.

chapter four

DIRECTOR NWABUDIKE MORGAN MADE LOVE TO A COURTE-
san on a massive mahogany bed, colored X-vapors
coiling from small metal pots at each bedpost. Jeweled lights shimmered around them, and her fingers tangled in sheets so finely woven that an individual thread would be invisible to the naked eye.

He studied her as she moved, taking deep breaths,
the two of them floating into alternate worlds on
the cloudy highway of the vapors. Her body was
young and firm, enhanced and improved by genetic technologies and a Morgan Superfood diet so
that it was hard to believe she was even real. A fine
dusting of light ran from her breasts down to her
abdomen; a pleasing pattern, it was a part of her
skin, created by a genetic tweak fashionable in the
time this young woman was born. Her eyes were
closed, enhancing the illusion that she was a material object.

He found his eyes wandering around the room.
Hanging around his bed at many angles were
translucent vidscreens. Some showed tasteful, erotic

programming, others showed less tasteful erotic programming, and one showed a rapid-fire stream of images from his newest Morgan TV channels. The light of the touchscreens melded with the indirect light of the room fixtures, casting warm tones on the woman's skin and the animal print sheets. He whispered a command and the lights abruptly blinked out. The luminescent patterns on her body continued to glow, and he could follow her movements by the indistinct patterns in the darkness.

It was too perfect, like a scene from one of his own channels. And yet he felt nothing. He moved, and his hips, though thin from age, were still tensile, and her lips parted in pleasure (or at least the illusion of pleasure), but he felt as if he were watching her from a million miles away. He had created a world for himself, and his citizens, where nothing was out of reach. And yet his hunger had only grown deeper with time.

He stopped abruptly and rolled out of bed, commanding the lights back on. She opened her eyes, heavy-lidded and smoky.

"I've had enough," he said in a deep, rich voice. Her expression crashed into an odd blend of fear and outrage, quickly masked.

Of course. Her reputation is at stake.

"Very well." She climbed out of bed, shaking her long, dark hair. Her expression had turned into a mask, her pupils wide and dark from vapor effects. "Then I'll bill your account, Director."

"Yes." He watched as she put on a thin golden belt and touched an activation key. Within moments a shimmering holodress had enveloped her body, leaving only the most tantalizing glimpses of her skin. Earrings that hummed with her movements cascaded from her ears. She was a creature of beauty, and he imagined that every layer he peeled back would reveal more of the same.

And in Morgan's territory, at the height of the twenty-fourth century, there were a thousand more like her.

He sat at a desk of top quality Gaian mahogany drinking a heady, concentrated chem beverage to knock the vapor thickness from his skull. Indirect light filtered through a small window; he estimated the time at almost noon. He worked while he drank, checking the exchange first, watching the flow of credits race between the factions of the settlements, responding to the unrest in University and Believer lands. Then he called up his advisors' most recent reports.

His first concern was the botched attack by Zakharov on New Jerusalem. Zakharov's trouble with New Jerusalem was trickling over into the other settlement territories, and he considered how he might profit from it. He knew Governor Lal wasn't pleased, with Zakharov having killed several thousand innocent Believers, and possibly Sister Miriam as well. In three days they'd heard nothing from her.

If so, good riddance. He had his own problems with citizens leaving his territory and going to New Jerusalem. It wasn't that he wanted to curtail his citizens' freedom, for they were free to spend at will. There was an active underground of J-freaks inside all of the larger Morganite bases, and they were active consumers of his Expanded Enhanced Holo-

Bibles, Gifts of Revelation, Archangel Rising games, and the like.

But when they left his territory, and went to Miriam's bases, he lost them as customers and as a tax base. Miriam took her asceticism seriously, which is why they could never truly be allies. Perhaps Zakharov would settle the problem for him. He nodded, slipping off a thick gold ring and tapping it on his desk.

His next order of business was his new foothold on the Hive Continent. His Morgan Minerals factory drew boatloads of minerals from the crust of the Uranium Flats, and he could almost feel the resulting energy credits gushing into his already massive accounts. Santiago, on the south end of that continent, was making noises about pushing into Hive territory, rattling her saber at Chairman Yang. How predictable. Santiago didn't understand human nature, and so she would never forge an effective alliance with the notoriously isolationist Hive.

He smiled and opened a secure vidlink. In something resembling a Gaian pleasure cove, a man writhed in the sand. Young, willowy women hovered around him, touching him and retreating, attaching various implements to his flesh, most of them based on erotic modifications of the basic nerve staple design. Behind him were more men and women, restrained by figures in heavy, dark armor, forced to look on . . .

Morgan closed the link. Let the Chairman have his privacy, and enjoy the fruits of their new alliance. He would be heading home tomorrow, ready to open his world to Morganite traders.

Morgan slipped the gold ring back on his finger. Finally there was the matter of the solar flares. They were imminent, and would no doubt disrupt communication in the settlements. He wondered if Zakharov would take the opportunity to attack the Believers again, or if the Hive might attack Santiago. Either would be to his benefit.

He would hardly have to lift a finger.

Above, from the surface of Centauri B, a great tongue of fire rolled, extending toward the red-brown sphere of Chiron like the tongue of an animal licking blood from a wound.

A burst of solar energy rushed into the ecosystem, knocking out the orbital satellites launched by Zakharov and bathing the mind of Planet in rich, hot energy.

In the xenofields, something stirred. From the deepest part of the fields of crimson, tiny creatures awakened, thousands and then millions and then billions of them, and they crawled their way up to the surface.

Once there, they spread their wings and took flight.

In UNHQ, the buzzing slipped into Pravin's consciousness, causing him to lose track of what he was saying. His top advisors, gathered in the room, stopped as well, glancing at each other in confusion.

It was Arthur who broke the silence. "Look outside," he said, pointing to the tall bank of windows on one wall. Pravin stood up and looked. Outside, it was noon, and the two suns blazed in the sky, hanging there with a scorching heaviness. The sky was white with heat, and the buildings of UNHQ looked harsh and edgy under the suns.

From beyond the far perimeter of UNHQ, where the tachyon field buzzed against the sky, a low rumble started. The rumble grew louder, echoing in Pravin's mind until it trembled in his core.

From out of the xenofields to the east of the base rose a dark cloud, an organic shadow that pushed up into the sky and then rolled toward the base like a vast stormcloud. As Pravin watched it continued to grow, a pillar of darkness rising and then spreading across the sky, a vast stain that blotted out the burning suns.

Pravin stumbled forward, knocking a crystal glass to the carpeted floor. His head buzzed with fury, as if a quantum drill had been placed on his forehead and turned on high speed, splitting his frontal lobe.

He heard the sound of crashing chairs as the vast shadow rolled across the window, chilling the air by several degrees. He felt something hit his eyes like slivers of hot glass.

He screamed. He knew he screamed, he could feel it, but he only heard the terrible piercing whine in his skull. It grew, louder and louder, driving spikes of pain into his forehead, his ears, his throat, his chest . . .

And then it was muffled in an instant, as if a mouth was covered by a thick hand.

He stood up, his hands shaking. Arthur and Blanca were climbing to their feet, their eyes wet with tears of pain. Outside the windows the cloud covered the entire city. On looking closer Pravin could see millions of tiny flying creatures, the same mottled colors as the mindworms.

"Locusts of Chiron," he said. They covered the sky like a plague. "The command center must have cranked up the tach field to protect us."

"We need some help here," said Blanca. Pravin looked over to see Beth still on the floor, her face scrunched in pain, gripping her head. Pravin hurried over to her, summoning medical help.

Outside, the clouds of locusts rolled on.

Zakharov, sitting on the observation deck by the Star Scope, received an alert from Daniel by quicklink. "What is it?"

"Solar flares, Academician, as we feared. The orbitals are offline. But that's not all. There are reports of native life activity."

It was then that Zakharov became aware of the humming that vibrated in the back of his skull. Here, in the mountains, they were relatively isolated from native life forms, mindworms and xenofungus and their ilk, the fascinating but detestable creatures that fed on the bedrock of the human mind. So it took him a moment to place the dull hum, which now rose in pitch.

It's inside my mind. He dropped his glass and hurried toward the door as the hum became a shriek, a hurricane scrambling his consciousness. He fell to one knee, his heart pounding in his chest, and he felt a warm trickle of urine on his inner thigh.

It's all just a physical process . . .

He turned his head in time to see something, a tidal wave of darkness rolling from the south, where the nearest patch of xenofields lay. What came toward him filled the horizon, filled his world . . . a cloud of native life, ready to devour him.

He clutched his head, resisting the sudden urge to claw through his eyes. *The tachyon field. The field will save us.*

He crawled forward and managed to fall through the metal door. The effect of the locusts seemed instantly lessened as if a damp towel had covered his face. By the time two guards had reached him he was composed, only the pale white of his face an indicator that he had been swept up in the locusts' cries.

"Are you all right, Academician?" Both guards looked shaken, young men with their weapons drawn against an unseen threat.

"Yes," he said, trying to calm himself as they helped him to his feet. His whole body felt clammy. "Did anything breach the fields?"

"We cranked it up to eleven, sir. It's keeping out the psi attacks." The guard stared at him. "I think we should get you medical help, Academician."

"Nonsense. I'm all right." But he took a moment to collect himself, and then he found himself slumping down against the wall. He tried to speak again, but his lips felt frozen, his skin covered in a clammy sweat.

What he had felt, when the locusts had first swarmed, was his own death, reaching out for him, ready to snuff the life from his mind.

Templars on watch saw the cloud of locusts boiling up to the west and sounded the alert in New Jerusalem. Although the base was in the center of the Great Dunes, and far from any xenofungus, the watchers on the base periphery could see the massive dark cloud hanging over the settlements.

Kola hurried up narrow, winding stone steps to the highest tower of the church, Kathryn with him. They stood in the narrow, round room and stared through vertical slits at the gathering cloud. It was as if the dust of a million marching feet was stirred up and cast into the sky.

"Almighty," said Kola. "What is this, Sister?"

"Locusts of Chiron," said Kathryn. She swallowed, her Empath nature trembling at the sight of the storm. "It's a form of native life. But I've never seen so many."

"How do we defend against them?"

"We gather inside the tach field. And we pray."

Kola looked at her, his brow wrinkling. Suddenly a message beeped on his quicklink, and he checked it. "Something is happening to the Ideal."

They hurried down through the church and to the Penitence Square next to the church. The square was hemmed in by tall buildings on each side, so that high stone walls choked the narrow square. About a dozen people were spread-eagled on large stone slabs, their arms, legs and necks held in place by thick stone brackets, and angled so that they stared at an iron cross towering against one wall.

Two Templars stood near one prisoner, about an arm's length away, staring down at him. As they drew closer they saw Adam, the Ideal, bracketed into place on the stone. He was a rod of tension, every muscle on his body standing out in stark relief, straining against his bonds. His face was flushed red, the veins on his neck and on his forehead standing out, his mouth open and eyes protruding. Kathryn was alarmed to see that his corneas had turned a blood red, and a foamy saliva dribbled from the corner of his mouth. His whole body trembled.

"He's hot," said one Templar, nodding to them.

"What do you mean?" asked Kathryn.

"His body."

As Kathryn approached, she could feel it. His skin gave off a sweaty heat that reminded her of the desert air.

"This is odd," said Kola. "Zakharov should have made him perfect for this world. Why would a native life attack disable him?"

"Perhaps it's a combination of factors. He's been out here for eight days." She looked at him, his eyes wide and bloody red, staring vacantly in the direction of the cross.

"Should we give him medical help?"

"He's an Ideal. He'll heal himself." She stared at him, thoughtfully, then turned to the Templars. "Keep watching him. When he calms down, take him to one of the Holy baths. Bathe him, cool him down. Then put him back out here."

"Yes, Sister." They moved toward him as Kathryn turned away.

Three days later

The locusts still covered the settlement lands. People stayed in the bases, protected by enhanced tachyon fields, and little by little became used to the buzzing in their minds, so that some could venture out.

Morgan counted his energy credits as the settlement bases burned power to maintain their fields.

Zakharov plotted another attack, unable to launch air strikes with his satellites down and the locusts choking the sky. He had already lost one pilot, who had gone down screaming, driving his needlejet into the red earth below.

In the Believer lands the locusts dispersed and returned, in rhythms only they knew. Time passed without Miriam's body being found, and the Templars and priests gathered, their faces shadowed by the power vacuum yawning between them.

On the third day, as another boil rolled in, two men continued to dig where Miriam lay buried beneath the darkening skies even as the other engineers fled.

"We got to go. We got to get out now," the first man, Greggor, called to his friend Lukas.

Lukas kneeled and dug, the gray dust covering his clothes and powdering his long hair. A sheen of sweat covered his face, and his eyes rolled to the sky.

"No! Keep on, Greggor. We pray. We're close."

The rock and rubble lay piled around them. They had cleared out a dark cavity, their instincts pulling them deeper into the heart of the rockslide, and they had already found the twisted remains of the rover.

"Can't take it." Greggor stood up, his body trembling. He clutched his head as if to hold it together, as if a screamsaw were cutting through his very skull.

Lukas looked up, refusing to hold his head, tears collecting in his eyes. The sky had turned the purplish color of a bruise as the locusts blotted the sun, some fluttering down to land around them. "Dig, man!"

Lukas jerked him hard back down into the cool dark cavity they had dug out. Greggor started digging again, throwing aside his shovel and pulling chunks out with his bare hands, until his fingers bled. His digging grew more frantic as the locusts called their shrill cries, like glass shards piercing his skull.

"Go! We dig for her! We dig!" He pulled a rock and another pile of gray pebbles slid down around his feet. He saw a flash of white, and for one moment the locusts' cries faded and the pattering of the stones filled his consciousness.

"Almighty!" he whispered.

Lukas stared, his hands slowly lowering. From the pile of rocks a white hand emerged, small and frail, one limp finger pointing toward the sky.

"It's her."

The news traveled throughout the packed base like summer lightning. Believers hurried from nearby to the spot where Lukas and Greggor pulled away the rocks, unburying Sister Miriam. They uncovered her arm and shoulder, moving the debris quickly but with loving care. They shouted when they saw the first strands of her white hair, and then her face, which emerged from the rocks like a moon from behind a dark cloud.

The entire base seemed to hold its breath. The dark cloud high above them registered as only a distant annoyance. As Lukas and Greggor lifted the rocks, and uncovered Miriam's body, their hearts rose in their throats as they watched her.

Her face was dirty, her eyes shut. "Sister, are you all right?" asked Lukas.

A long moment passed, and then the green eyes opened.

"I am," she croaked, and the news roared through New Jerusalem.

Believer medics pulled Sister Miriam from the rockpile and laid her out on the ground. Crowds of the faithful pressed in around her, while Lukas and Greggor tried to shield her, to give her air.

Four Templars carried her, the fragile figure in white, back to New Jerusalem and toward the church. As they hurried hymns and prayers rippled out from them, as the news spread—Sister Miriam was alive. The voices of the Believers lifted in harmony, rolling down the narrow streets. Finally, at the door to the church, she reached up and clutched a Templar's sleeve.

"Stop," she whispered. They stopped and waited. She closed her eyes and listened for a moment, to the hymn that pushed away the locusts' song. When she opened her eyes, the locusts that shrouded New Jerusalem from the sun whirled above her, gaps in the cloud allowing the hot rays through.

"Why did we wait so long?" she asked with wonder.

They took her inside the church, where she rested, and Leta tended to her wounds and told her about the attack and the locusts. Then she lay down and slept for a long time, while her faithful maintained their vigil on the streets outside.

The next morning

We prayed for you, Sister.

The hands clutched at her from the darkness, and she reached out to them, letting her fingers ripple across the thousand grasping hands. But her mind was somewhere else.

She touched her head again, feeling the shape of her skull beneath her fine white hair, where a new light burned the doubt from inside of her. Her heart started pounding.

Had God seen fit to release her, to extend her time in this world?

She awoke in blinding pain, the room around her filled with a piercing light. A high-pitched song drove needles into her ears, and she could feel a cold, clammy sweat all over her body.

She turned over, her heart pounding. The great cross above her bed loomed, a pale shadow on the blinding white wall. Sparks jumped in her vision, and she could feel water leaking from her eyes, unbidden, as if her body were squeezing agony from her skull.

"Light," she muttered, her breath coming in short gasps. She clutched the edge of the bed and stared at the cross, her only focal point in this sea of agony.

And finally, after long moments, the pain faded, and her room began to take shape from the white cloud around her. It took her several more long moments to realize that she still cried, the tears leaking from her eyes and running down her cheeks.

Three days, with nothing but her prayers and her faith to sustain her. But perhaps it had delivered her. She blinked the tears from her eyes and finally stood, crossing to the stone basin. In the still water she could see the hazy shadow of the settlements, mapped from afar, the leaders tracing political boundaries across the face of the world.

She touched the water, and it rippled, disrupting her vision.

"Leta!" she shouted, still staring at the water. A moment later the door opened and Leta entered, clutching her gray habit around her.

"Good morning, Sister. Should you be up so soon?"

"Yes," said Miriam. "There's much to do. I will take a bath, to wash the last of the grit from my skin, and then I'll meet with the high priests."

"Yes, Sister. Where will you meet with them?"

Miriam touched her face, and then touched the back of her head, feeling her fine, soft hair. It was not so long ago she had lain buried, a result of Zakharov's vicious attack, and she still felt that pain and anger.

"The war room. I believe it's time."

Miriam's bathing chamber was made of cool, plain stone. A small window set with a simple pattern of stained glass let a shaft of colored light slip down from high on the wall. One entire wall was dominated by a huge unadorned cross, and at the foot of the cross was a stone pool filled with water. The water was blessed but not heated.

Miriam entered, followed by Leta, who closed the thick wooden door to the room. Miriam stepped to one end of the bathing pool and undressed. She stepped into the pool, the shock of the cold water making her catch her breath.

Down into the pool she sank, her head turning up almost involuntarily at the intensity of the cold water. The cross loomed above her; it was as if she were a small child, staring at the face of a mountain. The shaft of dim colored light touched her skin and the surface of the water.

"Behold, I show you a mystery; We shall not all sleep, but we shall all be changed," Miriam murmured.

"Pardon me, Sister?"

Miriam smiled. "Nothing, Leta. Please be thorough today. This will be the last time."

"Ahmin, Sister."

Leta entered the pool, still wearing her simple habit, which floated around her. She began to scrub Miriam, using a harsh, crude sponge, some kind of hardened fungal bloom. She scrubbed Miriam all over, meticulously and hard, until tiny dots of blood stood out on her skin. Then Miriam let her head fall back, and Leta produced a silver blade that she used to cut the soft white hair. Miriam closed her eyes, feeling the cold razor rake her skull.

Once done, Miriam lifted her head and let out a sudden wail, a harsh, keening cry that seemed to come from the bottom of her soul and echo off the tiles.

Miriam turned and emerged from the pool, a step at a time. Her body felt electric, like a live wire with the cross behind her and water running from her skin.

"Bring me my purest white robe," said Miriam, "the one I wear under my ceremonial habit. Nothing more." Leta hurried to get the robe from a wooden cabinet, then helped Miriam dress herself.

"I'm going to the war room, Leta. I won't be needing this bath again."

"Yes, Sister."

Miriam watched Leta hurry for the door, and a part of her felt a wave of sympathy for the small and powerless, who would surely be crushed in the coming conflict.

She reached into her soul, seeking out that sliver of doubt that had plagued her, but it was gone, banished from even the darkest places inside her. What she felt instead was a steely anger at the senseless deaths of her people, and a growing fury at Zakharov and Morgan and all of the other leaders who had massed their strengths against her.

She touched her skull, bare now, shorn of its softness. Then she opened the door and walked out, heading for the war room.

The war room was a large stone room inside the church, with a high arched ceiling and elaborate tapestries hanging along the walls, depicting crucial moments of the journey from Earth to Chiron. A long wooden table dominated the center of the room, ringed by high-backed chairs.

Miriam's priests and advisors waited for her, all in their ceremonial robes, all standing by their chairs. Kola was there, and Pastor Prana and Kathryn and a few others who held her deepest trust, all shifting uneasily. A large, heavy touchpanel rested on the table. Miriam entered, walked to the head of the table and then spoke without fanfare.

"Things have changed," she said. "The hand of the settlements has dealt us the first of many blows. Chiron has moved against us, with these locusts boiling up from the ground to break our spirits, and men without souls walk from the labs of the University and through our gates. But the Almighty has given me a vision, and a way out of the darkness. So let me tell you what I saw those three days buried beneath the rubble.

The priests stared at her. In one corner of the room Leta had produced a small camlink and was recording Miriam's words, for entry into the New Conclave documents.

"We came to this land from the sky," said Miriam, and she pointed to a tapestry that showed a burning light, like a star, descending from the sky toward a desert on Chiron. "There was no rhyme or reason to this; it was only God's will. He cast us into this desert, into this most barren part of Chiron, and later we learned that other humans survived, and then thrived, and now drown themselves in material decadence."

"Ahmin," said two voices around the table.

"But our suffering made us strong." She began to pace, looking to each of them, her green eyes starting to sparkle with the rhythm of her speech. "God gave us only dust beneath our feet, and we fed ourselves with her word. God gave us two suns to burn our skin, but we pulled forth metal and stone and we built him a church. God gave us eyes to see, and when we looked we saw others, living in luxury, but we did not envy them, because we had the Almighty."

She pointed again to the tapestries, which depicted some of these events in elaborate, stylized detail.

"But now we have no food, and the people starve, and many voices are silenced. And we have stolen weapons from the unbelievers, but they make new weapons, and now they make people. *They make people*, to cast us down from Heaven. Though we have nothing, they move against us, and when we take from them they grow angry, as if *they* are the righteous."

"Ahmin." The voices were rising, and Miriam hushed them. She stopped and stared at one tapestry, one that depicted herself, her young self, leading blinded figures forth from a metal shell.

"I lay in that dark, cold stone for three days. Time stretched into an endless dullness, and I thought I might go mad. I prayed, and prayed again, repeating my words to the Almighty, waiting for her to bring me home.

"And then, after I repeated the prayer nine thousand times, and then nine times nine thousand, I felt the warmth of the two suns through the stone, and a light came down to embrace me, and before you pulled me forth I saw a vision. And the vision was this:

"The Tree of Knowledge. The Tree of Life. The Flaming Sword. When we possess these things, we will control the settlements, and we will never fear our enemies again."

"Ahmin," said the gathered, but Kola quickly cut in.

"What does this mean, Sister? These objects are from the Conclave Bible, but what is their meaning here?"

She gestured to the table, where the map laid out the settlement territories. "Academician Prokhor Zakharov holds the wisdom of the settlements in his datalink networks. If any holds the Tree of Knowledge, it's him, and he lies directly to our west.

"To our northwest lies the territories of the decadent Morganites. We have word from the faithful that they have created a powerful technology, codenamed Clinical Immortality, and this I believe is the Tree of Life. So we will move on the Morganites."

"This will be difficult," said Van Roken, her most cautious priest. He had gone pale, but the others ignored him.

"As for the Flaming Sword, the Almighty has not yet shown me where that lies."

"The Spartans are the most powerful warriors on Chiron," said Kathryn. "They must hold the Sword."

"Perhaps," said Miriam, appearing unconvinced, and unconcerned.

Kola spoke again. "Our warriors are full of strength and fire, Sister, but the settlements have weapons and defenses we have scarcely dreamed of. We must approach this carefully."

"Carefully? No. The time for carefully has passed." She pointed to the map. "Our assets are total faith, committed action, and the will of the world itself. While the locusts swarm, no air attacks can be launched against us. So we must move quickly. Observe:

"First we will take these two bases across the sea, one Morganite, one University. They won't suspect us. We'll ambush them and take their weapons, their vehicles, their ships, and bring them back to the Central Continent. From there we will join them with the faithful, every man, woman and child who can walk or carry a weapon.

"We'll strike deep into the heart of Morganite territory, taking the nearest large base, which is Morgan Solarfex, and then on to Morgan Industries, the capital. From there we'll take the Tree of Life, and then move here to Academy Park for the Tree of Knowledge. If we can do this before the locusts lift, we will destroy Zakharov's air power and be able to move against Santiago."

She looked at them. "We must move quickly. Assemble the Templars, assemble the faithful, and prepare to move. This is a crusade of vengeance, but also of survival. If we fail, our way of life is not long for this world."

The High Priests dispersed slowly, murmuring among themselves. Kola approached Miriam, who now sat at the head of the table, staring up at the tapestries on the wall.

"I must speak with you, Sister," he said.

She smiled at him. "Yes, Kola? Will the Templars be prepared?"

"We're always prepared to die for the cause, Sister. But I fear that's exactly what we'll be doing. I find this attack ill-advised."

"It will work, Kola. Have you no faith?"

He stared at her, wrestling with the question. Finally he let out a long breath. "I'm a warrior of the Almighty, but I'm a tactician as well. Morgan and

Zakharov have chaos guns, and quantum guns, and tachyon fields."

"And we have our faith, and those who follow us. And we have my vision." She touched his hand, and then stood up. "And since I will be leaving the Planetary Council, we have one more thing as well. Follow me."

They went beneath the church, down stone stairs and into the cool lower levels. The halls were as wide as any above, wider than the living spaces of most of the Believer citizens.

"It's peaceful down here," said Kola, enjoying the cool air under his thick robes and armor. Miriam didn't answer.

She passed through a gate, then down another set of narrower stairs and into increasing dark, crypt-like spaces. Finally she came to a metal door decorated with relief sculptures of the archangel Michael casting Lucifer down from the gates of Heaven. She pulled out a metal key and opened the door.

Beyond lay a long, arched room, with a raised platform at the end. On the platform sat an ark, engraved with images in gold, silver, and synthium, which glistened under the dim light in the room. The walls were decorated with mosaics in stylized form, meticulously detailed.

"Images of Armageddon," said Kola, and nodded.

Miriam closed the door and walked forward to the ark, and motioned him up next to her. She bowed her head, and he followed her lead. Then she reached forth and opened the lid of the ark.

Kola stared, along with Miriam. The ark was lined with silken cloth, and full of a number of strange globes, their surface rubbery, that seemed to shift with an imperceptible malevolence.

"Nerve gas pods," said Miriam. "The Council considers this an atrocity, a crime against humanity."

"But you said the Council means to destroy us," said Kola.

Miriam nodded. "If we wait, they will destroy us, now or in the next thousand years. These pods will clear our path into the first settlement bases. From there, we will bring their weapons across the sea to this shore, and launch our attack against the heart of the human settlements."

Kola nodded, as the cold eyes of the archangels on the murals around them looked on.

chapter five

On the Eastern Shore

THE MORGANITE ROVER CHURNED AGAINST THE TENDRILS OF fungus. Inside, the driver, Gerka, kept touching the pale blue band around his forehead; he was Level Three certified to resist the native life's psyche attacks, and he had completed the most advanced training available to a non-Gaian, but out here . . .

It was tough. The fungus rolled on for hillside after hillside, turning the horizon crimson. And the more Gerka looked at it the more he remembered that it kept rolling on for hundreds of kilometers beyond that, centering on the strange rock formation that some called the Heart of Chiron.

At least some Gaian fung-huggers called it that. He called it the Ass of Planet.

"Almost there," he said, more to cut his own tension than to engage his copilot, who sat there as silently as ever. Gerka glanced at him; the man, named Kras, was a new transfer from some other shithole Morganite base. He was tall and tough-looking, his face lean and tanned, but conversation

was not his strong point. Gerka had barely heard
him speak three words, and joking or carrying on
remained nonexistent.

It just seemed so damn un-Morganite of him.

"Hey, could you keep it down?" said Gerka after a
long, empty moment. "You're scaring the mindworms."

"I'm not," he grunted.

"Right. And they don't scare us, either." Gerka
stopped the rover, listening to the engine idle
down. Now he saw a visible trace of tension on
Kras' face, and it gave him a perverse pleasure. "A
little friendly advice here, Kras. You've gotta learn
to cut loose out here. Because if you don't, you'll go
crazy. Look at it out there!" He gestured to the scanners mounted in front of them, which were a wash
of blood red, the xenofungus stretching on forever.

"Let's get back to base," said Kras. He stared
straight ahead.

"Three, four, five words!" Gerka counted on his
fingertips. "That's the spirit!" He kicked the rover
back up to speed, talking all the while.

"Now listen, have you played Night Shift in the
holoworlds? *That* shit scares me. I have this Adult
Adaptor pack . . . jack that in and you've got naked,
and I mean dripping naked, vampire succubi chas-
ing you down the streets."

He chuckled to himself, but Kras seemed to have
retreated to a dark place. A moment later he
pointed ahead. "There."

Over the next hill of fungus they could see a
cleared patch, and past that the crackling tachyon
field surrounding the tiny Morganite colony. But
even a tiny Morganite colony was full of well-

stocked and ultramodern bubbletents, with food, wine, gaming tents, and holoworlds. He was trembling at the thought of another round of Night Shift. Made one forget the fungus.

He had almost forgotten their cargo, when the checkpoint guard came out to talk to them. "I heard you guys found a Unity pod."

"Oh yeah!" Gerka gestured back with a thumb. "Right there in the back."

"I don't believe it." The guard craned his neck to see through the small window into the cargo bay. "I thought those were all found. It's been a hundred years or more—"

"Buried in the fungus!" Gerka gestured to his comrade, who made no sound. "He saw it, and we dug it out. It's all burned black, and made of the old metals."

The guard just grunted, but Gerka could see he was intrigued. "Maybe I'll stop by and check it out later."

"Let's go," said Kras. Gerka and the guard trailed off, staring at the humorless man.

Gerka shrugged. "The guy's got to lighten up." He gestured straight ahead with a flourish. The guard nodded and the tachyon field deactivated between two posts.

The rover, carrying its new cargo, cruised inside the base known as Morgan Shores.

"You've got to admit he's a worker," said Gerka, taking a break with two of his friends as Kras, taller than most of them by six inches, helped three others pull the Unity pod out of the cargo hold.

Gerka held a small drink in a pale blue glass, with

a tiny umbrella. Actually the umbrella was projected from a holo unit in the glass, which made it even cooler. He drank and watched Kras surreptitiously, waiting for him to finish unloading before he went off break again.

Finally the pod came out in a rush. It was a sheath of jagged metal about the size of a small car, burned from reentry, replete with jagged connectors that had once held it onto the *Unity.* In the center of the connectors was a reinforced box of metal, and inside that, Gerka knew, would be potentially valuable datalinks from the starship that had carried humanity from Earth.

"Ten credits says that it's all just some news feeds, or some worthless tech," said the guard, who had wandered in from the front gate.

"Yeah!" Gerka fiddled with his hologlass, and suddenly it wasn't just an umbrella there, but an umbrella above a tiny beach, with tiny Gaian girls lying in the sun or playing in the water. He grinned, looking at the detailed scene.

And looking past the scene, he saw Kras, doubled over near one jagged connector from the Unity pod. Gerka watched as Kras stood up, clutching his belly, a thin trail of blood running down. Kras hurried for the door, waving off the other workers, and passed right by Gerka on his way out.

"Are you all right?"

Kras didn't answer. He just kept walking, doubled over, and no one saw what he carried.

Any modern base, Morganite or other, had a sophisticated ventilation system to feed oxygen-balanced air into the pressure domes that protected the bases from Chiron's not-quite-hospitable environment. And any modern base had several such systems, including backups.

But in a small colony outpost like Morgan Shores, the system wasn't designed to protect from sabotage.

At night, the location, with waves of fungus rolling to the horizons, made the pleasure-seeking Morganites exceedingly tense. And they blew off that tension not by staying in their small but well-appointed quarters, but rather by flocking to the main streets, the shops and recreation commons, to blow off steam. The center of Morgan Shores was jammed with these throngs, carrying elaborate drinks, watching giant vidscreens mounted on walls of the low buildings, jamming the doorways to the pleasure quarters, hologames, and other diversions.

Kras hardly ever came to the commons, just enough times so he wasn't branded a complete outcast. But tonight he did come. He wore a long coat that looked somewhat awkward on him, and he held, oddly, a cane. But on the stroll where men and women could be seen in everything from silk suits to feathers to only luminescent paint, he didn't really stand out.

He wound his way to the center of the commons, which was about a hundred meters long and lined with low bubbletents and buildings. The chattering of the crowd was loud enough to echo strangely off the spongy fabric of the pressure dome high above. A painted woman slid past him.

He thought back to an hour earlier, when he kneeled in his small room, thumbing his tiny touchBible, seeking solace in its pages as the black, malevolent bubble gleamed on the bed in front of him. He brought back to mind the chants of his fellow warriors, thousands of them in unison, and he imagined that the chatter echoing off the pressure dome was those chants, and not the chaos of shouts and laughter he heard now.

He looked at the pressure dome as he came to the central fountain, which was a stone statue of Director Morgan himself, dressed in fine robes, but reaching into those robes and peeing a stream of water that arced almost as high as his head. It was the colony governor's idea of a joke, and from all accounts Director Morgan loved it, and had ordered a copy for his own quarters back home.

Back home.

The fools of this base had let him carry a nerve gas pod right in, planted in the Unity pod that Miriam had preserved for just such an occasion. Now he dropped that pod from inside his coat, and glanced down to see it land, inert, at his feet.

He looked up at the pressure dome, and at the sky beyond, the stars and great Pholus. He sent a prayer to his brother warriors, for many would be joining him soon, he imagined, on the other side.

This stuff will hurt. It doesn't stop for gas masks, or filters, or stone, or metal. It only kills. That had been Kola's message to him earlier in the week.

He took his staff, lifted it up. A blond woman stopped in mid laugh to glance at him, her mouth open. He brought the staff down, and punctured the dark balloon.

One instant of burning pain ended his time in this world, and began his time in the next.

* * *

Zakharov's Marine Institute was a spindly research base constructed at the edge of a great freshwater lake, inexplicably formed at the bottom of the mostly unsettled Eastern Continent. The lake was far from the other colonies, including the ragged Believer bases near the shores to the north. It was also blessed by a safe distance from the locusts, which swarmed in the thick xenofields that choked the northern end of the continent.

It had once occurred to Isaac that Miriam should find the existence of a freshwater lake on Chiron an awe-inspiring kind of thing, perhaps even evidence of God's will, and the waters blessed and Holy. Isaac was joking, of course, but he had never understood Miriam's utter close-mindedness to the wonders of Chiron.

"Like the ruins, and the xenofields," said Isaac, drinking with Zakharov on the grid-laced metal platform atop the University Base. "How could she sit in her churches, preaching of God's will in the Universe, and not wonder if these strange rocky formations, dead center in a sea of living, mind-twisting crimson fungus, are evidence of the very mysteries she purports to study?"

Zakharov shrugged. "Perhaps she's just too narrow-minded, and seeks her answers in ancient philosophy."

"But people fall for it. She builds her world around an ancient set of values, and they follow her. Perhaps the need for a larger force is hardwired into us, and she understands that better than anyone."

"She doesn't understand anything. She's probably just afraid." Zakharov threw back a shot of expensive vodka, delivered by Morgan Vodkatonics. Why did they get everything, at least all the good stuff, from Morgan? Why didn't Zakharov just go to visit Deirdre Skye himself, and acquire the good vodka in simple glass bottles, rather than Morgan's holo-covered affairs?

"I think she's convinced herself she doesn't need to understand. To open the door any farther tha that . . ." Isaac lapsed off and stared into the sky. seemed to generally want to understand Miria while Zakharov felt her beneath his contempt. He opened his mouth to say so, but Isaac had lapsed into sleep, his portly frame sinking into his metal chair.

Zakharov took another drink and stared into t' sky, counting stars and classifying them.

Unlike Miriam, Zakharov did want to understand the world, and so had built the small colony outpost next to Freshwater Lake. It didn't take long t find the peculiar solidified patch of fungus throughwhich rainwater flowed, acting as a natural filter that purified that water. After that the station served as a general research facility, but also as a cation spot for burned-out University researchers There were recreation commons set up along thshore, and warm beaches of every variety catered to the often brittle tastes of University Talents in nee of stress release.

It was into this environment that the second nerve gas pod was released, at just the same time the pod was released in Morgan's base to the north. The invisible gas spread out from the punctured sac in a silent, deadly wave. The Believer agent died

first, collapsing instantly with a gout of blood staining the front of her shirt. Around her in the commons young, happy Talents in light clothing fell,
most with not even the time to scream. Windows
shattered from bodies that spasmed as they died,
and others in the base turned and stared vacantly
down the street as a wave of toppling bodies rolled
in their direction.

The devastation was almost instantaneous. Anyone outside, or anyone within a building that had
the slightest opening, was dead in seconds. Even far
away, down the beaches that were still within the
pressure domes, it took only five minutes for
bathers, bronzed and nude under the sun and with
their eyes closed, to spasm, vomit, and die without
opening their eyes. Swimmers sank without a trace,
and no one was left to pull their bodies from the
bottom of that clear lake.

Simultaneously, Believer warriors, hidden in
great pockets in the hills out of sensor range of either of the bases, surged forward to overrun the
damaged bases before any reinforcements could be
sent. Stolen and out-of-date rovers roared across
the surface of Chiron, each one packed with lean,
fanatical Believers, so that barely a square cen-
timeter of space remained. Behind this advance
wave came hordes of Believers on the ground,
moving in a jittery line north and south toward
the targets.

They reached the Morganite base first, and as
they arrived a second agent, sequestered deep inside
the base and wrapped in an airtight blanket with a
tiny oxygen supply, made her way through to the

gate guard post. She used explosive charges to get inside the smallish guard post, and there she shut down the tachyon field.

The first Believer hovertanks with their pock-marked, dented shells arrived, and out poured an impossible number of the faithful, pulling penetrator rifles from a storage locker on the side of the tank. They entered the city, wearing unwieldy gas masks, and walked down the streets.

Some still lived at that point, the Morganites sequestered in sealed buildings or underground facilities, who worked frantically to contact the Morganite headquarters. But within hours, every one of them was dead, and bodies were carried out and piled in the central square, where the tall statue of Director Morgan stood.

Templar Trayne, who coordinated the attack, stood in the center square and watched the Believers hauling bodies, their backs bent under the weight of dead Morganites.

"Pure, crystallized decadence," he said, shaking his head. On the Morganlink screens overhead, suggestive video clips played to pounding music, while his warriors carried half-naked partygoers down the street and out to the gate. The Believer War Chant had started simultaneously, and everyone now joined their voices to it.

A Believer carried a young woman and man with silver glitter in their hair, wearing only a kind of shimmering paint and tiny scraps of fabric. He averted his eyes; their faces looked blue and cold in death.

"Destroy that," Trayne said, motioning a tough-looking faithful to the vidscreen. "Get a task force and round up everything . . . drugs, pornography, access to the links. We must destroy any form of temptation."

"What about weapons, and ignition keys to the rovers and gunships?"

"Gather those in this tall building near the docks and load them up. We'll certainly need those."

"We don't have much time." Miriam's voice was almost a whisper over the quicklink. "What weapons and vehicles did you acquire?"

Trayne nodded. "Twenty Recon Batteries, three Chaos Tanks, a lot of Q-guns and Gatling lasers, more than we could have hoped. The mindworms and the small Gaian colony nearby made them paranoid. But we did get a true gift from the Almighty . . . a quantum transport."

"That's what we needed. Morgan and Zakharov will be sending reinforcements quickly. Get your best people, everyone, loaded in those foils and get underway immediately. Leave that base empty, and get back to the main continent with the new weapons. You are to return to this continent, rejoin with the army from New Jerusalem, and take Morgan's Solarfex base."

"What of the Believers left here, in our other bases?"

"Send the foils back for them, as quickly as possible. But Morgan's Solarfex base is the target. Our agents inside the base will help you. Solarfex will be our new base of operations, and I'll join you there."

She made to sign off, but Trayne caught her attention first. "One thing, Sister. There is the matter of this small Gaian base here, not a hundred kilometers away. I wonder if we might send some over to take it." His face, as calm as ever, masked a growing hunger for conquest that Miriam was pleased to see. But not now, not in this way.

"Forget the Gaians. Morgan is our worry now. I'll join you at Solarfex."

She broke the link.

And in that tiny Gaian colony, with crimson fungus pushing in from all sides, a handful of Gaian Empaths gathered at a simple table set in the middle of a lush, dewy garden of hybrid Earth flowering plants. The Empaths, mostly women but with a few men, wore simple green clothing with a yellow cord around their necks, from which dangled the golden rose of their rank.

They sat in silence for the most part, letting emotional currents shift back and forth across the table. There was fear, and concern, and the emotional residue of the deaths of nearly every soul in the Morganite colony.

"Should we flee?" asked Julia, the lead Empath of the group. The words fell like stones into the middle of their quiet circle.

"We're the eyes of the settlements here," said Xenia, the youngest of the Empaths there, but also the most serious. And the tallest, as the modern genetic treatments had blessed her with the build of a willow. "We should stay."

"But the garden variety citizens can go," said Muir. "We can't put them in harm's way here."

Julia nodded. "We'll evacuate them by foil, but we'll stay."

"We have no tachyon field defense," said Muir.

"If the Believers come this way, we will be hard put to hold them off."

"Why would they come here? Conquest lies on the far shore. We will be ignored."

They all nodded in silent agreement, while around them flowers bloomed and lush green plants bathed in the sun, all as beautiful as Eden itself.

Back on the Central Continent, news of the two-pronged attack rippled across the settlements, still buried under the hovering storm. Morgan was the first to hear, sequestered as he was in his quarters inside Morgan Industries, which was still wrapped beneath the dark blanket of the locusts. The alert shook him out of a vapor-induced reverie, and he stared at the damage reports.

"How could this have happened?"

The woman, one of his many advisors, stared back at him from the quicklink. She had beautiful, soft brown skin, and her face was a little odd, her eyes set too far apart. She fell just short of the perfection that the typical Morganite aspired to. "We don't know much. It appears to be a nerve gas attack from inside the base, and then the Believers came out of the hills." She blinked at him.

"Are you sure it wasn't the Gaians?"

"There was no activity from the nearby Gaian base, and it's too small. Besides, the Gaians wouldn't be caught dead in those scruffy brown robes." She suddenly smiled. Morgan felt the vapors still clouding his thinking.

"Send needlejets across the sea immediately."

"It's too risky, Director. The locust cloud is interfering with our air communication. The first pilot that flew steered his jet directly into the ground when he got near a locust cloud."

"Then send foils. Just get them over there and report back." He stared at her eyes, which seemed deeper, browner, and farther apart than ever. He believed her name was Tani, and he vaguely remembered that she was the great-great-granddaughter of a previous advisor of his. That thought filled him with a delicious sense of perversion.

She nodded. "Yes, Director."

"Excellent. And perhaps we can meet later to discuss future plans."

Zakharov learned of the attack on his base and felt the shock go through him like cold water. As he watched the reports of the dead pour in, he could feel his hands shaking. Not since his Theory of Everything had been downgraded to the Theory of *Almost* Everything had he felt this angry.

"They used nerve gas on us!" He was outraged, but the outrage was gradually overtaken by a realization. The use of nerve gas was utterly forbidden by settlement convention and the U.N. Charter. With such an atrocity, it was quite possible that he could wipe her out without guilt. How satisfying and proper that would be, for the last holdout against science, the dead backwater of the anti-intellectual, eliminated by his hand.

"She's sending foils back across to this continent," said Daniel. "We can't launch an air strike or drop troops against her, at least not until the locusts dissipate. But we're massing our ground troops, and it would only take two days to reach New Jerusalem at top speed."

"And where is her horde from New Jerusalem?" He closed his eyes, preferring to lay out the coming battle in his mind; it helped him to see layers of strategy and abstractions that the cold reality of the tac table didn't always highlight.

"We're unsure, Academician. But her foils should touch shore around Port Grace."

Zakharov opened his eyes. "That's closer to Morganite territory than us. And she attacked a Morganite base overseas. Could she be moving on Director Morgan first?"

"That's possible, Academician. Our sensors show no activity on our border."

"But we're her enemy. We attacked her."

"Maybe she considers Morgan the easier target."

Zakharov nodded. "At any rate, this looks like the makings of a full invasion. Given that, I don't think we'll need Council permission to commence our attack." Daniel shifted uneasily. "Assemble the ground forces and await my command."

The Believer hydrofoil stolen from the Morganite base skimmed the water like a seabird. Navigation was by instruments alone; the sea below was a blue blur, the clouds above appearing and receding on the horizon. To each side of the foil stretched a dozen more, each one loaded to the hilt with stolen weapons for the faithful back home.

The ship had been modified by Believer technicians and was now piloted by another Believer specialist, a tall woman who manned the controls with rough hands and piercing eyes. She, and the techs who modified the foils, were Miriam's secret pride; they pored over stolen information and equipment obsessively, rather than spending their time in ritual prayer.

Now the captain watched the nav charts and responded to the signal to decelerate; they were nearing the shore of the Central Continent. Her shields were on full, but scans showed no one awaited them. The settlements were still organizing after the unexpected attack.

So much the better. Whether she died on this rocky shore or on a place far inland mattered little to her; she set aside thoughts of her own death as inconvenient. Life blurred into afterlife as sea into sky.

But the Believers needed these weapons. Of that she was sure.

They touched the shore. Fifteen Templars waited, and behind them a mass of Believers, a dark wall of force, mirroring the dark wall of locusts on the far horizon.

The Believers worked quickly, offloading stolen tanks and rovers, combining them with the fleet of older vehicles they already possessed. The Recon Batteries, now outfitted with nerve gas pods to make them X Recon Batteries, mingled with Believer shock troops and laser tanks. The soldiers boarded transports, forcing themselves into tiny spaces without complaint.

Kola strode out to the shore, where frothy waves hissed on the sand. The foils turned in the deeper surf, ready to head back to the Eastern Continent for more vehicles, but the assembled army was enough.

"Into Morgan territory," he said. "To Morgan Solarfex Base, and may the Almighty be with us."

*   *   *

Morgan's Solarfex base, being one of his more recent, still had that fresh new smell in the clean white hallways, and the metal tables in the mess halls were silver and pristine.

It also had only a Mark II tachyon field installed, and a handful of hovertanks to protect it, thought Hooper as he loped down the hallway. Red lights flashed at intervals, a muted siren rose and fell in the background, and his quicklink spooled with messages, most of which he ignored.

He got the gist. *Invasion.*

Though why Miriam was attacking this base, and not the University bases some thousand kilometers to their south, was beyond him.

The locusts made communication difficult, so it wasn't clear what the enemy force comprised. Apparently there were stolen weapons among the outdated Believer forces? He couldn't get a straight answer. All told, he would rather be in the research labs burning his holo fantasy books into layers of the new experimental crystals he had developed.

He reached a low metal door and stooped his large frame through, then turned and ran down a short, narrow hallway to a ladder. He pulled himself twenty meters to an upper deck that felt a bit claustrophobic. Someone was already there, a guy who wore a generic gray maintenance coverall, and who smelled oddly sour.

"I'm your co-gunner on this deck," the man said, and extended a hand. "Name's Pix. You're Hooper. Looks like we're working together here."

"Where's Riehl?" he asked. She had been his co-gunner on every previous drill.

Pix shrugged. "Reassigned. I think she got expert

marksmanship, got assigned to the upper turrets. Away from the action." He grinned and gestured to the metal hatch that led to the gun emplacement. "You first, Hoops."

Hooper, feeling a little out of sorts, folded his tall frame into the gun deck, which was a cramped, two-level affair. He sat in the top gunner seat and put in the earlink, then attached the sensors that would turn the gun into something close to an extension of his mind and muscles. The chair spun as he acclimated himself, and then he heard the whirring of Pix's gun below.

"We got to work together on this one, Hoops." That was Pix's voice in his earlink. Hooper tensed at the nickname. "I want us having the highest kill ratio on the perimeter, right? 'Cause I want a promotion and transfer to the special tac team."

Great, this guy saw the battle as a way to a pay raise. "Whatever it takes," he said.

"You'll have to do better than that, Hoops! Come on, man, visualize it. Highest kill ratio, highest kill ratio . . ."

Pix discharged a shot. Looking out the rounded synthglass porthole, Hooper saw the quantum bolt, a compact fist of humming force, blast a chunk of the red terrain into rubble. The cloud of red dust rose up against the barren, slightly sloping terrain.

You just lowered our kill ratio, friend.

Still spinning his chair, Hooper surveyed the terrain. As he had already noticed, it was all barren red rock, sloping up outside the base, typical of this area. He could see a few small outpost buildings, and a decent forest seeded from Morganite genetically modified hybrids rather than the good Gaian stock, but the thin gray trees seemed to be growing well. He would try to resist firing in that direction unless necessary.

"Do you know anything?" asked Hooper finally, wondering at the long silence of his comrade. He could hear the servos below whining and stopping, whining and stopping.

"Believers," said Pix. "Hovertanks coming, some stolen from our own base overseas. And beyond that a horde of J-freaks on foot, but we'll take care of—"

"J-freaks?"

"Jesus-freaks. Jesus, the main man in the old Conclave Bible that the Believers follow. A Middle-Eastern miracle worker."

"Ah." Hooper wasn't closed to other ways of thought, but he also found great pleasure in his crystals, and desired little more than getting lost in the beauty of their abstract patterns.

"They're trying an all-out invasion. I hear that they've abandoned New Jerusalem, that they're all coming at us."

"All?"

"All! Anyone who can walk! That's what I heard, anyway."

"Sync up," came the calm voice in Hooper's ear-link. He felt his chair leave his control and spin to a point on the horizon, and he knew that all around the perimeter the other gun chairs were doing the same.

A silence descended, and Hooper felt the hairs on the back of his neck rise. He could hear the breathing of Pix beneath him, echoing in the small metallic gun cell.

There was a light on the horizon, over the hill. And

then there were hovertanks, sleek and silver with the Morganites' own insignia blazing from the front, and columns of white fire pouring from the back.

"What the fuck?" shouted Pix, and he fired his first shot, which sailed under the lead hovertank as it caught air, cresting the hillside at phenomenal speed and sailing as high as the tops of the walls.

The hovertank landed, and more white fire poured from the back. It crossed the plain in two seconds or less, and Hooper felt the gun chair wrench as he tried to track the speeding vehicle.

"H-tanks don't go that fucking fast!" said Pix from below.

"Not stopping. They're not stopping," Hoops said into his link, as calm as he could manage, as a fan gun opened on the top of the hovertank. Small missiles streaked out in every direction, and the tach field crackled as shot after shot struck it, not crude Believer weapons but Morgan's own Q-gun technology. One missile penetrated the tach field and struck the perimeter. Hooper's head whipped sideways from that impact and banged into the metal shell around him. The world shuddered as he waited for the ache to subside.

He blinked, and a hovertank was only meters away, heading directly for the tach field near him. It hit the field and exploded, and he heard the sound of metal twisting and rock shuddering, and a wave of heat went out in every direction.

"They're suicidal! They're goddamn freaks!" Pix was spinning his cannon and firing at the horizon randomly, a stream of curses accompanying his fire.

Over the hill came three more hovertanks.

* * *

Up in the command tower, Commander Riehl felt her shoulders tighten as more reports came in. Three more hovertanks had hit the fields, each one spraying missiles and energy weapons at impact. And as the field flickered, they were able to fire a bevy of missiles into the base, getting closer and closer to the field generators. Fifteen of the thirty manned gun turrets had been destroyed, plus over half of the fifty autoturrets along the wall, and there were now gaping holes in the perimeter.

Her hand drifted down to rest on her round belly, where her child waited in gestation . . . the old way, rather than the artificial wombs that more than half of settlement citizens now used. She chose this way because she felt more in touch with the child and her body, in good ways and bad.

And in this case, her body told her in no uncertain terms that they may want to abandon this base.

Another breach in the perimeter, and a wave of "D and D's:" damage and death reports, lit up her touchscreen.

"They've burned out almost all of the hovertanks they took from the other base," said Riehl, and her co-commander, Gakky, nodded in terse agreement. "But it looks like it might pay off. They're hammering the field generator."

"I'm going to deploy the blink hovertanks to the front," said Gakky. "Without a tachyon field defense we might as well send them out into the field."

"We should send those tanks away," said Riehl suddenly. "We can't let the Believers get them. They'll just use them against the next base, right?"

Gorky locked on to her with an arrogant stare. "They are not going to take this base. They may be willing to kill dozens of their warriors, but our technology is absolutely superior. They have no chance here."

Riehl felt herself bristle at Gorky's tone, and it seemed only to increase her resolve. "I command here. If many more Believers arrive, we could have serious problems." She looked at the feeds, and saw another of the turrets go down, and three more deaths. Plus the approaching horde of Believers was not so far behind. "Prepare to evacuate."

"On what grounds?"

"On the grounds that this is a command decision, and I'm the commander."

"Show me an analysis of this battle that indicates in any form of logic or reason that we should retreat from this attack." She could see a little bead of spittle forming at the corner of Gorky's mouth.

There was no report she could show. An analysis of the odds would never dictate a retreat. But she could see the videofeeds of new high-powered hovertanks that the Believers had slammed into their perimeter, and her instincts told her that these ferocious warriors might soon occupy the very room she stood in.

"Prepare the retreat," she said.

Hoops received the retreat message in his earlink. Below him, in the can, Pix had settled down somewhat and now fired his turret gun calmly at the next wave of attackers, now a few hovertanks (that hung back and fired streak missiles and Q-guns at the perimeter) and a lot of rovers, which skidded toward the walls. So far the rovers hadn't gotten close, but from each one that was hit and not destroyed completely, Believers boiled forth, scattering instantly in every direction.

Even as he watched, Pix hit an old rover that took a tight turn. His distributed Q-blast shredded half the rover to atoms, and the other half flew apart into scraps of fiery metal. But still dark figures, like shiny beetles, struggled to their feet and ran toward the base. One managed to pick up a small missile launcher and fire into one of the other turrets, and Hoops heard two more death tones in his ear.

"The retreat code!" said Hoops. He looked at his quicklink to verify it. "Command has ordered a retreat!"

"We stay," said Pix. "No way I'm leaving."

"We do stay, to cover the retreat," said Hoops. "But why retreat at all? We've taken damage, sure, but they aren't getting close."

"More of them. Ha!" That was a bark of laughter as he fired a disruption blast across the increasingly littered terrain.

"Ours again. Stolen." Hooper swiveled his cannon chair, feeling the servo assist lock on to the closest rover. He tightened his finger on the fire button . . .

. . . and the chair suddenly jerked away, sending his shot wide.

Commander Riehl was monitoring the newest wave of rovers cresting the hill when she heard an angry voice behind her. She turned to see Gorky at a touchpanel, with a security command feed showing. He stared at her with a kind of edgy malevolence, like a scruffy dog that had stolen a bone and awaited a beating.

"What did you say?"

"I've raised Morganite command and showed them the battle stats. They have something to say to you."

Her stomach fell as she looked at the screen. A tough-looking senior official was there, staring at her with his stern demeanor. She hurried over.

He wasted no time. "I've seen the battle stats and conferred with my command staff. Why did you order a retreat, Commander?"

"My personal analysis of what I see on the field, General. As commander, I must use my discretion—"

"And what of the valuable weapons and equipment in the base, Commander?"

"We'll retreat to Morgan Industries, General. It can't fall into enemy hands."

His eyes flared like dark suns. "Exactly!" he almost hissed. "These Believers have embarrassed us once, and they won't take a second base of ours. Now stay and fight. Reinforcements are on the way."

"Yes, sir." Riehl felt numb. "Does Director Morgan support your position? And what about the approaching horde?"

"He supports it, Commander. Now belay the retreat order and get your things in order." He blinked once, and she could see his fury now, just below the surface. "I want you to destroy them all." He broke the link abruptly.

She turned to Gorky, who stared at her with his hands on his hips. "I'll deal with you later."

"Don't like my initiative, Commander? Fine. But you don't run the territory, and don't bother ordering me out of your sight. You need me here."

"Then get on your damn console, Lieutenant. And if we get through this battle you won't see the rec commons until the next double eclipse."

He turned smoothly to his console, but she could still see the smug grin tightening on his lips. A moment later, his voice came back to her, wary. "Another problem."

"What?"

"The rovers stolen from our other base . . . they've figured out how to use our battle transponders. Our guns won't target lock on them."

Another chill rolled down her body as she stared at the screen. Fifteen rovers headed right for the base, as shots flew wide around them.

"Deactivate the transponders remotely, if you can!" Riehl shouted. "How did this happen?"

"They must have reactivated the transponder codes in the rovers," said Gorky, his fingers flying on a touchpanel.

"How long?" She watched as they struck the tach field, one after another. The field weakened and a dozen missiles rocketed into the base, and then a dozen more. As she watched several hit the field generators, consuming them in fire.

The tach field winked out, and the edgy buzz of the locusts overhead tickled the back of her mind.

"They're in," said Gorky.

There was a knock on the door. Miriam, deep in the world of meditative prayer, slowly returned to the real world. She felt like a tiny beacon rising from the ocean depths, and breaking the surface into a world that was real, and solid, but less comforting than the silent world left behind.

Kathryn entered, wearing clean white robes, her hair pulled back and bound with green cords. Her usual warmth was absent, replaced by a cool businesslike demeanor.

"Kola has taken the Morganite Solarfex base, Sister. But we had a lot of casualties, more than we could have anticipated."

"But we have the base." Miriam touched her smooth skull, staring at Kathryn. Kathryn shifted away and nodded. "Agreed, but there are rumblings among the Templars. This attack is unsustainable."

"And what do the people say?"

Kathryn folded her hands lightly in front of her. "They're overjoyed. Those who live can fight again, and those who die go to the Almighty."

"And what does the Almighty say?"

Kathryn paused. Finally she shook her head, her robes rustling. "I don't know, Sister. The Almighty doesn't speak to me as she does to you."

"Ah." Miriam stood up and crossed to Kathryn. She leaned in close, taking Kathryn's arm. "Go to the Templars, and tell them I want Morgan Solarfex base cleaned out. We will use that as a temporary headquarters. I want it blessed, and I want all weapons rounded up. Let everyone left in New Jerusalem go there, and replenish the attack force. Our next target is Morgan Industries."

Kathryn leaned away, her arm slipping out of Miriam's grasp. She turned to face Miriam head on. "That's what I'm trying to tell you, Sister. Morgan Industries is the headquarters base, fortified and surrounded by a full Mark V tachyon field. We can charge with all our faith, and we'll only burn on the field outside."

"You forget the faithful, Kathryn. The faithful are all over, inside and out. A tach field can't hold out an idea. Go and do as I have ordered, and know that Morgan Industries will be ready for us."

"By faith." Kathryn brushed back a stray strand of her dark hair.

"Yes. I'll send out the word. Go tell the Templars that."

Morgan entered the NuSpace for his prearranged meeting with Zakharov. Since he had requested the meeting, he chose the program that created the environment they met in.

As he often did, Morgan ran a modified Teahouse program, so that he appeared in a small, nearly barren room, with only a low wooden table on a tatami floor and simple shoji screens around the wall. After the opulent materialism of his base, it somehow pleased him to meet with the other leaders in such an austere setting.

His projection wore a sleeveless black vest and matching pants. Zakharov appeared, looking like Zakharov. The two men greeted each other, and Zakharov sat on the floor on one side of the table while Morgan floated a little above the tatami on the other.

"What do you need, Director?" asked Zakharov.

Morgan slid open a recessed place on the table and pulled out a clay pot of steaming ocha, green tea, which he poured into delicate ceramic cups for the two of them. On the cups flowers slowly bloomed and decayed, the patterns shifting and merging.

"Miriam has attacked two of my bases, Academician, as you know."

"She didn't just attack them. She overran them." Zakharov gripped his teacup. "But I lost one as well."

"Yes." Morgan nodded, took a long sip of tea, closed his eyes and opened them again. "Delicious. It looks to myself, and Pravin Lal as well, that Miriam means business this time. Of course I can handle her, but I also have Santiago to worry about on the far shore."

"Why don't you just pull off of that shore, Director? Save yourself the aggravation."

"Because I won't." He grimaced. "I want to wrap this up, with both Santiago and Godwinson, so I can get back to the things that matter. Miriam has cost me."

"We lost thousands," said Zakharov. "She's using nerve gas. I want to eliminate her as well. But she's in your territory now."

"Yes. And since you and I both have interests in eliminating Miriam, I would like to trade with you for some of your newest weapons."

"What weapons are those?"

Morgan shrugged. "I heard you have something new. I know you have the best research minds on Chiron. I have the energy credits. It would be to both of our benefits if we could eliminate Godwinson." He considered for a moment, taking a sip of the tea. "Some of your plasma shards, perhaps? I could give you some of the technology that goes into my matter transmitter."

"We already are working on that technology, Director. In fact, I gave you the technology that led to your research."

"You haven't seen it deployed like we're going to deploy it, Academician. I have every scientist in—" He stopped, about to mention a base name. "Every scientist possible working on it."

"Wait."

Zakharov's figure froze in mid gesture, as Zakharov departed the projection program to return to his base and check some fact or figure. Morgan sighed and looked around the small room, then studied Zakharov's frozen figure. He leaned forward and looked at the skin . . . there were hairs and freckles and age spots, and complex wrinkles that wrapped his face.

"Amazing," said Morgan. "I don't know why he goes through the trouble."

"To show off!" said the Zakharov projection, moving again. He stood up and walked over to one of the shoji, still deep in thought. He tore one of the rice paper panels, revealing a black, clear night sky that stretched on in every direction. "I have a new weapon. A gun, powerful enough to destroy Miriam's army without doing much harm to your buildings, as long as she's in a confined space."

"Such as my Solarfex base?"

"Yes." Zakharov turned back at him. "This weapon can wipe out an army while sparing a base. It will damage Morgan Solarfex, but not as badly as a planet buster."

Planet buster. Morgan kept his eyes on the thin green tea in his cup. He remembered the last use of a planet buster, by the Hive against Santiago, some forty years before. It had resulted in absolute destruction, an entire base destroyed, a smoking crater left in the ground.

"If it's that powerful why don't you use it?"

"She's on your land. The gun is powerful, but its range is limited. Besides, she attacked you, and occupies your base. You have the moral high ground."

Morgan looked up. "I suppose that's worth something. What do you want in return, then?"

"I've heard reports that you have rooms in your bases where your most valuable citizens are held in a state of longevity far beyond the Gene Baths I produced. That they can live forever."

Morgan cleared his throat. "That's true. Clinical Immortality. But they can't move, Academician. They are held in stasis, and interface with the world only sporadically. It's kind of . . ." He wrinkled his brow, looking for the right words. "It's kind of sick, really."

"But I have a use for it. Is it a deal?"

Morgan considered, drumming his fingers on the table. "How will we use this gun?"

"I'll lend it to your army. It won't function without a code stream from my base. We'll have to transport by ground, after you send me the Clinical Immortality."

Morgan nodded. "You have a deal."

Zakharov stepped into a coded elevator and performed a flurry of security checks, from retinal scan to fingerprint analysis to DNA testing. The checks complete, the secure elevator rocketed at a rapid pace into the earth, and Zakharov felt his stomach rise. It was a lonely journey in this tiny elevator; it would only carry one person down at a time, deep into the mountain.

When the door opened he went through another security checkpoint, including a robot that watched him with an almost human awareness and a beefy guard that checked his credentials robotically. He finally stepped past the checkpoint and through a thick metal door into the Green Rooms, so called because of the pale green light that illuminated the hallways. These were his most private labs, where only his top people were allowed.

He opened a door labeled with only a yellow circle and stepped inside. The room was empty, but lined with large touchpanels on which figures and interface elements interwove in a complex dance.

On the other side of the room was a thick synth-glass window, and he peered through it. In a sealed cylindrical chamber rested a sleek black base with an odd, cannonlike implement on top, the barrel intertwining crystalline fibers and a deep burnished metal. A deep throbbing permeated the room, thrumming in his chest.

He could almost feel the light being sucked from the world around it and into that dark thing. It was his finest accomplishment to date, a cannon powered by a singularity.

Singularity. An artificial black hole, generated in a stasis field, its awesome power harnessed for human gain. It was the most powerful weapon in the settlements, and no one yet knew about it.

The Sin Gun. Let Yang hide his planet busters in

the ground, and Miriam push her angry horde across the red earth. This weapon would decimate Miriam, or Santiago, or anyone else. He stared at the long barrel, and the stasis field, and felt it drawing the light from his very eyes.

chapter six

PRAVIN SAT IN HIS CHAMBERS IN ONE OF THE TALL, GOLD-domed towers of UNHQ. He had dimmed the light, and music piped through an array of hidden speakers, a new piece by Bolorav, the famous University composer. The notes had a wonderful mathematical symmetry, but were informed with a deep passion. He remembered that Bolorav had loved a Spartan woman, and had pined away when she was killed in a mindworm attack. Yet her death had left the world this legacy.

He lifted a crystal glass from the table next to him and sipped fine xenowine, Deirdre's best. As he drank he caught his own reflection in the shimmering surface of the touchpanel in his lap. His face looked long and narrow, his expression sour.

The conflicts in the settlements lay on him, thick and heavy. He hardened himself to the chaos, knowing that the weakening of Morgan's power could ultimately benefit him, but every death was like a sliver of glass in his skin. Even now the fighting raged, underneath skies choked with the locusts.

Zakharov and Morgan would eject Miriam from their lands, and Pravin could only ask that they be merciful, although he wasn't sure that Miriam deserved such mercy. When the locusts cleared and Council reconvened, she would be arrested and sanctions would be levied against her. She had started this conflict.

He shook his head and tried to clear his mind. He took a sip of warm tea and let the steam rise around his face as he closed his eyes and wished that a certain loved one could be with him again, a buffer against the injuries of the world.

He thought of Miriam, who seemed content to find perfection beyond the world, rather than in it. He thought of his own past, and the most satisfying relationship he had ever experienced. He still reached out to that time, across hundreds of years, and feared sometimes that his mind had created something that was as unreal and ephemeral as Miriam's Heaven.

He took another sip of wine. Modern life, with all of its choices, created more problems than it solved.

A series of tones sounded at the outer door, and he issued the open command. The doors opened down the hallway, and he could see a shadow in the foyer. He stood up and set down his mug, then surreptitiously wiped his palms free of sweat.

The shadowy figure stepped forward into the room, hesitantly. She was a younger woman, about twenty-nine, a little short but with a curvy body that pleased him, as it had so long ago. Long black hair fell down her back, shiny, rich with wavy curls. The soft brown face looked almost as it did so long ago.

She stood there, her hands folded, not speaking. She looked at him once, then looked away. He took a step toward her.

"Pria . . ."

After greeting her, he walked past a divider into a small kitchen area and prepared a mug of tea for her, just like his own. When he walked back out she was sitting on a broad white couch, silhouetted against the window.

She wore a pale white dress, strapless, that showed her shoulders to good effect, a body part that his wife had made full use of as well. The dress fell to knee length, and he noticed her smoothing it constantly. She hadn't turned back to look at him.

He walked out and sat near her, setting her mug on the low table near the couch.

"Thank you," she said quietly.

"Is everything all right? Do you have everything you need?"

She turned to look at him, and the sight of her face, of those soft planes and wide dark eyes, stopped his heart for just a moment. "They give me whatever I ask for."

He nodded. She was looking down at the mug now, but didn't pick it up. "Do you enjoy coming here?" he asked.

She gave a warm half-smile, gracious. "I don't mind it so much. I'm sure there are far worse jobs in the settlements."

He felt as if something had struck him at the base of the spine, sending a wave of dull pain up his back. "You don't have to come if you don't want to."

"Please. I don't mind." She looked at him, searching his face. He remembered words she had shouted at him years ago, when she had been young and rebellious, striking back against the forces that had created her . . . which meant him.

You don't think I know who I am? Who I'm supposed to be? I hear things. I know you had a wife, on Earth, two hundred years ago. So who am I?

But in recent years she had become calmer, quieter. She even requested to meet him sometimes, rather than the other way around.

"You look tired," she said.

"It's been difficult." He gestured outside. "The locusts, the perihelion. Things are getting unstable. It's a constant balancing act between the ideals we founded this world on, and the cold reality of life."

She smiled. "If you close your eyes, the locusts teach you things."

"What?"

"The locusts. If you relax, they fill your mind."

"Like the vapors?" Pria had never taken drugs. Pravin wondered what they were giving this New Pria.

"Try it."

He closed his eyes. The buzzing tickled the back of his brain, and his mind started to fill with sensations, colors that resolved into misty scenes. The image of the woman who sat next to him, and her elegant perfumes, crossed into that misty world with him.

He saw Pria, his first wife. He saw her smile. He saw her stoic, lovely face, and heard her words.

Embrace the world, Pravin. Someone must, and if not you, then who?

He opened his eyes to see her double, eyes closed,

a small half-smile on her face. He could see her drifting into another world. He stood up and walked to the windows, talking to her without looking at her.

"If you want to go, Pria, you can. Anywhere in the world, with anyone you choose. I won't stop you."

He heard her voice float from behind him, and he had the impression that her eyes were still closed. "I don't know what I want, or need. I've lived my life sequestered, watched over, tagged and tailed. Things were never what they seemed for me."

He turned back to look at her. Her eyes were open, and she stared at him.

"You'd better get back," he said finally. "I have to return to the command center."

"Can I stay awhile? I'd like to finish my tea." She hadn't even started it. She looked at him, and he had the impression that she was searching for an answer in his face, something that he held but didn't know it.

Pravin nodded. "Stay here, then. You're welcome to anything I've got. But I'd better get to the command center to make sure everything is all right."

He left the room, glancing back to see her looking after him, empty and silent. Still as a ghost.

Miriam Godwinson walked slowly through the great arched halls of the captured Solarfex base. Her people hurried back and forth through the base, tearing down anything deemed overly "secular" by the pastors in their white robes and tossing them into the massive burn piles located in the central courtyard.

There was a lot of it. Networks full of pornography, all manner of crude material goods, the kinds of things that would distract anyone from the Almighty. It was a firm belief of hers that an ounce of prevention was worth a megaton of cure, so she would make sure that her people would never see these things, and thus never be tempted by the lure of the flesh.

She turned up a sweeping staircase with sleek metal railings that took her to a balcony above the great hall. Her people were tearing huge vidscreens off the walls and driving jagged holes through to the outside. They would quickly smooth these openings and then her finest craftspeople would turn their heat guns on delicate borders of metal and powdered synthglass, filling this hall with lovely stained glass murals.

Then they would lock the Morganite prisoners away, with some food and touchBibles. "Bread and God" as she liked to think of it, although the bread and water would be withheld for two days. Suffering could lead to transcendence, as she herself had learned so well.

"I don't think it will work."

She turned to see Pastor Prana, his small hands folded into clean white robes.

"Why not?"

He shook his head with a jerk. "These Morganite people. They're as far from God as I could imagine. They are fat and furious, as if by taking away their media channels and luxuries we're depriving them of the very air. Morgan's brainwashing has taken too well."

Miriam bit her lip and looked at her people in

their simple robes, smoothing the windows. "If it doesn't work, it doesn't work. But we have to try."

"We'll just have to be careful of a revolution. I suggest smaller sway groups, say half the size, and leaving them bound and gagged. Letting them talk will only keep them in their mass hypnosis."

She nodded. Prana was clever, and he knew people. She would follow his lead. "See to it, Pastor. Almighty."

"Almighty."

Director Morgan sat cross-legged in a large bed, in one of the pleasure hotels that dotted his far-flung recreation bases. Across from him lounged Tani, leaning on one arm. Between them rested a low table on short legs. Two glasses of fresh mango juice and chem-X rested on opposite corners of the square, and a metal burner in the center released vapors into the air.

"Zakharov won't deploy his new weapon until he has the Clinical Immortality. Apparently he needs the technology for some purpose."

"Give it to him." Her voice was like a series of musical notes. She was in every way more elegant and composed than her great-great-grandmother had been. "It will be worth it to get Miriam out of our hair."

He nodded, staring at the polished surface of the table. "A lot of Morganites will die. She has them in that base."

"You ran your spreadsheets. There is no other way. Our ground forces can't get near Solarfex with those Believers in the hills around it. It would take a Santiago army to get through."

He looked at her. "Perhaps we've spent too much time expanding and too little money on our army."

"If we have, we have. There's nothing to be done about it now. We're getting Zakharov's weapon, and we're expanding on Hive Continent. Miriam is just an annoyance. Solarfex was running in the red anyway." She reached over and took a sip of mango juice. He grinned and moved toward her, twisting sheets around them. She embraced him fully, which sealed their plans.

Later that evening, Director Morgan sat at a table laboriously crafted from a rare Gaian tiger which had then been coated in a solid glassine substance, freezing the living beast forever. What pleased Morgan most about this particular piece was that he had purchased it from a desperate Gaian merchant; Deirdre never would have allowed such a blasphemy if she had known.

But right now the cool touch of the table didn't do much for him. He threw back a shot of brandy, trying to sense its heat in his bones, but he could feel nothing of the sort.

He looked back to his bed, where Tani lay. He couldn't remember when he had last spoken informally to his other advisors, but now Tani was his go-between. He enjoyed mixing business with pleasure, and the cycle of discussion, eating, decision making, and lovemaking had its advantages.

But now he just felt tired again.

He tapped his fingers on the table and thought about Zakharov's transport, waiting in his cargo bay. He would have to load it up with the Clinical Immortality specimens soon. He shuddered.

Now was as good a time as any for a final visit. . . .

He left the bedroom, with Tani sleeping there, and went through hallways lit by elaborate metal sconces to a terrace. He paused there to look over the glittering towers of his Morgan Industries, the lights gleaming from everywhere, citizens moving about even at this late hour, intent on drinking in everything Chiron had to offer, even under the roiling skies. He could feel the pulse of their energy, their sexuality, their relentless pounding against the walls of time, boredom and fate.

If only Miriam could see this. This is what it means to be human.

At the periphery of his great city the tall capacitor towers rose, and he could almost feel the electric energy suffusing them and bleeding over into the streets. They loomed above the city, a symbol of what he and his citizens believed in.

Anything on Chiron he wanted, he could have.

He turned away and continued down to the lower floors of the base and out to a wide, tiled street. Lights blazed everywhere as a hoverlimo pulled up and his driver opened the door for him. He sat in the back and gave the driver an address.

The hoverlimo whisked him through the streets, past recreation commons with their blazing lights, past well-dressed citizens staggering drunkenly through the streets, high on vapors or chem-X drinks. Morgan TV was showing everywhere, even on the surface of the street itself; as they drove you could look down and see vidfeeds playing in the translucent street surface.

Finally the hoverlimo stopped at a tall building that had the rich, conservative look of one of his banks, though all the lights were dimmed at this late hour. Morgan got out of the car and used a DNA scan to enter the huge glass doors.

Once inside he took an elevator up to the top floor, and from there he passed through a set of double doors into a series of offices. The offices were nondescript and cluttered, with stim cans everywhere and touchpanels scattered across large tables. They were dim, no one working, most of the top people on this project transferred elsewhere. The silence clutched him like woolen fingers.

In the back of the offices were a set of double doors that opened onto a glassed-in hallway, set with heavy stones. It was ornate, not at all like the sleek modernism that was currently in fashion. He walked down the synthglass hallway, and noticed for the first time that most of the city wasn't visible from this location, though the lights dimmed even the night sky of Chiron.

At the end of the hallway was a tall tapestry of Adam and Eve from the Garden of Eden, strangely baroque-looking. Eve held out her apple, and its luscious richness brought Deirdre Skye to mind. Serpents twined around the two figures, hiding their nudity in lieu of fig leaves.

It was an odd painting, though it made sense in retrospect. Turk, one of the project leads, had defected to the Believers, making the journey by hovercar in the dead of night. He was one of the few to do so, but his eccentric brilliance made it excusable. Kind of.

He entered a code into a hidden DNA detection

plate. The mural slid up with a heavy sound, as if pushing up the weight of a mountain, and then a thick door beyond that opened as well.

The room inside was dim, and there were no attendants. One of the points of this experiment was that no attendants were needed.

Banks of equipment ringed the walls, and lights winked on them. The light to the room had a bluish cast, making the equipment look heavier and more shadowy, like things crouched against the wall. There was a hissing breath that echoed in the room, perfectly rhythmic, and the sound of bubbling fluids underlay it all.

Morgan, who felt little of anything these days, felt a chill go up his spine, being alone in this room in the presence of . . .

Death? No, it was actually Life, but not a bright or fulfilling life. The room was steeped in malevolence.

His eyes adjusted to the darkness, so that he could see the five small glass cubicles that ringed the room. Soft white lights shone from beneath each tank, and next to each one was a piston of sorts, hissing its oxygenated air into the tanks at regular intervals.

How Zakharov had once laughed at the crudeness of his experiment. *How typical of you,* Zakharov had said, *to try to extend life from a purely material perspective, when real life, the life that matters, exists in the mind.*

How would you do it? Morgan had asked defensively.

My senses, Director. Downloading my mind, saving it, expanding it. In fact (and here his eyes lit up as if from within) *what if I could take your mind and make it believe that five minutes were an eternity? Would that be eternal life?*

The conversation had degenerated from there. Director Morgan decided to stick with his way, the "materialistic" way, and this room held the result. And now Zakharov wanted it? *What had caused that shift?* he wondered.

Five citizens, all volunteers (in fact, the lottery had swept every Morganite base and taken over the link channels for six solid months). He walked up to the first one, an economic wizard who had developed a new method of valuing energy reserves.

"How is it in there, old chum?" asked Morgan. Inside the dimly lit tank, a spine was suspended, fibers drifting from it like jellyfish tendrils. At the top of the spinal column was a fleshy blob, wrinkled with cerebellum, and from that drifted one eye, held in tiny robotic carriers that let it swivel at will.

Not much to look at now. After Turk had defected, the project had faded into the background. There were support staff, but they didn't always bother to position the touchscreens so that the minds, the preserved citizens, had something to look at. They had found it impossible to communicate with these minds in the tanks, to accurately know what they wanted or needed. Other concerns had taken over.

Like a tiny submarine, the one eye cart hummed and rose a little, then advanced toward the edge of the tank. Morgan stared into the black pupil . . . what was it thinking? Did he sense that malevolence again, or was it his imagination?

Let Zakharov figure it out. The technology in this room could allow a human body to live for a long, long time, but what was the point of it?

The death, the stagnation in this room, suddenly sickened Morgan. Tomorrow he would ship two of these to Zakharov, and await the weapon Zakharov had called the Sin Gun.

Zakharov's Academy Park

Jynna Sol, a technician at Zakharov's Academy Park, treated each movement as a meditation, even while twiddling the quantum burners at her unremarkable lab job. A job so unremarkable that a robot could have done it, simply taking random genetic sequences and inserting them into tiny one-celled creatures, then monitoring the results. If anything remarkable or dangerous emerged, the creatures were held in the same small container that spawned them, their "blue box." Each blue box was a completely enclosed cell, about half a meter on each side, made of a clear icy substance. The box would remain their entire world, cradle to tiny grave.

Yes, a robot could have done this job, but one of the Talents had a new theory about Chaos Intuition that she was studying. The Talent, Sandy Jacobs, believed that human beings processed even meaningless information on some deep, subconscious level and that if given a task, even one with almost infinite choices, beneficial patterns would emerge as expressions of the subconscious. Jynna had been considered, after a battery of tests, to be the person with the "emptiest mind," most adaptable to choosing sequences of genetic codes effectively.

So she carefully used the extension hands to select the gene codes, building on her base of scientific knowledge coupled with raw intuition. The work suited her, because she had come to treat each movement of the siphon arm as a meditation, and had found a prayer that lasted just the right amount of time.

She was a quick learner and a faithful one, which was why she had been chosen by her Believer high priest to operate with a probe team infiltrating Zakharov's second largest base. They had brought her in as a child, created a false identity for her (surprisingly easy in Zakharov's domain, where information possessed a chaotic life of its own), and she had studied genetic science from a young age.

She had studied the Bible, too, schooled in the "club" that her parents (also Believer agents, known affectionately as "probe parents") took her to each week. And oddly, she saw patterns in the words of the Conclave Bible that resonated with her just like the patterns of genes and cells. After all, it was all God's hand in the end, from her own body, to the genes that formed it, to the machines that analyzed these same genes right in front of her.

And most oddly, after all that, her pseudo-random selections had bred a one-celled creature that held all the qualities of a killer virus . . .

- It spread from human to human in a matter of mere seconds.
- It incubated for several hours, virtually untraceable, so that it wouldn't alert the authorities too soon, at which point . . .

- It killed whomever it touched, instantly and violently, and . . .
- It dispersed quickly, for the invading force to follow in safety.

It had been quite a discovery. She looked across the cool white lab to Sandy, so tall and lovely, with long blond hair and the body of an Amazon. A true Talent, all genes, no soul. Sandy smiled and gave her a head tilt, then looked away quickly.

Hey, I'm your Chaotic Intuition theory, living and breathing! I'm your ticket to a top academic post!

Fact was, Sandy probably thought Jynna was stupid, a blank slate, which she was, but on purpose. She had been taught to clear her mind of all but the prayer, and when the Word was needed, it would come.

Such as now, when the sequence she had created over four months ago, the fifteen pronged sequence that had created the killer gene (whose records had been whisked away from her the instant it had been verified) rose up again in the blank slate of her mind. As casual as could be, she created the creature again.

And there would be no way to get to it, in its solid blue prison, except that yesterday she had snuck into the storage room with a young researcher, and had gotten hopped up on some chem-X with him, and while they both lay there in a pleasant daze (all for the Holy, and not so different from that rapture, really), she had acquired one of several flawed blue boxes, waiting in the discard queue.

With the help of her parents and a chemical compound, they had exploited the tiny flaw, opening it up. Just a hair. And during each experiment there was a moment, if you were quite subtle and sneaky, when you could switch a box, after it had been scanned and before it got locked into the creator mechanism.

So while Sandy smiled at her, Jynna worked, while in the blue box, with its tiny flaw, the one-celled killer grew.

Her parents had gotten the order yesterday. They had been so stoic, their backs so straight as they sent her to work that day! She saw one tremble of her mother's lip, but that was all.

And now she fell into the haze of prayer, letting it carry her. The extra dose of chem-X she had palmed didn't hurt. Her mind bathed in the chaos.

She leaned forward, or she fell forward, into that blue glass box with its hairline crack. The virus had reached the incubation stage, so she bent to the tiny crack, and she breathed in. She could imagine the tiny coil of air she inhaled with its tiny, living wind surfer, whisking out of the blue prison and into the wide, wide world.

After all, God had made even this tiny creature for a reason. She was just helping to deliver it, and this entire base, to its final purpose.

Zakharov sat deep in thought, up on his observation deck in University Base. Miriam's image tugged at him . . . the ridiculous NuSpace program, the way she taunted him. He thought of her, and then he thought of the Sin Gun, and he considered turning it against New Jerusalem after Morgan had used it. A fitting use for it.

Annihilation of an entire base . . . as bad as the

planet busters, but even more powerful and flexible. He was on the razor's edge of this decision. He knew he could eliminate Miriam physically; that was a given, despite her string of good fortune. But to eliminate her intellectually was just the sort of challenge he craved.

He stared up into the sky, and was struck by the thought of Miriam staring at this same sky, *his* sky, from inside one of the captured bases. The thought annoyed him and made it all but impossible to enjoy the night.

He went down into his base, and decided to try the NuSpace connector. He would broadcast a call to Miriam to meet again, and see if she would dare to meet him.

He logged into the access room himself, and found the origin of Miriam's last connection. He selected his own default program for the meeting room, and hoped that somehow she would receive the alert to join him, and would have the courage to meet him face-to-face.

He connected, and found himself in an empty shell of a room, waiting alone.

He looked around, bemused. Rather than the clean elegant space of Pravin Lal (with windows and an azure sky, no less!), or the lushness of Deirdre's Garden program, or the sparseness of Santiago's War Room, he found himself in a featureless gray cube. There was no furniture, no doors, no windows, nothing.

He had never selected a program, a default space, of his own!

Thinking back, the early test runs had been in

rooms hacked together by his young investigators, little more than joke spaces, with smiley faces on the walls or disco balls (to test light projection) or rubbery chairs (to test textures). Then, he always waited for the other party to select the meeting space, projections of their own beings.

But this . . . was this him? He felt the rage leave him suddenly, almost inexplicably, and a deep emptiness descend, accompanied by a mind-numbing claustrophobia.

And at that moment, a star of light burst in the center of the room, and Miriam appeared.

She was cloaked in a wrap of white that gave off a light that filled every corner of his gray cube, much to his annoyance. Now he could see dark stringy webs in the corners, sending down gray broken strands. Where did those come from?

She looked around and smiled. "So this is the mind of Zakharov."

He struggled to reconnect with his anger, and the video feeds from the attack on Marine Institute helped him do that. With sudden inspiration, he jacked out quickly and redirected the feeds from the central datalinks and into the NuSpace, onto the walls of his cube.

When he jacked back in, he and Miriam stood in the center of six walls of carnage, as images of his dead citizens churned around them.

"Have you no mercy?" he asked; in fact, the words popped out of his mouth.

She, her projection, arched an eyebrow. "Mercy? On you? I have no mercy on my own people. Why would I have any on yours?"

"Is this the real face of the Believers, Sister?"

"I don't hide this face, Prokhor." She stared at him, ignoring the chaos in the video feeds around them. Oddly, it was Zakharov losing his bearings, feeling nauseous as the vidfeeds jumped from scene to scene, with fire and smoke and violence crossing the walls. "My people know that only God is their final arbiter, and only he can show them mercy. They know they will go to a better place, and the sooner the better."

"You mean that you've *convinced* them that they can go to a better place, Miriam. You've filled their heads with comforting illusions, and clouded their view of reality. You've sold them a lie."

She laughed then, and somehow, in his plain cubespace, the laugh sounded like quiet wind chimes. Even in her projection, her eyes had taken on a complex green light. "There are no lies here, Zakharov. Lies are a product of an intellect that thinks it knows a truth, and then contradicts it; a lie is fundamental arrogance. I, and my people, *believe.* We *know,* with a certainty that you could never possess, what the truth is about the world. For you, doubt lies beyond the next hypothesis."

"You act against a thousand years of science, that has pulled us from an age of darkness and intellectual waste."

"And into this?" She motioned around. "You stand here in a world that doesn't exist except in our own senses, and tell me what is real and what isn't?" She smiled. "Faith can move mountains, Zakharov. You've heard the saying?"

"Science can move mountains more easily than faith, Sister. Or your Believers wouldn't be starving and half mad."

"Maybe so, Zakharov. But faith can certainly move bases, wouldn't you agree?" She gestured to the video feeds, and Zakharov felt the rage boil up inside of him again.

"You kill your people for nothing more than a foolish cause. You can't win against the combined might of the settlements. Why are you doing this?"

Miriam seemed to take a long breath before her next words. She nodded. "We die in great numbers, that's true. But imagine three small spheres, touching each other but otherwise unremarkable, except for a small explosive charge placed in each. The charge lies dormant, and the spheres remain at rest."

"I take your metaphor."

"Strike these balls and the charge detonates, the balls rocket off, full of power now. And they strike other groups and each of those explode, and then more and more. Magnify this a thousand times and send it into every dimension your science has invented for itself, and you will understand the power of my Word."

"It's a hydrogen bomb, I understand. Or it's one Holy pyramid scheme."

"Except the charge I speak of exists in everyone. It's inside our genes. Your intelligence and reason is a blip on the evolutionary radar; us, our bodies, our cells, and our secret dreams have been with us since the Garden of Eden. You give people a means to live, but I give people a reason to live, and that makes all the difference."

What could he say to this single-mindedness? What could he do, but ignore it utterly, or eliminate it completely?

The sad truth was that if he did capture her and put her in the punishment sphere, she probably would hold on to the belief that she was going to a better place. Internally, she was an unassailable fortress, though if he could breach her faith, show her how small and pathetic she was, how worthless to a large and uncaring universe, it would be his ultimate triumph.

He made up his mind then and there to do it. So elated was he at his newest challenge that he ignored her, and jacked right out of the NuSpace.

Once out, he looked at his quicklink, where a priority diplomatic message awaited.

You'll be back, it said, and he smiled. Because on that they agreed.

Jynna took the broken blue cube and wrapped it in her lab coat, and then took it back to the storage room. She smiled and waved to Sandy Jacobs as she walked by; Sandy was on the other side of the lab, but crossed over to talk to her.

"How's the work going?" Sandy was tall and calm, her clear skin giving off a healthy radiance even after all the time she spent in the lab. Jynna knew that Sandy often went to the Marine Institute for recreation and tanning, and despite her calm demeanor the Talent beachside parties were famous for their debauchery.

"It's going all right." Sandy's eyes started wandering down Jynna, toward the bundled lab coat she had under her arm. "What do you think of the Marine Institute?" Jynna asked impulsively.

"You mean the Believer attack? Horrible." Her face twitched for a moment, the perfect smoothness flickering to concern and back to calmness. "Why do you ask?"

"I know you go there. You might have been there."

Sandy nodded. "I don't go that often. But still, you're right."

"Do you think the attacks will go any farther? After all, the Morganite territories aren't so far away. Are you worried?" As Jynna spoke she felt an odd churning in her stomach. Nerves? Something else, like a mutant virus?

She had to hold it together. If there was even the slightest hint of illness in the lab, it would all be shut down, and everyone, even the Talent, put into quarantine.

"I'm not worried," Sandy replied. "The Believers are disorganized and primitive. Their ridiculous little raid will be stopped, and even if they do get here they'll never breach the tach field—"

She stopped, frowning, as an alert came over her quicklink. Her face grew troubled. "I have to go," she said, not looking at Jynna anymore. She turned away but Jynna reached out quickly, grabbing Sandy by the arm. Sandy turned back, looking annoyed, and Jynna leaned in, smelling the subtle and expensive perfume Sandy always wore, and breathing a soft breath into her face.

"Be careful," she said.

Sandy pulled away and walked briskly across the lab. There was a genetic scanner at the door that was supposed to be used on everyone as they left the lab, but it took thirteen minutes and Sandy was in a hurry. The Talents were gathering.

So she nodded to the attendant and walked right

out. She would head for the busiest section of the base, and she would meet with the other Talents, probably about the Believer invasion, and those Talents would scatter throughout the base.

But Jynna wanted to lie down, because to pass through the scanner was too risky. She might talk to the attendant before his break, and she might meet her latest suitor in the storage room and let him kiss her right before he left for the day. She would hide the blue box, which would be discovered eventually during the accounting process, but by then it would be too late.

She had done well today. She looked up at the featureless ceiling, and gently reminded her vengeful God that she had earned her place in Heaven.

Miriam stood on the battlements and watched her faithful mill around on the streets of her new Holy Sword Base, which had once been Morgan Solarfex. New Jerusalem and her other bases had little more than a skeleton crew, and all of the faithful who could walk and carry a weapon had been transported (on stolen, ultrafast transports) to locations suitable for the next wave of invasion.

Kola came through the double doors to the balcony and stood next to her. He didn't look down, but focused on her, his face stern. "We've come far, Sister. God has smiled on us. And we've made a discovery."

"What's that?"

"Blink displacers." Kola's nostrils flared at the mention of them. "They can vanish and reappear several hundred meters away in an instant. It's very advanced technology . . . we can use them to penetrate the tach field at Morgan Industries."

Miriam nodded absently, staring at the locust cloud overhead. "Do the clouds seem thinner to you, Kola?"

"Perhaps. But I must tell you, Sister. They're going to come after us. We've made our threat known, and taken three bases now, and used nerve gas."

"Truth," she said.

"The Council will meet. They'll coordinate against us."

"Kola, I don't listen to the Council. And though I value your advice and company, I don't listen to my advisors either. I listen to the One."

She pointed her hand up into the sky. Two suns blazed off the dome, and as he so often experienced with Sister Miriam, Kola found himself seeing things in a new way, bathing in the glory of common occurrences.

The dome did glow. And Sister Miriam, in her simple white robe, glowed as well.

"We're going to keep moving. If they attack us, we'll smite them from behind, because we will already be deep into their heart. I want Morgan Industries, and I want University Base."

Kola swallowed, and his mind raced with how he would dispute his leader's ambition. But Miriam turned to him first. "Besides, it will be dangerous to stay here. Even with the locusts we'll be a target for Morgan and Zakharov."

"We've suffered many losses, Sister. It wouldn't be prudent to move again."

"Prudent?" She shook her head. "I want Zakharov's bases as well as Morgan's. The Almighty has shown me that both are within our grasp."

Kola shook his head, his eyes wide. "It isn't possible, Sister. We'll be lucky to take Morgan Industries, even with the new weapons we've found here. We must focus our attack."

But Miriam's eyes had softened, and she touched her chest. "Here is our focus, Kola. If we send out the word, the faithful will respond."

Kola nodded, his neck tense. "You are the voice. But I must protest. It will fail. They will come back at us with everything they have, and there won't be enough of us to resist."

She turned to look at him. "Still, I want you to take half the remaining army and send them north. Take the blink displacers, and when the locusts lift, as they will, use the displacers to hide from Zakharov's air strikes. Go into the mag-tube tunnels if you must. But we must get to University Base. And we must abandon this base now, and make our way through the mountains to the next targets. We don't need these walls to hide."

"We're far outnumbered. We'll fail."

"We have the faithful, Kola. Haven't you learned? Morgan and Zakharov's bases will fall from the inside, and the army will simply occupy the shell they leave behind."

Zakharov believed in the machine as an extension of his mind, and even the opposite . . . himself as an agent to assist his great machines in doing their work more easily. It was this mindset, which made the most sense for human survival in almost any conceivable situation, that allowed his science and research to thrive.

It had created the Sin Gun, and the Gene Bath . . . the very technology that Miriam had stolen and used to extend her own life!

And now it alerted him to new conditions in his domain. He had helped to design the system itself . . . a thinking mind that monitored events throughout the University territory, tried to explain any deviations based on other deviations (so that a new Morganite luxury car might explain unusual spikes in spending, for example). Anything else it spit out to him, so that his human mind could analyze it and take appropriate action.

In this case, productivity had slipped in Academy Park, suddenly and noticeably. At least, noticeable to a computer that monitored the tiniest activities on the smallest scale.

Of course, the Believer invasion might explain it. Were people upset, spending too much time talking around the water cooler, staying home to contact loved ones?

Perhaps, but he also noted a slight spike in hospital admissions, and on further scanning he noticed that these admissions were mostly among the drones.

The drones. The weak, the stupid, the genetically unfit. And in this case, quite possibly, they were the canaries that would warn his perfect Talents of impending trouble.

He began to rock back and forth in his chair as thoughts and associations crashed through his brain. What had Miriam said?

And they strike other groups and each of those ex-

plode, and then more and more. Magnify this a thousand times . . .

She was talking about the Word, or "God's Pyramid Scheme" as he had cynically thought of it. But the mechanism, the *transmission* of something from person to person . . .

A wave of panic washed over him like a sheet of ice. He opened an emergency feed to Daniel.

"Where's the Believer army now?"

"Still in Morgan territory. The Sin Gun is on its way."

"Trigger a Genetic Alert in Academy Park. Quarantine everyone until we're sure that nothing has happened inside the base."

"Yes, Academician. But before we start a panic there, what is the evidence?"

"Just do it," Zakharov snapped. Truthfully, he had little evidence . . .

. . . just one big feeling.

The Genetic Inspectors swept through the base, their filter masks and rubberized suits in place. Bursting through doorways, they surfed a wave of information and panic that swept through the base, over quicklink and MorganLink TV.

They went to the hospitals and began initiating genetic scans on the most recently admitted drones, though it would take some time. Worried doctors looked on, wearing masks of their own.

Citizens returned to their homes and closed themselves in, as they were ordered to do, and turned on the links to get the information they needed.

Genetic Inspectors went down into the labs and did an immediate check on all current genetic experiments, and it didn't take long to find the missing blue box in the labs of Talent Sandy Jacobs.

Those labs became a nexus of activity. Genetic Inspectors took every worker there and hustled them into long white boxes, like phone booths, for an immediate trip to the gene lab. The checkpoint attendant, who had gone off duty, was located in the rec commons, drinking at a long bar. The bar was closed and he was loaded into his own box, and the other patrons were held inside. Most waited calmly, somewhat puzzled, and the few that had the urge to lash out saw the weapons at the Genetic Inspectors' belts, and remembered they were authorized to use them.

Two Genetic Inspectors burst into the second storage room in Sandy Jacobs' lab, in search of the missing blue box, which all of them felt, on some level that sent a nervous electricity through the spaces beneath their skin, was critical to what they were doing here.

They found the box, wrapped in a white lab coat. It was being used as a pillow by a young blond girl, who shuddered gently on the floor, and stared at the ceiling with blank, shadowed eyes. She seemed to have no conception of the gout of rich red blood that rolled slowly down from her nose and spread across her white shirt.

The alert rippled out across the base, staining the lives of everyone who heard it. Moods changed from breathless curiosity to sudden, bone-deep fear. Talents who had maintained a calm mood their whole life suddenly felt the animal inside of them start to thrash, knowing that their lives were in jeopardy, that it may already be too late.

All traffic in and out of the base was immediately closed. Bodies were analyzed, because within minutes of the blond girl being discovered there were others, who lay down for a rest and spasmed the last moments of their lives, to people watching the links for further news who suddenly felt a pale, cold hand clutch their chests.

Zakharov, receiving the news in University Base, trembled with rage. The video feeds came as a confused jumble on the tac table in front of him, as if he had broken an expensive vase and now stared helplessly at the shattered pieces. "What has she done? Genetic warfare!"

Daniel simply stood by quietly as the death stats rolled in. The virus had taken the entire base in the space of an evening, choking the hospitals. Talents were whisked in past drones and hapless Ordinaries into the back rooms of the one nanohospital, where nanosurgeons worked furiously to rebuild shattered respiratory systems. Several riots broke out, with dying, bleeding citizens storming into hospitals and tearing the masks from top surgeons.

Daniel conferred with Zakharov. "Shall we airlift people to the next base?"

Zakharov shook his head. "By the time we get sufficient help there, this virus will have run its course. Do what you can, but we'll maintain strict quarantine. No one enters or leaves that base."

A priority link came in, and Daniel took it.

"Chiron!" he shouted when he had read the news. He turned to Zakharov, as pale as the white wall behind him. "A transport left Academy Park this morning, within the incubation period of the virus."

Time seemed to stop for Zakharov. He felt his mortality again, closing in on him, his death closer than ever. He swallowed.

"Where was it going?"

"Here," said Daniel, and it looked as if his body would fall, like a sac without support. "It arrived one hour ago."

Zakharov sat on the observation platform, his mouth thick with the taste of chem-X. Up here the air was cool and refreshing, and the sky open above him. It was a welcome change from watching people in his base rounded up by the masked Genetic Inspectors and taken into holding cells below the base.

He took another drink, his hand shaking. Miriam's face kept appearing in his mind. His belly twisted with a bitter cocktail of anger and shame.

He stared at the second chair, where Isaac sometimes sat, and longed for his company. He remembered a time the two of them had been working on an experiment that required a finicky burner. Zakharov had been eager to begin the experiment, but the burner control had been jammed. Isaac had gone to get some lubricant, but Zakharov had twisted at the knob, frustrated that he couldn't begin the experiment immediately.

The knob had broken. He grabbed a laser cutter, intent on slicing off the broken stub and attaching a replacement, but the twisted metal stub was at the wrong angle. By the time Isaac had returned, Zakharov had run a gamut of emotion, from impatience to anger to a creeping feeling of revelation.

This knob, this tiny, insignificant knob, was going to ruin his experiment.

"You see, now," said Isaac, who had been watching most of the drama from the doorway. "When your mind seizes on something that is not real, that is not based on the hard evidence in front of you, it only takes you *farther* from the truth. You underestimated the importance of this little knob . . ." He held it up. "And of big Isaac, who had the lubricant the whole time!"

Zakharov felt the same growing realization he had felt when staring at the broken knob while his experiment crashed around him. He had completely underestimated Miriam and her importance.

One thing was certain: he now saw Miriam for what she was . . . a creeping virus, reaching across the settlements. The question now was what to do about it.

He thought of the Sin Gun. He thought of his own death, which haunted him constantly. And he thought of a project he had been working on, and what the Clinical Immortality could do to finish it.

chapter seven

GRAND ADVISOR MIA YANG OF THE HUMAN HIVE SAT IN A plush silken chair and waited for her husband, the Chairman, to return. Her hands were folded lightly in her lap, and a glass of crimson wine, the finest from Deirdre Skye's gardens, sat untouched on the carved planetpearl table next to her.

She shifted, just slightly, on the chair. The patterned silk that covered the chair had been made the old way, by dedicated Hive craftsmen working hand-extracted planetsilk on fine looms. It was an antique; the Chairman had since filled the Hive with fabricated Morganite imports, and a chair such as this would now be made in Morgan's factories, by mashing the worms in great machines and extracting the raw silk with chemicals. Her husband had been so excited to show her this on his quicklink.

And now our people follow the Morganite traders through the hallways like lost glowmites, thirsting for new luxuries while their spirits wither.

The trends were everywhere, from the bodies

packed into the shadowy new gamelink rooms, to the seedy LinkBars springing up on the periphery of the territory, to the citizens crossing the sea as stowaways to the Gaian and Morganite lands.

The Gaian lands. Her own husband had dallied there for a month, on his way to visit Director Morgan. What had been an investigation into Morganite trade practices had turned into a ten-month sojourn.

At any rate, she hadn't been idle.

She glanced at the two Hiveguard behind her, with their thick black armor and the jade dragon shoulder insignia that denoted them as her personal guard. They were carefully selected from the stock of the genejack factory, processed in the cloning vats, and trained in the Death Tunnels of the Human Hive. Only the top two percent could become the personal guard of the Chairman, or the Chairman's wife. She felt their awareness on her, silently enveloping her every move like a fine mist.

She reached up and touched the back of her neck, which was slightly damp in spite of her hair being pinned up with jeweled hairpins. She was over a hundred and fifty years old, but the genetic treatments had been kind to her. Her skin was still smooth and radiant, her body slender, and her face held a powerful gravity. She attributed it to clean living and a strong spirit.

Today she needed that spirit. The thick ceremonial robes were hot and awkward, making her feel like a doll. But she had chosen this outfit for that very reason; not to help her feel strong, but to make her *appear* weak.

There was a mild commotion on the other side of the room. The double doors there, made of synth-gold acquired from her husband's Decree of Open Trade, swung open, and she felt an unexpected tension roil her stomach. She used one slender hand to smooth her robes as she stood.

Two Hiveguard entered, like shadows stretching into the room. Behind them came two advisors in red and gold robes made of some kind of shiny material. Three children followed, their faces solemn, their role unclear. And then came Jin, now Chairman Yang. Her husband.

She stepped forward and extended one hand to him, tiny rings glittering there. He nodded to her, then smiled as she noticed who walked behind him.

It was a young woman, her face smooth and tan. She wore a tight-fitting wrap, black and sheer, the design from one of the Morgaia design houses. Tiny diamonds glittered in her long hair.

"Hello, Mia," said Jin. "It's good to see you."

"And you, husband."

He touched the woman's arm lightly and guided her forward until they were two steps away from Mia. "I'd like you to meet Sada. She's our trade liaison to Director Morgan. Sada, this is Mia Yang, my advisor and wife."

Mia reached out to take the woman's hand lightly. Things had changed, in just a single moment.

"I'm putting Sada in the common apartments. I hope you don't object." His tone suggested he didn't care whether she objected or not. He hurried

down the hall, tossing back the words as Mia struggled to keep up in her voluminous robes.

"The common apartments between our rooms,
Chairman? Does that mean she'll be dining with us
as well? Bathing with us?"

"I'm sure she'll use the utmost discretion." He
smiled back at her, then quickened his pace. "At
any rate, you won't see her much if you stay in your
rooms."

"I'll be in the central ministry most of the time,
Chairman. Have you forgotten who keeps the Hive
running while you're on your diplomatic mis-
sions?"

There was a pause that lasted just a heartbeat
longer than it should have.

"Of course not," he said.

"Stop walking, please." He walked on, ignoring
her. "Jin Long!"

That stopped him. He turned back, his face ever
so slightly flushed. She walked toward him, studying him.

Jin Long was his given name, his name when he
had overthrown the first Chairman Yang, her father, over a century ago. He had since taken her as
his wife, and thus taken her father's name. He had
her name, and she borrowed from his power, a marriage of convenience for both. But he squandered
his gift, while she nurtured hers, in the dark places
behind Jin's sprawling government.

"What do you want?" His voice trembled with a
suppressed rage. The Jin that had left a year ago had
the thin, smooth body of the other extended lifers,
and near-perfect control over his emotions. The Jin
she saw before her had a puffy face, and though still

thin he had a small protruding belly, like a ball. He also appeared to be more rash, more given to emotional outbursts.

She smiled. "I want to know my husband's thinking, bringing a Morganite liaison into our midst. Aren't you worried that she might be a probe?"

He puffed out his cheeks like a plump fish. "Director Morgan is our link to the settlements, Mia. To settlement power, and settlement luxuries. We have to widen our hallways."

"Widen our hallways?"

Jin chuckled. "You've heard the saying, from our citizens. We have to let in some settlement ideas, even if it means changing our way of life."

"Ah." But what he didn't know was that the saying was coined by Director Morgan, and spread to her citizens through a popular Linksong. Pure corruption.

Jin glanced back at the Hiveguard, two pairs, one for him and one for her. "Look at them." He shook his head. "Why does my wife need her own elite Hiveguard, shadowing her through the tunnels, guarding her chambers? When we're together it makes us look like fools."

"There are many secrets that live in these tunnels, Chairman. The guard is for my protection."

"If there are secrets, root them out, Mia. You took on the duties of monitoring the underground after your father died. You're the one who talks of spiritual pollution." He shook his head and started off again. Mia hurried after him. "No, Director Morgan has opened my eyes. It makes no sense, such resources spent on the likes of . . ."

But Jin didn't finish his thought.

They reached a wide silver door. The door slid open, revealing an elevator that led down to the complex of chambers they shared: rooms for him, rooms for her, and the common rooms in between. Mia caught the smell of Gaian flowers wafting from the elevator.

Jin stepped in, then his Hiveguard, then Mia and her Hiveguard. The door whispered shut, and the elevator carried them down.

As they descended her mind whirred. Her husband didn't love her, but he never really had. Yet now he didn't *want* her, and that was unacceptable for this night's plans.

Ironically, the hallways of the Human Hive *were* wider, she reflected as she walked toward her private chambers after parting with Jin. They both had worked to make the environment more pleasant after her father's overthrow. Hallways were wider and brighter, and some extended to low aboveground complexes. Bright full-spectrum lights were everywhere. They were generous with the rec chits . . . *too generous,* she thought.

On the upper common levels you couldn't walk ten meters without passing a rec commons from which the babble of speech and laughter emerged. There were the sounds of Morgan's gaming channels, all screened and approved by the Ministry of Trade, of course. Some of the rejected channels from MorganLink were . . . disgusting. Yet competition was fierce to be on the screening committee!

So what was wrong?

She entered her private chambers, nodding to the additional Hiveguard stationed at the door. Inside her two escorts took up their posts as she stepped behind a sheer curtain and changed from the stifling ceremonial garb and into a comfortable wrap, putting it carefully around her body. She was much older than the child her father once knew . . . well over a hundred years older, in fact, though her body had not yet suffered the thin, pale look of the other long-lifers. Her face was wrinkled, but still had the glow that poets had written of from the time she was born, an aristocratic look that seemed out of place in the communal Utopia she helped to rule.

She almost laughed. She might be part of the problem! Young girls had once dressed like her, mirrored the split gowns she had worn as a rebellious young girl, studied the tapes of her sparring with Spartan warriors. But now they imported black market MorganLink tapes, and graffiti on the walls of the Hive bespoke a new kind of restlessness.

"Cassie," she said, talking into a touchpanel mounted over a simple red desk. Cassie came on, smiling as always, even in the dark cubicle where she spent most of her time monitoring the Hive's central nervous system. She had a young, fresh face that belied both her age and her formidable intelligence.

"Yes, Grand Advisor?" Cassie smiled, her cropped black hair held back by a series of tiny clips. It was far from regulation Hive wear, and in anyone else Mia would take it as more of Morgan's corrupting influence, but Cassie was one of the genuine intellects that stretched beyond the boundaries of her immediate world, and thrived in that freedom.

"Where's my husband now?"

Cassie blinked once and checked several readouts. "He's in his rooms, using the virtual world."

"And where is that new woman, from the Morganites?"

Cassie bit her lower lip as she checked some data. "She's being shown around the Hive. Her itinerary is full until late this evening."

"When she'll no doubt find her way to his bed," Mia said. "Could you please send me feeds of what the Chairman is watching in the virtual world?"

"That could be difficult, Grand Advisor." But she smiled.

"That's why I'm asking you specifically, Cassie."

She nodded. "Anything else?"

"Tell me when he leaves his chambers. I want to be apprised of his movements. And I don't want anyone approaching my quarters without my knowledge."

"Of course, Grand Advisor." She nodded and vanished.

Mia stared into the mirror again, slipping the long golden pins from her hair, which had turned a beautiful silver color that caught the lights in the room. Since their marriage, one of Jin's primary recreations was trying to talk her into his bed, a game she played for her own purposes. But now he looked at her as if she were a moth resting on his favorite tapestry. And she thought she knew why.

After a short time, Cassie beeped her back. "Here's the information you requested, Grand Advisor."

Mia looked over the information. Jin used the virtual world all the time; he was most likely addicted to it. In the early days, he had watched Chairman Yang's stored virtual world creations religiously, running them over and over until he could duplicate them perfectly. In that way he learned the thoughts that had governed the formidable mind of the original Chairman.

But lately . . . nothing. In fact, he seemed to be accessing educational shows repeatedly. The one he screened now was called Day of the Locust.

Did he take her for a fool? She entered the reference code and jacked into his experience as an observer. On the touchpanel, nude bodies curled in a Gaian pleasure palace, while a shadowy man watched from a golden chair above it all.

"Ah." She continued to watch, looking past the writhing bodies and into the larger patterns of what Jin was seeking in this particular holo. The activities onscreen degenerated into realms beyond mere sexual pleasure. The pinkish translucent field of a punishment sphere glimmered in the background. And then she saw a figure she recognized, held fast between two faceless men. A slender woman, with an ageless face.

Her face.

Suddenly, the holo winked out. "What happened, Cassie?" she asked, her mind spinning. *So there is weakness there, after all.*

"He's finished with it, I suppose. Security sensors indicate that he's opened his closet."

"Where to next, I wonder?" Mia asked, the rhetorical question floating into the ether of her link with Cassie.

"After similar exertions, do you know what I like to do, Grand Advisor?"

Mia nodded. "I believe I do."

*   *   *

Mia pinned up her long hair and stepped into the warm pool. The pool was lined with stone tiles, and the bathing room pleasantly lit, but there was no abundance of luxury. Several more hot pools, smelling faintly of sulfur and heated by a hot spring, sent their vapors wafting up to a high, dark ceiling. It was a simple room that performed a simple function: relaxation.

It was also one of the communal rooms she shared with her husband. She sank into the warm waters and waited.

The double doors opened on the other side of the chamber. Jin entered, wearing a golden robe and followed by his two Hiveguard. He stopped for a moment when he saw her, but then nodded graciously and walked to a pool near hers. Through the steam she watched as he dropped his robe to the floor, revealing his body that looked more gaunt than ever, but with his belly puffier than before. He entered the pool, then took a white towel doused in cold water and set it on his head to keep him cool.

"What are you doing here?" he finally asked, his eyes closed.

"I'm bathing, Chairman. It's been a long day."

"Indeed."

She shifted in the water, creating pleasant sounds. He didn't move, but she could tell he was listening.

"I don't know why I bother," he finally said.

"Pardon, Chairman?"

"Trying to relax in these pools." He held up one hand and peered at it from beneath his towel, which covered his eyes like a large white brow. "I've got the look, from the Gene Baths. Hollow."

"Not at all, Chairman."

But he did. She stared at him across the damp stone, her eyes wide in the dark room. She was never so sure that he was going to kill her.

She stood up suddenly, propelling her slender body from the pool. His head turned to her the instant she moved, and she quickly padded five steps to his pool, intending to slip into the water.

As her foot touched the water she felt a cold grip close around her wrist. She looked around to see Jin's Hiveguard, springing from the shadows at her sudden movements. And her own guard had a Q-gun out and against her aggressor's helmeted head. Everyone stood still, and the moment stretched on.

Jin looked up, pulling the towel off his head. She imagined the scene from his angle . . . her tall, naked body above him, held by the Hiveguard. Even through the steam she could see the crooked grin on his face.

"What are you doing, Mia?"

"I intended to share a bath with my husband." She shifted and tilted her hips, just a few millimeters, but the effect was one she had practiced for a lifetime. He put the white towel back over his head.

"Let her go."

The cold grip left her. Angrily, she motioned to her other guard, who quickly pulled her wrap from a metal rack and brought it to her. By the time Jin looked up again her body was vanishing into a patterned robe of blue and silver.

"It was an intriguing game we used to play, Jin, before the Morganites got to you."

He laughed without looking at her. Her body hitched as she took deep breaths, feeling the hot vapors at the back of her throat.

Jin settled back into his pool. Mia watched him for a moment more and then turned away. She was over one hundred years old by the calendar, although she had access to most of the best genetic technologies. She didn't have the perfect body of a young Gaian courtesan, but she was slim and beautiful, and moved with a practiced grace.

Jin's voice floated to her as she reached the door. "Come to dinner with me tonight, Mia. Two hours from now. We haven't spoken in such a long time."

She answered without turning back. "Yes, Chairman."

Jin was rich and powerful. He only wanted what he couldn't have. And now he could have almost anything, except for her.

One hour before the dinner, Mia lay in her smallish bedchamber under layers of soft colored light. The chamber was more luxurious than any normal citizen possessed, but it was a far cry from the boundless luxury Jin hoarded for himself in his "pleasure complex."

She stared at the ceiling, but spoke to the shadowy form next to her, who served as a soothing tonic after Jin's excess.

"He's done with me. This Morganite slut will take my place at his side. Another marriage of convenience."

"But you control the Hive. He just doesn't know it yet." The voice was soft, like a warm breeze that brushed past her face. Mia nodded.

"He's gone soft, Cassie, but paranoia can substitute for wisdom, and brutality for righteousness. He's cunning. He might know my plans."

Next to her, Cassie's face turned toward her in the darkness, like a moon rolling over the sea. "Perhaps tonight is the wrong time."

"It's the only time. We can read each other too well. He won't let me near him . . ." She trailed off, feeling Cassie's fingers touching her back. She sighed a tiny puff of air.

"He likes his games though, Mia. And you saw what he was watching in the virtual world."

"Yes." But she was thinking of her father, who would never have opened himself to this sort of attack. Her thoughts drifted back over a hundred years, to Jin marching along the hallways of Hive Central after her father was taken prisoner by the settlements. She remembered the things she had to do to preserve her own life, and eventually to convince Jin to take her as his wife.

She looked over at Cassie. "Are you ready with the feeds?"

"Yes. I have several of him in the Gaian pleasure gardens. We may have to add an onscreen counter to tally the number of Gaian sluts he dallies with." Mia could hear the undercurrent of disgust in her voice, and it pleased her greatly. It was real, as real as the stone around them. She reached out and gripped Cassie's hand, which was small and hot in the shadows. The girl seemed to run on double speed, even at rest.

"I'm going to him, Cassie. Think good thoughts for me."

"Yes, Grand Advisor."

* * *

Mia moved into her dressing chamber and sat in front of a circular mirror. She opened a small lacquered case and examined the bottles and brushes there. The bottles and containers were each a small masterpiece, handcrafted by Hive artisans and then filled with the finest cosmetics from the Gaians, and then packaged and resold by the Morganites, of course.

She picked up the first tiny bottle and opened it. A kind of glittering rouge filled the inside, and a subtle scent of flowers wafted up. There were also tiny brushes for her eyes and lips, and a large container of a shimmering opaque substance that could be used anywhere on the body, another fashion statement from the decadent Morganites.

She slipped her robe from her shoulders and began smoothing scented lotions into her skin. She followed carefully with applications of makeup to her eyes, widening them, giving her a more innocent look. She made her lips fuller and then began to work on her hair, pinning it up in a style popular among young Morganite debutantes.

Finally she dressed in layers of sheer, patterned fabrics that blended on her body in a most tantalizing way. And before leaving the room, she took a small contraption from a black box and held it up to the light.

It was a small round cylinder with a kind of mechanism on the side, a work of fine craftsmanship in miniature. Its function was so secret that she had killed, with her own hands, the man who made it.

She sat down in front of the mirror again, turning her head to look at herself from various angles. She reached down and parted her robes, and then pushed her hand up inside of them, her expression in the mirror never changing.

When she entered the dining hall, she could see the flicker of desire in Jin's eyes, even from across the long, low-ceilinged room. Small spherical glowlamps floated over a table so long it barely fit in the room, the lamps sending light that barely reached the walls, making the lush tapestries that hung there look subtle and mysterious. She caught the scent of spicy foods.

A citizen in a simple gray-green tunic pulled out the chair at the near end of the table and ducked his head to her.

"My wife," said Jin, his voice utterly devoid of meaning. From the far side of the table he lifted a large crystal goblet full of some kind of amber liquid. The glowlamps floated at a level that obscured his face. Still, Mia was pleased. She knew the lighting in the room caught in her layers of sheer clothing, wrapping her in provocative shadows.

"Thank you, husband."

She sat down and heard the chair scrape as the citizen pushed it back in. The sound grated on her nerves. Her two Hiveguard waited in the back corners of the room, and she could see Jin's two in the far corners.

"Let's eat, then," said Jin. The place settings glittered all around her, and there were more utensils of obscure purpose set in front of her than there were dishes on the table. Faceless servants moved back and forth in the shadows, carrying food and drink.

Mia stared down the table at Jin, but he seemed too busy eating to notice her. Finally she spoke. "So why did you come back?"

"Mmm?" He stopped and stared at her, a tangle of strange noodles, dripping sauce, dangling off his fork.

"You were enjoying yourself overseas, Chairman, if the reports I've heard were true. So why did you choose to return to the Hive?"

He set down his fork and leaned his elbows on the table, then let out a long, deliberate breath. "Do you really think I would leave matters here unattended?" She let her silence answer him, until he nodded, a squat figure surrounded by food. "And the locusts concerned me. But I also came back to talk to General Kwan."

She forced herself to take a small bite of plantelope and chew deliberately. "So you have military concerns, Chairman? Is it really time to deal with the outsiders?"

A short bark of laughter answered her. Finally he shrugged as he started in on a thick cakelike dish. "I welcome the outsiders, Mia. What I need the army for is an alliance. Our new friends need us on the other side of the world."

Mia took her napkin and dabbed her lip. As she did she glanced at her bracelet, which had a built-in security monitor. The monitor scanned for odd frequencies, long-range waveform attacks, metal and explosives, and poisons. The small monitor stone flickered a dull black, which meant nothing threatened her at the moment.

"It seems to contradict the spirit of the Hive, husband. Are you toying with me?" Her voice sounded thick and throaty, as if she had lost control, but of course that exact tone was her intention.

"You're no toy, Mia." He stared at her, his eyes gleaming from the far side of the table, meters away.

"Rumors are that Director Morgan has a punishment sphere, and he uses it on his courtesans, Chairman. Is this the man you want to ally with?"

"Ridiculous!"

She slipped out of the chair and walked down the length of the table, using a slow, sensual gait she'd perfected over the years. Jin had stopped eating to watch her, suspicion on his face. She let her face run a short play of emotions: challenge, longing, fear. Her body shifted and swayed under her veils, with the promise of decades of learned sexual technique.

"Stop!" he barked, when she was five steps away. His Hiveguard had moved forward from the shadows, and she could feel the tension like black threads choking the air between them. Without looking, she waved her own Hiveguard back into their corners, never taking her eyes from Jin.

"I'm no threat to you, Chairman." Her words were no more than a whisper. She was close enough to see his face now, his lips moist from drink, a tiny flake of something at the corner of his lip. One hand pointed at her, a fork trembling slightly in his grip while anger and curiosity traded places on his face. He wore a silk lounging robe, decorated with complex patterns of gold and black. The scent of expensive cologne mixed with a tainted sweat drifted toward her.

"Just stop there," he said, and swallowed the

piece of meat in his mouth. He tapped his own security monitor, which glowed a deep purple. "You must think I'm a fool."

She glanced at his monitor bracelet and laughed. "It's picking up my jewelry, Chairman. What are you afraid of?" She showed him her fingers glittering with rings.

"Paranoia has brought me this far," he muttered.

"I'm your wife, Jin. And young enough to be your daughter."

"You have enough years on you, Mia. You're no child."

"Once something is gone, it's forever beyond your reach." She whispered the words, but he looked up in momentary shock. Her pupils widened and a flush came to her cheeks and her lips, reddening them just slightly. She shifted so that one leg emerged from the folds of her veils.

"You've certainly brought a thrill back to the Hive, Chairman." She twisted her torso and reached over to pluck a glowlamp from the air. It was a smooth ball, surprisingly cool to the touch, small enough to close her hand around it. She could feel its tiny servo motors trying to push it out of her hand, like a small animal struggling against her. She moved the light, letting the light and shadows shift across her veils, and then released it. The lamp floated back to its position.

"I don't want you standing there, Mia."

Her bare feet gripped the cool stone. She held up her fingers, where five rings glittered. Coincidentally, there were five steps to Jin. She slipped the rings off her fingers, one by one, and set them on the table.

"There. No rings." She took a step toward Jin. A cunning smile broke on his face for just a moment, the smile of a man who relishes a challenge, and then it was gone. He stood up, moving away from her. She saw his robe open a little and caught the flash of a knife there, a knife she knew he always carried.

"She has something on her." That was the voice of one of the Hiveguard. The two of them had advanced on her, and they now formed a triangle of balanced forces, their strong darkness against her pale sexuality.

"Yes." She kneeled down, letting the robes shift around her. She could sense Jin move, changing his angle to keep her in sight. From her bare feet she took a toe ring and a silvery ankle bracelet, then she stood up and dropped them on the table. "A killer toe ring." She glanced at each of his Hiveguard, but then her eyes widened a little, as if in fear. She caught the glimmer of interest from Jin, though he had trained himself to hide such emotions. He glanced back at her Hiveguard, whom she had ordered to stay against the wall.

"And there's this," she said quickly, reaching down the front of her robes to pull out a chain of synthium that hung around her neck. On the chain was her Hive seal, a translucent pendant with a tiny jade dragon inside, its silver eyes glittering. She set the seal on the table and stared at Jin, her face flushing with defiance.

"There's more metal," he said. He took the knife and gestured to her with it. "Search her, head to toe," he said, and she could hear the hoarseness underlying his voice now. "Leave her with nothing."

She arched one eyebrow. She felt the hard grip of one guard on her right wrist, and then the two hands of the other reaching around her waist, pushing into her clothes. The guard found one of the tiny metal clasps she had used to secure the wraps.

She kept her eyes fixed on Jin, whose smile began to widen as the guard yanked the metal clasp and began pulling veils from her body. He pulled the first one off her shoulder, and then from around her waist, revealing new layers of cloth that shimmered in new colors. Every time he pulled a clasp she caught her breath.

Two steps lay between her and Jin. As the guard began pulling the wrap that covered her breasts, she stepped forward, pulling away as a leaf might pull from a tree if carried by a breeze. The veil slipped away, remaining in the guard's hands. Another veil began to slip down from her hips.

The guard holding her wrist grunted and yanked. She stopped again, and the second guard pushed her feet apart and then snatched the thin metal belt from around her waist. The last veil slipped down past her hips and fell to the floor.

She flushed, still holding Jin's eyes. "I'm your wife."

He smiled. "I'm not nearly as soft as you think I've become, Mia." He nodded to the Hiveguard. "Let her go," he said, his voice thick. Mia heard the Hiveguard retreat, leaving a bruise on her wrist.

Jin came at her, the knife glinting in his hand, and she wondered if she would end up breaking his arm while his two Hiveguard killed her from behind. But then he was on her, a sweaty, lustful wave, his robe falling open as he came at her.

"Chairman . . ." she said, but he grabbed her shoulders, hard, and pushed her back on the table. She didn't resist. She had watched copies of the illicit holos Jin had ordered, and she knew his tastes, and his weaknesses.

He kissed her, his lips puffy and hard. She brushed her hands along his sides, kissing him, hearing the clink of silverware behind her as he moved her hips back on the tabletop. Then she saw his hand moving toward her thighs, his monitor bracelet nearing her . . .

Not now!

She let her hand slip and sprawled back on the table, hearing glasses tumble over and shatter. At the same moment she gasped, turning the accident into a moment of passion. She caught a brief glimpse of one Hiveguard, the dark mask staring at her, and then Jin leaned in, grabbing her shoulders, his breath hot and smelling of nectar.

"Now," he grunted. She slipped back toward him as he heaved his body up on the table. The white tablecloth felt rough against her back, and his pale, small belly pressed into her. Then he entered her, and she opened her mouth and gasped.

"Ah, Mia," he said, looking down at her with a smile breaking across his face.

There was a subtle snicking sound, perhaps so quiet that she didn't actually hear it at all. But Jin's eyes widened as if he had reached into a pillowcase and found a scorpion.

His back arched as the poison raced through his body. She had chosen it carefully, to paralyze his muscles but to give him a few last moments of life, to take it all in. From the other side of the room she heard the quiet whisking of two poison darts, crossing the table from her Hiveguard to his.

She pulled back from her husband's body, staring into his eyes. At last, she smiled. "You're not my father, Jin. You never were."

General Kwan lifted the girl and carried her across his sprawling chambers, toward the bed that waited on the other side. It was a large bed, covered in sheets as red as blood, and golden lamps threw light from the huge stone headboard. It was a warrior's room, he reflected, a successful warrior's room, and he liked it that way. It had a chaotic feel, with mirrors and crystal and stone everywhere, as if decorated from the spoils of a hundred hard-fought wars, though in fact it was decorated from a dozen hard-earned expense accounts.

He tossed the girl up and caught her, and she giggled. Her short cropped hair was held back by a tiny clip, and he took that in his teeth as if he would tear it from her. She giggled again. "This place is magnificent!" She clapped once.

He tossed her on the bed, and watched for a moment as she bobbed there, her body a jumble of arms, legs, and curves. She laughed and sat up. She wore a simple blue sleeveless top and a skirt, and she seemed oblivious to the way her skirt rode up her thighs.

He grinned. This girl was a free spirit, and free spirits were hard to find down here in the Hive tunnels. "This is the new world you see," he told her, gesturing to the room. "Riches from the settlements, all to be enjoyed by those who reach out and ask for it. Director Morgan will treat us well."

"So we may all soon live this way? I'd like that."

"Not all." He picked up a crystal decanter and poured a chem-X drink into two glasses, then he ran and jumped onto the bed, like a young child. She bobbed up and down.

"Lights!" he said, and the lighting changed, dimming. Soft patterns bloomed on the walls around them. She took a glass from him and gulped it down as he stared at her. "That's powerful stuff," he told her. "You should savor it."

She laughed and threw the glass away, and he heard it shatter somewhere. He tensed and started to say something.

But then she rose up on her knees and peeled her shirt off, revealing small, firm breasts, and he lost interest in worrying about his silk rug. He set his own glass on the elaborate headboard and moved over to her, reaching out his hand, sliding it up her leg.

"Let me help you with that," he said.

She laughed. "Just wait! Let me . . ." She rolled away from him, and fiddled with something. The skirt slipped down around her hips, and now he stared at her naked back, slender, with the bumps of her spine tracing a line from her slender neck to the light swell of her buttocks. He shifted over toward her.

"Cassie . . ."

She turned to him, and her eyes were as wide as two boreholes, staring up from hidden depths. She moved in and brushed his face with her lips, and the last thing he felt was the sting in his belly, stealing his pride.

* * *

Mia took Jin's lounging robe and wrapped it around herself as if against a chill. Nearby his two Hiveguard lay dead, their gold leaf insignia gleaming from their shoulders. Her own Hiveguard watched her expectantly.

"Close these chambers off, and Jin's private rooms as well. Kill all of his Hiveguard on sight, and lock up that Morganite woman as well. We'll not be using his rooms anymore."

She hurried down the hallway, back to her own sleeping chambers, and from there to another, smaller room hidden behind a tapestry.

Here she waited as the reports came in. The wave of assassinations spread quickly and quietly through the Human Hive, targeting the top supporters of Jin's increasingly decadent regime. Men and women were struck down in their sleep, or as they lay in the stupor of the vapors or in the embrace of the holoworlds.

There was a soft knock at the door, in a coded sequence. The panel slid open and Cassie entered, wearing a blue vest and short blue skirt. She looked tired, her face shadowed by fatigue. She sat down at the edge of the bed while Mia monitored reports from a touchscreen.

"So far it's going well," said Mia, her eyes glued to the screen.

"It should. You planned it so perfectly." Cassie sighed and lay back on the bed, stretching her arms out behind her head. "I left Kwan in his room. He had some pretty nice stuff."

"We'll collect it all later. We're going to search all the bodies, and all of the rooms, and then the rooms will be dismantled and turned back into quarters for the citizens. I want every trace of Jin's corruption eliminated. We must shock our people back to their true natures, the way my father envisioned it."

"A good battle could do that as well."

Mia smiled and looked at Cassie. "You know my plans. Morgan and Santiago will be forced off this continent within three years."

"Sounds good to me. Morgan first?"

"Yes. We won't fight a war on two fronts, like foolish Morgan would." She stared at Cassie for a moment more. "I want you to spend some time on my investigation teams, but as an undercover agent. Make sure they're doing their job."

"Identify the future rebels? Seed some paranoia?"

Mia nodded. "A little paranoia is healthy for the soul. It encourages right action."

"Yes, Chairman Yang. I won't argue there."

chapter eight

DIRECTOR MORGAN BLINKED AGAIN AND STARED AT HIS touchscreen. He shook his head, tapped his fist on the edge of the touchpanel, and waited.

No reply. Locusts swarmed, Miriam still occupied Solarfex, and now this.

"Tani?"

Her face appeared in holo, floating just in front of the touchscreen. She seemed tense, perhaps busy, her wide eyes shadowed. "Yes, Director?"

"I'm trying to reach Sada and she's not responding."

She glanced off to the side, apparently checking something. "She should be in the Hive. The ship arrived two days ago. But I can't get her, either." She frowned.

"Is it the locusts?"

"Well, the channel is clear at the moment. And she left no Away message."

"Then what's wrong?" On a hunch he punched up Chairman Yang's priority frequency, but no one answered. Instead the image of a woman appeared, ancient and beautiful, wearing a dynamic red dress.

The message under the holo said "Chairman Yang is unavailable. Please try again soon."

And even in the image, her eyes seemed to study him, sparkling with some private joke.

"Beautiful."

Mia Yang, now Chairman Yang, stood in front of a full-length mirror as her citizen tailor put the last touches on her new ceremonial garb. Rather than the elaborate robes she and the other Grand Advisors had worn under Jin's regime, her new clothing was lean and functional, while still evoking the early history of the Hive. There were no traces of the casual and expensive Morganite influence, but she still looked the way she felt: beautiful and dynamic. And in the grand spirit of her father's ideological warfare, she had holos of herself taken and leaked to the MorganLinks. Soon all the settlements would see this vibrant new persona who led the Hive. Maybe Morgan would even make an action figure.

Cassie bounced into the room, wearing a simple knee-length skirt that had a dark blue-green hue. It looked sturdy and plain, but still let her youthful buoyancy shine. This pleased Mia as well.

"What news, Cassie?"

Cassie sat down in a wooden chair and set a small touchpanel on the round table next to it. She began scanning reports.

"We've assembled the army, and stepped up the pace of the genejacks factory. I've relayed your order to the Minister of Genetics to lower the error rate in the warrior clones to less than eight percent, or to consider a position for himself on the Drone Lines."

Mia laughed. "That wasn't how I put it, Cassie."

"But that's more or less what he needed to hear," she said. "We'll march on Morgan and drive him out of the Uranium Flats. The fighting will rally the citizens, and give them something to concentrate on."

"Or smoke out the loudest dissenters. Good."

"Chairman . . ." Cassie trailed off. Mia turned quickly to look at her, attuned to every emotional quirk in those around her.

"Tell me, Cassie. Don't waste my time."

"Morgan is embroiled in this war with Godwinson, it's true. But I worry about Santiago. She occupies this land, and she's Morgan's enemy. She may want the Uranium Flats. She may want this land. And she may know that we're going to come after her next . . ."

"Hush!" Mia looked at the tailor, who kneeled on the floor, eyes carefully downcast. Mia regarded the woman for a moment, who seemed to shrink even farther into herself, like a dark puddle being sucked down through a drain in the floor.

Mia calmly reached down and brushed the back of the woman's neck with her thumb. For a moment the tailor remained still, and then she fell over, collapsing on the floor.

Cassie stared, wide-eyed, as Mia slipped something off her thumb and put it on a small table. "It's not altogether your fault, Cassie," said Mia quietly. "I don't want our plans circulating so quickly. Santiago is a dangerous woman, and we must strike quickly, and secretly."

Cassie finally nodded. "With the strength of her

soldiers, it must happen quickly, or she will destroy us."

"Santiago," said Mia, stepping over the tailor and slipping quickly out of the new red ceremonial dress. She stared at a rack of dresses in many colors. "She'll be formidable. But Morgan is first."

"Speaking of Director Morgan . . ."

"Yes?"

"He wants to see you in the NuSpace."

Mia entered the NuSpace and found herself in Morgan's Teahouse program. He waited by one wall, looking guarded, though she remembered from reviewing tapes of Jin's meetings with him that they sat at the table like gentlemen.

She smiled and walked carefully to the table, then sat. Two cups of tea rested on the low table, sending their steam into the air of the projection.

"What do you want, Director Morgan?"

He rubbed his hand along the surface of his gold and black robe and stepped over to the table. Instead of sitting he remained on his feet, looming over her, but that made her smile, too. Did he think such crude psychological games would work on her?

"I want to know where we stand. Your predecessor signed a treaty with us, and I want to assure you that I have every intention of honoring it."

She picked up her cup, took a small sip, and set it back on the table with a click. Suddenly she was on her feet again, her long, willowy body rising up from the floor. Her red robe seemed to pulse in the dim light of the teahouse.

"My husband met an unfortunate end before he

could get all his affairs in order. The Hive is under new management, so to speak. Naturally there'll be a housecleaning."

"Of course. But the treaty is still to your benefit. We can help you expand your influence throughout the world, introduce more goods into your bases, please your citizens—"

"I don't need material goods to satisfy my citizens. That was a fallacy of my husband's thinking. The Hive remains independent, and with good reason. I've seen what your corruption did to Jin, even in the short time he was in your territory."

Morgan stopped short. His projection seemed to shift ever so slightly, melting into itself for a moment and then reforming again. "If you mean to break our treaty, the consequences will be severe. I won't relinquish the Uranium Flats."

She smiled. "Really? As I said, there's no treaty. But I can offer you the safe return of your citizens in exchange for the Morgan Minerals base itself. We're taking it back."

His eyes flashed at her, and the walls of the Teahouse seemed to warp for a moment, as if mirroring his anger. "That's a Morganite settlement, built by me. The Council will not stand for such a blatant—"

"That land belongs to the Hive, the Council be damned. The Hive stands alone, Director Morgan. You vacate the Uranium Flats in five days, and no blood will be shed. Let that be the end of this." She extended a hand to him.

He lifted his own hand, tightening his fist. A complex chain of emotions washed across his projection, and then he brought it under control. "I won't allow your representatives into Morgan Minerals. We have a treaty. I suggest we wait for Council mediation."

"The Council can't meet because of the locusts."

"It won't be long. Lady Skye says they'll break soon."

She stared at him for a moment. "We can wait five days at most. But I assure you the end result will be the same."

Once out of the NuSpace, Mia gestured to Cassie. "Get the playback of that session. Let's go back in together and analyze it."

Once back in, Mia and Cassie floated in observer mode, shifting their angle, stopping and pausing the scene. Mia thought nothing of watching herself, or her projection, talk to Morgan, though Cassie took a momentary delight in swooping her tiny pointcam around Mia's frozen body.

"I want to analyze one sequence. When I told him we were going to send representatives to the Hive, he had a very complex reaction, one he failed to mask." She ran the projection to that point, and then slow-mo'd it. Glowing text spooled down in space, from an adapted Gaian Empath program that helped in psych analysis.

"Anger, not surprising," said Cassie. She watched Morgan's face as the projection advanced slowly, turning his expression into a tumbling slow motion avalanche.

"Look at his projection as well. The edges fray for a moment. He remembered something important. A moment of shock, and a flurry of responses."

"Then a quick flash of elation, and he gets it together again."

"What a foghead, to have let himself slip so badly. He doesn't want us in Morgan Minerals. He has something to hide, something that might help him."

"So we go in now?" asked Cassie.

"Yes. There won't be a better time. Send the army in full speed ahead, and cut off all Morgan transports to these shores."

Morgan tensed his arms in fury as he waited for Tani to lift the NuSpace rig from his head and torso. As soon as it was up he pushed his way out of the booth.

"She means to betray me." He paced back and forth, his arms trembling. "She's broken our treaty and threatened Morgan Minerals."

"There's little we can do about it."

Morgan turned on her. "There are ways to get troops there. Even across the world, remember?"

"Have you forgotten the Believer troops are only one base away, Director?"

"We can spare some of ours. Take a fifth. Pull them back and send them to Morgan Minerals."

"A fifth won't be enough, here or there."

"Do it! We can't give up our foothold on the far shore so easily." At that moment he received a priority link. The Sin Gun had arrived at Morgan Industries.

He and Tani went to watch as the secure magtrain pulled in from the gold line that ran from Morgan Industries up to University Base. The line spanned a series of checkpoints, and the train that arrived was sleek and black and held several transport and cargo cars.

Two dozen University guards got out, along with four technicians in their clean white tunics. The four University technicians greeted Morgan and Tani and then waited calmly while the small yellow cranes moved the reactor base and wide barrel into position on a transport elevator. While they waited the head tech, Natasha, reviewed a holographic contour map.

Morgan and Tani stared. The base unit was a monster, an imposing cylinder made of a smoky gray glasslike metal, over ten meters in diameter. Into the top they slid a long silver tube, and when it clicked into place Morgan had the odd impression that the whole world had shifted, just a millimeter out of sync.

"That is the fuel for the singularity," said Natasha. "It's a one-time charge, and it will be consumed during the operation of the gun."

"Can you use it against their army?" asked Tani, but Natasha shook her head.

"Godwinson has them all spread out across the land. We could take out some of them, but it would be a waste. But the forces they've assembled in Solarfex will be destroyed."

"Since we're going to do this, can we get a vidfeed of the target?"

Natasha nodded and had her techs bring over a large touchpanel. A long-distance scan showed the dim shape of Solarfex, the sleek buildings touched by the silvery light of the moon, Nessus.

"Peaceful," murmured Natasha. The technicians

had set up the Sin Gun barrel itself, a short stubby affair about two meters long clamped to the top of the singularity cell. It was made of the same smoky glass as the base unit, but inside the glass they could see a sheet of synthmetal.

"Is that it?" Morgan asked, cupping his hand to peer through the translucent surface. Indeed, the gun looked strangely nondescript. There were no blinking lights, no phallic cannon thrust into the sky, nothing.

"What you're seeing is pure function," said Natasha. "Are you ready?"

"Yes," said Morgan. Tani nodded.

"If you please, give us the order to destroy the base."

"I order you to do so," he said.

Each of the four technicians pulled out a small back control disc and plugged it into sockets around the perimeter of the Sin Gun base. As Morgan watched they each entered a code, and then Natasha said "Activate singularity."

From deep inside the glassy base there was a flash of something, and for a moment the world blackened before his eyes, and the stars seemed to jolt.

"A singularity is smaller than the eye can see," said Natasha. "This base is mostly a stasis field. It holds a force as powerful as this base's output for a half year."

"What if the field were to break?"

"There are safeguards." Natasha stared at a readout on her touchpanel. "It's going to fire."

From the barrel of the gun emerged a ball of darkness that Morgan could barely see against the night sky. He felt something buffet him, like a great wind that pushed the air from his lungs, and then it was gone, a black spot crossing the vast distance beneath the mountaintop. On the touchpanel the silvery lights of Solarfex flickered.

And in the next instant, they were gone.

He stared at the monitor. The buildings of the base stood, and there were still a few feeble lights blinking, but it was as if a giant wind had come through and knocked the people right off the streets. There were vehicles overturned and smashed into walls, and bodies lying like ragged leaves against the walls of the highest buildings. The pressure dome above the base was shattered and deflated. Morgan could see no other movement.

"One more for good measure," said Natasha, her voice even. Another burst swallowed the base for a moment, and then Morgan could see some crumbled buildings, pieces of steel and cement gusting down the street. Debris lay scattered in an eddy for kilometers behind the base.

"That's it," said Natasha. She turned to Morgan. "What did you think?"

"Amazing. I can't say more than that. I don't suppose you'd sell me one?"

Natasha laughed, and the four technicians pulled out their activation keys. There was a series of cracks and flashes, and Morgan jumped. "What was that?"

"The fuel cell is spent, and the interior automatically disintegrates after the gun is used. We can bring up another, but this one is useless."

"Very good." He found himself easing away from

these four, as if they were an extension of the force he had just seen. "You're welcome to come to my rec commons for some relaxation."

Natasha smiled, her grin unusually toothy. "Thank you. But we have to return the gun to University Base immediately. Perhaps some other time."

Inside Morgan Industries; some time earlier

Bhara Dov of Morgan Industries Base had grown tired of the fads and the funkiness that swept through Morganite society so quickly and constantly, with no relief.

One month it was eye piercing, the next it was transmutable skin, and then shimmering body paints, 40 cm shoes, electric fingernails, Recon Rover Rick holovids, toys and clothing, Linksongs and ReconRaves out in the xenofungus fields that left half the participants in a gibbering nightmare state until the meds showed up and reinfused them, on and on until the next fad came.

It was a dizzying array that kept her sad, empty and lonely, as if she were the lone rubber bumper in a pinball machine, while silver balls and flashing lights ricocheted around her and shook her very foundation.

She wasn't a Talent, which was part of the problem for sure. She didn't have the two-meter height or the long, lean build. She had once seen her friend, a muscular construction worker, insult a Talent who looked as beautiful as any SuperHoloGirl, and the woman had taken her tall, lithe form and forced her stocky friend into the street, where she threw him, quite literally, into a gutter.

They were tall and fast and healthy and gorgeous, and she couldn't keep up. Standing on her 40 cm shoes and staring at her friend, lying in the gutter holding a bloody nose, she had felt like a ridiculous toadstool as the Talent fixed her with a glance as cool as a Silver Ice, the popular new drink that left her with hammers in her head every morning.

Wobbling her way home that night, she had taken her friend and tended to him, massaging his wounds and his ego. And they had made love, him pulling off her fashionable shift to expose slightly plump flesh, and he had turned on a holo projector on the bed, masking her. As he thrust into her from above with angry grunts, she had looked into the mirror to see the holo, and it was a Talent, two meters tall, just like the one that had humiliated him that night.

Despair washed over her and she pushed him off. His flash of anger faded into a look of sullen bitterness. Then he had grabbed his clothes and left her tiny, expensive apartment.

As the city flashed its lights outside her window, she had surfed the links into the night, getting into darker and darker spaces, trying to find holos of Talents in the most degrading situations possible.

She read in the links that the newest super drink, the same Silver Ice she tried to drink every night at the bars, had been specially formulated to the typical Talent genetic profile, and in the others, the Ordinaries, it was closer to a poison.

She read that there were Talent sex rings, where clones of the most beautiful women and men in the settlements were kept for the wealthiest.

She read that some wealthy Talents kept punishment spheres in secret chambers in their bedrooms, and acquired drones to torture inside, though the use of the sphere had been outlawed by U.N. Charter.

She read of a world that was fast-moving and ultimately sickening.

And gradually, on the great uncontrolled mass of the Morganite datalinks, she found a Voice that promised another way.

The Voice, she learned, had grown slowly but surely, sweeping through a select and largely silent minority, like a fad that had grown deeper and more slowly, rather than burning out and fading away.

The Voice was small, but it was everywhere. The Voice spurned the rampant materialism of the Morganites, and whispered of an abiding faith in the human spirit. As she came to explore the Voice, she learned the method of "singing prayer," of filling the mind with a long, ever-cycling hymn to the glory of what they called the Almighty, who was something she understood as a part of her, but much bigger. Bigger than the world, or even the universe. Bigger than the Morganites, certainly.

Some scientists believed that the universe was nothing more than a quantum flux of energy, spawning the illusion called Time, and that it would all vanish when this energy was spent. The Voice said that only a flawed invention of the equally flawed human intelligence could imagine its own demise, or its own irrelevance. When had God ever imagined her own demise, or a world in which she had no relevance?

The Voice made sense to Bhara. Gradually she distanced herself from her family, whom she felt now stared at her through bars of their own making, not realizing it was them, and not her, inside the cage.

Slowly, as the veil of materialism was lifted, she began to see the Voice at work in the Morganite bases. The Freq Freaks who shambled the streets in their odd brown robes, ignoring the fickle flow of fashion, they were extensions of the Voice. Some of the filthy outcast drones who slept outside the power capacitors on Energy Lane were of the Voice too, because she saw the way they set tiny rocks in a pattern she had learned to help identify the faithful.

The Voice embraced her, because she embraced it. When her boyfriend shouted at her and shook her, it was as if he moved underwater, because the flow of the Word swept his words away the instant they left his lips.

She met others of the Voice, in tiny offices rented from the big Morganite Industry buildings. There they talked about the Word, and drank soothing, warm beverages and came to believe, in so many ways, that the frantic, helpless people outside would be much better served when the system of culture that enslaved them had ceased to exist.

Days went by in her job, monitoring security at the second tallest tower in the base, and the days flowed so easily, since she imagined herself one of the protected and the Holy. When the leader of the Voice, a tall man with hooded eyes, asked her to transfer to a lower position, a position monitoring the great capacitors that fed the city, it was an easy change for her, like switching seats at a holovid theater.

Until yesterday, when he had called her to him again, while the locusts swept back and forth across the settlements. The mood of the citizens was dark, even the usually hard-partying Morganites subdued and staying indoors.

It's the perfect time, he said. *Tomorrow, here is your task, for the glory of Sister Miriam and the Voice. You know the power equipment as well as anyone. You have their trust. Now here is your job.*

Something inside of her, a tiny, prickly worm that had never quite relented to the Voice, jolted in alarm, but it was easy enough to ignore.

The next day she went in to work, and she used her pass to walk on to the power fields, where the great capacitors bathed in their endless riches of energy. She had grown peaceful and more lovely since embracing the Voice, and she smiled at the guard as he checked her credentials and waved her right in.

A small cutting tool got her through an obscure, forgotten hatch and into the main power grid of the energy feeds to Morgan Base. She stared down at the underground grid, deep and vast like a small city in itself, as the energy crackled in her ears and pulled gently at her hair.

The Voice had told her where to land, a juncture point between two of the main capacitor feeds. She was aware of alarms, and flashing lights. She said her last prayer, and jumped.

Her body, which was only flesh and muscle and fat after all, landed at the juncture point and fused to it instantly. The silver cross she wore around her neck melted into the lump of burning flesh she had become.

Two capacitors emptied into each other like two

giants battling on a mountaintop. Energy backed up and discharged and then every capacitor shut down, and the mighty energy nexus of Morgan Industries went dark.

At the same moment Bhara crossed the capacitor feeds and sucked the life from Morgan Base, a series of Believer agents infiltrated the relatively unguarded power feeds to the main nanohospital and shorted them out. Still another set blew open a toxic sludge tunnel, feeding it down into the water supply, until the filters whined with effort, while others rerouted the noxious output from a small factory into the air filters.

With the capacitors drained and emergency power split between several critical sites, the tachyon field around the base dimmed and reduced itself, so that it no longer extended beneath the earth. Which meant it no longer extended to the deepest part of the river.

Not so far away, on a rocky mountain pass that overlooked the Industry River that fed its glimmering waters into the heart of this Morganite base, a man waited with his group of huddled brothers and sisters under the dark skies.

The man, Ezran, held a long penetrator rifle bristling with hooks for hand-to-hand combat, not that he expected any. "I can see the field dimming," he said.

Noah, his second in command, surveyed the rocky terrain below and nodded. "The sensors will be out as well."

Ezran's eyes rolled in the darkness. They had

all studied the glorious attacks on the other Morgan outposts, but this attack was on the heart of Morgan's territory itself. Thousands of Believers counted on them to get through the flickering tachyon field and into the base, to throw down its walls.

He looked back at his party, huddled in their brown robes, stoic and unflinching. Every face seemed chiseled in the moonlight, expressionless, fearless. He knew his own face looked the same, but fear did turn at his belly, and that made him ashamed. Miriam's War Verse rolled through his head unbidden.

"With the power down, the tachyon field will no longer extend below ground level. That means there is a way in, through the river. We go now, and I will see you all again, in this world or the next."

"Ahmin."

Ezran stood and pulled off his brown robe, and the others did the same behind him. The silver cross, smeared with a black oil to keep it from glinting, still hung around his neck, and his body was smeared with camo oil as well. From a pouch in his clothes he took a small rebreather that Kola had given him.

Naked except for a loincloth, his skin dark against the rocks, he crept along a path and to a short outcropping that thrust out over the river.

It was a drop of about fifty meters, but this was the best chance of avoiding detection from the darkened base that lay a few hundred meters down the river.

He closed his eyes and reached deep into his soul

for the prayers that he repeated, day and night, for the twenty years of his life. He felt the resonance of thousands of his brothers and sisters chanting with him; strength surged through his muscles, and he felt as if he would shout from the mountaintops. He let the energy build; he could see only the light of God even on this dark night, and he could see the pale white form of Sister Miriam raising her staff above the gathered masses.

He might have shouted, or not, he no longer cared. He hurled himself off the cliff, and felt the elation as he fell, until he crashed into the waters below.

The world shifted from light to dark, hot to cold for Ezran. He knifed into the water, hard, and a small part of him thought he might have broken bones. But his exhilaration continued, and he could feel a Holy power in his limbs.

He pushed his way through the cloudy water. He could taste blood in his mouth, but he had clenched his teeth hard on his rebreather and hadn't lost it. He followed an internal light now, a raw wave of intuition and feeling that told him to swim down, hard, until he could feel the cool mud of the river bottom. Then he let the current pull him, and he pushed with it, toward the tachyon field.

Even with the cloudy water he could smell and hear the tachyon field. The water washing through it boiled, and he could feel its heat on his skin early, as he started pushing down to the bottom of the river. He touched the river mud and then he pushed forward with all his strength. He could feel boiling water from the weakened tach field on his back, and he clenched his teeth on his rebreather.

But even as pain rocketed through his body it triggered a light that surrounded him, as neural pathways built on thousands of hours of meditation guided him to a Holy place, beyond the pain.

He pushed, feeling the blisters rise on his back, and then he was past it all. A last blade of pain scraped across his legs, and then he pushed up.

He kicked to the surface and dragged himself to the riverside. The base loomed dark around him, the stars barely visible above. He was about a hundred meters away from a side street lined by two-story buildings, the lights all out. Down the river he saw two people, soldiers on a nervous patrol.

He was inside Morgan Industries, and thousands of Believers would soon follow.

Director Morgan stared at the display readout, stunned. It was as if his very lifeblood was draining away before him. The energy reserves for Morgan Industries, gathered and hoarded over decades, were vanishing before his eyes.

"Sabotage," he croaked, through lips gone suddenly dry. And this, on the heels of discovering Jin Yang of the Human Hive was gone.

Tani, lurking behind him like a dark shadow, finally stepped forward. She nodded as if satisfied with the answer to a problem.

"Believers, I'll bet. Better check the tach fields." She stepped forward and started punching up the readouts in the base. "It says I have to go through the Morgan Security uplink, and check in with them. But with the power reserves down, that's difficult. And the sensors aren't working, either."

"They're coming," said Morgan. He sat down in a large, thick chair, but his mind was already racing, trying to find the way out, a way to turn this situation to his advantage. "We have to contact Zakharov. No, the Council! She's gone too far this time. Anyone can see it."

Tani was already on her quicklink, summoning escorts; at the same time she gathered items from around the room, such as a string of brilliant sapphires that snaked its way across a night table. "We need to leave," she said. "With the tachyon field breached, the Believers will get in. We'll go to another base, or even to UNHQ. Pravin is more centrally located, and much safer."

"Of course." Morgan stood up and walked slowly to the broad windows along one wall. The touch of a sensor opened the blinds, and Morgan was surprised to find light flooding into the room. He blinked against the sun and the hot blue sky.

"The locusts are dispersing," he said. He watched as the dark clouds moved westward, tapering away into thin trails. A weight seemed lifted from his mind.

Tani walked over, stuffing several small lacquered boxes into a black silk bag. "Look there. The sun glinting off those hovertanks. It's the Believer army."

Morgan looked out and saw thousands of scraggly Believers, with stolen hovertanks and speeders. Believers on foot, great silver crosses among them. He could see his own Morganite tanks rolling toward the perimeter in a somewhat organized fashion, a bolt of blue-white fire crossing the vast distance already. He nodded.

"We'll leave immediately. This can't be good for business."

Zakharov clattered up the metal stairs to the observation deck, his heart pounding. He pushed open the door and was greeted by the sight of the clear white sky overhead, the two suns hanging there, and the locusts dispersing like smoke in the wind.

"Daniel!" he barked into his quicklink. "Tell me more."

"They're dispersing, sir. All over the settlements, apparently. The sky is opening up, but the orbitals aren't back online yet."

"Still, we can send out needlejets in short excursions. Prepare them. And I want those orbitals back online. That very instant we'll launch the counterattack on Miriam."

"Yes, Academician. Also, the comm lines are all open again. The Council is gathering."

Zakharov entered the NuSpace into the program for the Council meeting chamber. This room resembled a large domed room, glinting with gold and platinum highlights, the chairs of the Council members elevated so they appeared to float in a vast space. He could almost hear the heavenly choir as he ascended to his spot, although the irony of the space was that there was no one to actually look down on; except for the Council members, no one else occupied the room.

Pravin already waited there, in his white and blue

robes of state, occupying the central chair. Zakharov had long ago determined that Lal made his projection slightly bigger than life, but he never exposed the small deception. Indeed, he admired Lal's resourcefulness in altering the program just that much.

Santiago waited there, in her crisp uniform, her breast ablaze with medals. Deirdre Skye waited there, her green robes flowing about her, her expression pensive. Morgan was there too, dressed in expensive, tailored clothes, but Zakharov could already feel the nexus of rage from Morgan's seat.

Zakharov crossed to his chair and sat down. A glass of crystal water, so pure it didn't even look real, which in fact it wasn't, shimmered in the light in front of him.

"We're all here, then," said Pravin. "Except Miriam, of course. Let me call to order this meeting of Council. The purpose of this meeting is to deal with the Believer threat."

"She leads an army of barbarians with an unnatural amount of luck," said Morgan. "She's occupied two of my bases now, and she's heading for Morgan Industries. My home!"

"They're more than barbarians," said Zakharov, and was surprised to find that his own voice was tight with a rage he hadn't fully expressed. "They have weapons now, and vehicles, and a supply line."

"What are we talking about here?" asked Santiago in clipped, professional tones. "Full disclosure. What weapons do they have, and do you have any video feeds or sensor information showing the composition of their force?"

"Does this mean you would help spearhead an attack against them, Santiago?" asked Lal.

"I want to know what they have, before they get to me. That's all."

Zakharov sighed and linked the information to the others on weapons and vehicles that he held. Morgan finally did the same.

"This isn't all," said Santiago.

"That's all my material from the Marine Institute and Academy Park," said Zakharov, and Morgan remained silent. The issue of the Sin Gun hadn't been broached.

"This is what she has now," said Santiago. "I want to know what she'll have when she enters University lands!"

"She won't enter my lands." Zakharov slammed his hand down on the table as his anger caught up with his words. "She doesn't have the resources, or the means. Nothing she has could breach the field around University Base, and the weapons I have there—" He stopped short, looking at the others. "They're more than enough. I just want retribution for Academy Park."

Morgan stayed silent, not looking at any of them.

"All right," said Pravin. "Miriam has used nerve gas pods, twice, in clear violation of the U.N. Charter. Will we attack her, and take her out, together?"

"I say we use nerve gas back at her," said Morgan. "A couple of capsules, delivered properly—"

"I will veto any such attempt," said Pravin firmly. "They are religious fanatics, and they're under the sway of a charismatic leader. We won't slaughter them all, along with the remainder of your citizens taken hostage in these bases."

Morgan lapsed into silence.

"But we will band together. Santiago, will you assist?"

"I'll send troops to rendezvous with whatever Zakharov has at University Base. Deirdre can send her sprouts to meet Morgan. We can squeeze the J-freaks from north and south."

Pravin nodded. "Gather your armies. We'll have our tacticians coordinate the attack on Believer lands, and Miriam's army. We meet again in one day. Agreed?"

They all signaled their agreement, and then jacked out.

chapter nine

Pravin stared at Pria, who stood silhouetted against the high windows of his quarters as the rain lashed the building. The form was as he remembered; seeing her like this, as a shadow on the glass, it was as if his wife stood there and no time had passed.

He cleared his throat, and she turned. He saw her body stiffen from tension, and he looked away, staring at the reports on his table.

Damn. She got like this sometimes . . . nervous and edgy. And it made him edgy. Why did she even come here?

Again he examined the feeds from the University satellites, and the reports from Morgan and Zakharov. The virus was sweeping Academy Park and even University Base itself. Even the locusts' lifting worried him, knowing that it would soon allow Zakharov to mobilize his air forces for an attack on Miriam and her followers.

And now Morgan Industries, gone dark from sabotage.

"She'll never make this work," he said aloud. He

tried not to pay any attention to the way that the woman in the room inched her way around the perimeter, sticking close to the windows, and far away from him. But finally he became annoyed. "Stop that!"

She froze. "Am I bothering you?" The voice was a hushed whisper, with a throaty undertone. He felt a chill go up his spine.

"Why can't you relax a little?" He waved his hands at her in frustration. "Sit down. You can have anything you want or need. Why do you spend every evening creeping around the walls like a spider?"

"I'm sorry." She came slowly to one of the low stuffed chairs and sat down in it, but her body was still stiff as a rod. She folded her hands in her lap and waited.

He stood up and paced, trying to work the knots of tension from his shoulders. Finally he went to the small food prep area, which lay in shadows, but he could see light glinting off the smooth steel surfaces.

He ran warm water to wash his hands, a habit when he was nervous. And there he saw, in the sink, a white mug.

Why didn't the maid clean that up?

He shook his head in annoyance, and then he noticed the tiny rim of lip coloring on the mug. Pria, or the woman he called Pria, had drunk from this mug the night before.

He picked up the mug and stared at it, and suddenly it was as if he existed in two worlds, one in which his own Pria lived, and drank her ginseng tea, which was her favorite, and held this white mug and laughed with him . . .

And that world bled into the real world, the here

and now, in which a woman he barely knew wore pale rose lipstick and drank . . . something. Tea? A different kind of tea? Did her Pria genes actually influence her tastes?

No. Because Pria loved ginseng tea since the time we had shared a mug at the tiny cafe in New Delhi. We bought it because of the funny drawing on the box, a little kung-fu man. From that time on she drank the tea, and it reminded her of home. Of our home.

He opened a cabinet, pulled down another mug, and filled it with a jet of hot water. A metal canister in the cabinet contained tea pellets, eight different flavors. He had been serving her the ginseng, just like Pria used to drink.

He stared out past the kitchen divider and into the dark living room. The woman sat there as if on trial, her hands still folded in her lap. He felt a sudden empathy. Slowly, he walked to her, then presented her with one of the mugs. "Would you like to drink?"

"Thank you." She took the mug in both hands, nervously, and then as he watched she brought it to her face. A look of confusion crossed her features.

"It's hot water?"

He kneeled down in front of her and held out the tea canister. "I thought you might like to choose." He held it out. "Whatever you like."

She looked into the canister, and finally picked out a reddish pellet. "Lemongrass," she said, as if apologizing, and dropped it into the mug.

He got up and sat in a chair a few meters away, not too close and not too far away. He picked the same flavor and put it into his own mug, and drank deeply. Finally he looked at her.

"You don't have to stay here. I'm sorry for the trouble I've given you."

She took a sip and swallowed, then looked at him. At the sight of her brown eyes, his heart leapt into his throat. "Where should I go, then?"

"You can go back to your quarters. You can stay here, too. I won't tell you what to drink anymore, though." He laughed a little, to himself. "You are always welcome here. To me, you're like family."

She set down her mug on a glass coffee table, the clink loud in the darkness. Then she looked at him. "I don't want to leave. It's lonely in my quarters. But you're busy."

"Not so busy."

He took her hand and led her to the couch. They drank their tea, and talked awhile. Later, he stayed in the darkness for a long time, his work momentarily forgotten, as a tiny sliver of hope grew inside of him.

Cassie watched over the Hive army, as the soldiers massed in the long staging tunnels of Watcher's Eye, the northernmost Hive base. The staging tunnels were tall enough to stack ten needlejets, and so long that they had their own horizon, one end scarcely visible from the other.

Huge camouflaged hatches on one end of each tunnel led to the surface, the tunnels sloped in such a way that needlejets could launch right through them. Other hatches led to a series of smaller tunnels, these lined with massive Hive drills that could extend the tunnels in any direction.

Standing on a railed viewing balcony halfway up one massive wall, Cassie felt swallowed by it all.

Thousands of Hive soldiers lined the floor beneath her, all in black armor and looking like carefully positioned ants. The army had grown soft under Jin, but Mia's physical education programs were changing that. Those that refused to follow them answered to a hierarchy of enforcers. The army had doubled in size almost at once.

She could see the newer soldiers below, their formations loose. They would march in first, and the better soldiers would mop up afterward. An advance strike force would clear the way for everyone.

A loud humming sound echoed through the hall. Cassie looked to see a large hatch opening, leading to a newly drilled tunnel, which in turn led to Morgan Minerals. She checked her quicklink; the advance strike force should be hitting soon, and the army would follow. She signaled the new general below to move them out.

Slowly, in units, the Hive soldiers started their march.

Morgan Minerals was a compact, efficient base that existed for one purpose: to suck every particle of rich, mineral-laden soil from the so-called Uranium Flats. The Flats were a vast swath of land on the upper end of Hive Continent, gray and featureless beneath any combination of Centauri suns, that held abundant heavy minerals in the soil and crust.

Director Morgan entertained no illusions about a utopian, materialistic lifestyle on this side of the world. Morgan Minerals was mostly functional, small and well-defended, with as many soldiers as miners. It was his biggest foot in the door on this

continent, and transport after transport departed
for the settlements, loaded down with chemically
extracted minerals. The men and women who
worked the base were strong and humorless.

Not so long ago, the number of transports had
lessened severely. When pressed for an explanation
by Jin, Morgan only said that his mineral produc-
tion was stable, and that he didn't want to deplete
the Uranium Flats, which were "as valuable and
striking a part of Chiron as any of Deirdre Skye's
luscious gardens."

Even so, the land around Morgan Minerals was as
close to a wasteland as anything Deirdre could have
imagined. Vast craters and long pits had been
gouged from the ground with various chemical and
machine extraction methods, and a cloud of noxious chemical byproduct hung in the sky. A borehole punctuated all of this, the deep shaft into the
earth topped by a huge metal cap that emitted
steam, more gases, and the occasional gout of
flame. Every so often a spark would ignite the sky itself, the clouds of chemical byproduct bursting into
a flame that could be seen for hundreds of kilometers, scorching the ground.

The Hive advance strike team decided to use this
peculiar environmental hazard to their advantage.
Captain Hung, the leader of the fifteen soldier
squad, moved up behind a low rise of grayish rock.
Quiet and fast-moving, their presence masked by
sophisticated sensor jamming equipment, the strike
team had seen no sign of Morganite soldiers. Now
they stared over the rise at the long gray flats and
the dark, squat shape of the Minerals base in the

distance. The chemical soup churned in the air above the base.

Hung looked back and signaled one of his soldiers. She pulled a sleek "pyro" hand-held missile from a pack on her back and handed it to him. He adjusted the flight parameters on the missile carefully, aimed it across the dull gray plain, and hurled it into the air.

The missile fired, streaking toward Morgan Minerals. It was small and not meant to penetrate any defenses. Instead it sailed toward the base, a tiny spark in a dark, hazy sky, and burst. From that the chem-choked sky ignited, haloing the Morgan base and its outposts in clouds of red fire that seemed to reach to the twin suns themselves.

Hung turned his head away and felt the heat on the side and back of his armor, then he and his fellow soldiers were hit by a wall of hot wind and knocked down the hill. When he recovered he stood and signaled the others to regroup.

In the distance alarm claxons went off. "They'll call all the workers in and monitor damage to the base. They won't know that was intentional for hours. By then, too late."

The others nodded their assent in typical Hive fashion, preferring signals and visual communication over voice. Hung linked to command.

The main Hive army was streaming through a tunnel below them, heading for the Morganite base.

Hive foils, cleaned to perfection by the hands of the soldiers that manned them, raced across the sea, hopping high above the white-capped swells. Captain Schiller stared across the water, enjoying the spray on his face. He had come up on deck to get away from the stifling heat of the transport hold, loaded with silent Hive soldiers.

His gunner scanned the horizon as well, and then suddenly she pointed; at the same instant an alert went off on his sealink.

A Morgan transport ship, foolishly silver and glinting in the twin suns, powered away from the shore to their left. It had obviously left Morgan Minerals recently, and was now gathering speed for its journey to the far shore.

"Get it," said Schiller.

The foil changed course smoothly. Sea warfare in the modern world was a war of vectors; ships raced at blinding speed across the sea, powered by advanced quantum engines, and the key was intercepting the enemy by calculating probable course changes.

"Morganite vessel, prepare to be boarded," he said over the appropriate channel, making sure to use the neutral, emotionless tone befitting a Hive soldier.

"Negative, Hive vessel. We're a supply transport, protected by treaty and settlement law. Stand down, you will not board this vessel."

"Sorry," said Schiller, and checked the count-down. It should be moments before the attack was launched.

"Sorry, you didn't mean it, or sorry, you're going to board us anyway, Hive vessel? Please clarify."

He closed the link. The Morgan vessel had kicked its speed up a notch and started evasive action, its massive hull gleaming as it turned in the water, exposing half its belly. But Schiller knew the Hive tracking and seeking algorithms were the most sophisticated on Chiron.

"Fire at will." The words were like a fine Morgan wine, which, since trade with the Morganites was to be suspended, he hoped to find on yonder ship.

His gunner checked some tracking readouts, adjusted her weapon, and fired. A bolt of hazy light rocketed across the deep blue-green of the sea, even as the Morganite ship receded from them.

A moment later there was a shock that rocked his boat, and a column of smoke rose in the sky. His ship changed course and headed right for the Morganite vessel, the gunner unloading several more shots to cripple it further.

They pulled up alongside the ship. A handful of Morganites stood on the smoking deck, their hands raised. Morganites never liked to go down fighting, but rather seemed to welcome arrest and expected prison cells more luxurious than a typical Hive citizen's home. Schiller dispatched several guards down to the deck to take the Morganites prisoner.

He followed, heading for the cargo hold. Several Hive soldiers gathered around him eager to see the booty, though it would no doubt be a hold full of featureless mineral blocks.

They blasted open the locks, and he punched the key that opened the hold. Massive cargo doors opened to reveal . . .

Nothing. The hold was empty, and perfectly clean.

"Empty?" repeated Cassie, reviewing reports from the field.

"Yes," said the captain, staring into the link with

his ruddy face. "We've seized three cargo ships now, and they're all empty."

"And these ships left Morgan Minerals *before* our invasion began?"

"Yes, Grand Advisor."

"Why would Morgan be shipping nothing across the sea?" Cassie thought of the time, about four months ago, when the transports leaving Morgan Minerals had slackened. "Something's going on in that base. Continue your patrol, and I'll inform the Chairman."

In digging vast pits and filling the sky with fire, Morgan had left his Morgan Minerals base open to the Hive engineers' main strength, which was drilling. As Hung monitored the battle on his tiny touch display, he saw the progress of the lean silver drills of the Hive slipping through the rock like fish through the ocean.

"How is it?" asked his lieutenant, Francis.

Hung nodded. "The drills have almost reached the base."

"His tach field could extend underground, though."

Hung packed up and signaled his squad to move back to a low hill, beyond which a small drill would soon open a pathway connecting with the main tunnel. "We're not going in just anywhere. We're going in through the borehole at the center of the base."

"We?" The lieutenant motioned toward the squad.

"Do you have anything better to do?"

* * *

One of the drills pushed its silver nose through the hillside exactly on schedule. Hung could see the whirring drill front, letting it cut earth like butter. It quickly retreated, leaving a narrow opening that sloped down.

He and his squad jogged down this opening, which was as smooth as if it had been cut by a laser, and about two meters around. It soon joined a larger tunnel down which a long line of Hive warriors flowed, like black ants following a trail of sugar. Hung led his squad down this line, pushing his way toward the front and moving quickly.

The Hive warriors marched next to him, all in their black armor and all carrying Q-guns in a ready position across their chest. Even with the numbers in the tunnel they moved with an eerie silence.

Hung ran on, until the tunnel opened into a wide staging area and he started to smell burning flesh through his pressure mask, feeling heat on the front of his armor. Squads of Hive warriors lined up in this room, all silent, and he could see piles of bodies at the far end, under the harsh light of large glowlamps.

"We're close. Let's go!"

He ran to the other end of the staging area. There were Hive bodies, charred or almost disintegrated from Morgan Q-guns, and then the contents of the piles gradually shifted to the Morganite defenders. Some of the bodies still smoked, and resembled dark lumps in the harsh, stony light.

An impassive Hive lieutenant saw Hung's rank and waved him on. Hung ran across a makeshift metal platform and into the borehole shaft.

Hung clattered onto a metal platform, and felt

tremendous heat even through his armor. He stood on a round platform attached to the edge of a deep shaft, and he had to stop and stare for a moment.

The shaft was narrow, much narrower than he thought: about twenty meters across. Metal platforms ringed it at intervals, and he could see sealed lifts that moved between the platforms. Above he could see artificial lights outlining the shape of the metal cap, and down below the shaft vanished into absolute darkness.

"Is this the borehole?" he asked. He felt cramped and hot and suffocated. It wasn't at all what he'd imagined.

"This is just a maintenance shaft," said a Hiveguard, approaching them. "What's your final position, sir?"

"Up there," said Hung, pointing to the metal cap. "We'll join the fight where needed."

"It was a complete surprise attack." The Hiveguard showed no emotion, although Hung thought he could see a glimmer of pleasure somewhere behind the faceless mask he or she wore. "Take this elevator, sir."

The Hiveguard led them to an elevator emblazoned with the Morganlink symbol. He jammed himself inside along with five other of his squad, and the elevator started up.

"Chiron," exclaimed Hung. One whole wall of the elevator was thick, reinforced synthglass, and through it they could look into the real borehole. It was dark and round, some forty meters across. Equipment and scaffolding lined the shaft in places, but there was no human life, nor did he imagine any human life could survive in there.

What he could see, and feel, and even smell through the glass was the heat, rushing up from the core of the world in shimmering waves.

Many settlement bases had boreholes, but Hung had once seen a work vest worn by the Morganite mining engineers. It said "Wider and deeper," and staring down this shaft that reached into the center of the world, he knew what they meant.

The elevator pushed Hung's gut into his shoes as it rocketed up and then quickly stopped. When the doors opened two large Hiveguard pressed in, strong and threatening, and then eased off as they saw Hung's sigil of rank.

He stepped out and looked around. They were in a large room, basically a huge, plain cylinder that surrounded the cap on the borehole. At one side were large metal doors, like cargo doors, now opened. Hiveguard were dragging bodies into a large pile in one corner.

Hung located the ranking officer, a swarthy man with sweat running down his face, who held his helmet mask in his hand. "What's happening here?" Hung asked.

"We've about taken the base," said the man, and the sweat gleamed from the large banks of lights on the high ceiling. "They didn't expect us to come through the borehole, and we hit them from the sea as well. Except—"

"What? Where?"

"There's a heavy knot of fighting in the center of the base. They have turrets in the hallways, security systems, and a mass of soldiers that won't give up. We keep killing them, and they keep coming."

"Thanks. Put your helmet on." Hung set off at a run, using his quicklink to guide him through the base.

The base consisted of large hallways, all heavily reinforced. The walls were made of some shiny gray metal that caught the light in interesting ways. Lights were everywhere, banks of them illuminating from walls and floors, as if the entire base were a jewel of energy that never stopped sparkling, sucking Morgan's energy pipes as if the supply were bottomless.

Even in this functional base he passed doors made of a crystalline glass, and rec commons full of modern gaming equipment and vidscreens the size of hovertanks. Along the hallway lay scattered bodies, but he hardly looked at these.

The Hive soldiers didn't use the death tones that Zakharov and the Peacekeeper soldiers used. What was another life lost? The Hive was many, and deep. But as he neared the nexus of fighting, Hung found himself wading through a sea of bodies, Hive soldiers, many cut clean through by a cannon of some kind. He could see more Hive soldiers up ahead, and he heard shouts and the fire of a variety of weapons, from penetrators to Q-guns.

"What now?" he asked rhetorically, ducking behind a pillar. The supports around him seemed thick and strong.

There was a whining hum, and then a blast of energy from the hallway. A flash nearly blinded him, and as he jerked his head away he felt something heavy slam into him.

He blinked, then looked up to see what had hit

him . . . a Hive soldier, blasted by a Morganite impact weapon. The woman's bones seemed twisted into a hundred different angles. The whine started again, and this time he looked up.

A single bank of lights on the ceiling dimmed, right before the gun fired.

"Boost me," he ordered Francis. Francis got on his hands and knees, lifting Hung toward the high ceiling. He pulled out a laser cutter and sliced down a bank of lights, giving him access to a crawlspace in the ceiling just as the lights dimmed once again. Below him he heard the weapon fire, its blast dying out to the screams of more Hive soldiers.

They're powering the weapon from the power feeds.

He pulled himself up into the crawlspace. Thick cables snaked around him, the arteries and veins of the base, bathed in tiny green lights. He took his laser tool and started slashing indiscriminately, even as he heard the weapon charge itself again.

A cable snaked toward him and touched his arm, and he felt a force like a powerful wind jolt through him. Every muscle in his body jerked and he shouted in agony as his own muscles hurled him backward, down to the ground below, unconscious.

Miriam traveled by armed escort to Morgan Industries. As her armed vehicle, which Kathryn jokingly named the Holy Rover, approached the conquered base she stared out a small porthole, taking in her handiwork.

Morgan Industries was as close to a crowded, dirty, bustling city as Chiron had. Tall buildings of glass and metal reached to the sky, but now the windows in these vast buildings were dark, making them look like forgotten monoliths. Smoke rose up and there was no flicker of the tachyon field, making the whole city look strangely exposed to the barren hills around it.

Great pressure cages had been set up, and she could see her Believers, most filthy and many wounded, herding captured Morganites into these secure shells. Large crosses had been driven into the earth in random places; "Believer terraforming," as Miriam liked to call it. She could see her elite squads heading up into the distant mountains to round up any Morganites at the boreholes and elevated solar arrays. If this were a painted landscape, smoke, crosses, and darkness would be the primary themes.

"It's become real," she said to herself, and then let that thought fade into the course of prayer that hummed through her brain. The light that had descended to her on her last day of burial pulsed inside of her. She realized again that the old Miriam, the one who doubted, had died on that day.

Her vehicle crossed a loose perimeter that her people had set up, and she saw a tall man with blood matted in his beard stare at her window and then prostrate himself. Then they were past the perimeter and finally in the streets, which were wide, paved, and strangely deserted. Bits of ash blew down the streets, and the streetlamps were dark. They rolled across a long bridge that arced over a wide, slow-moving river.

Pastor Prana met her at the foot of a tall building that looked like another bank. He bowed to her as she stepped from the armed rover.

"Where is it?" she asked. She could feel the power

of the Almighty prickling the hairs on the back of her neck.

"Top floor," he said. "May this be the end of our quest."

"Almighty. Take me."

Hung floated toward a gray haze that gradually lightened as he approached, until it opened up into the world of consciousness. With that world came pain, in his bones and back, but he shook that off, willing himself to focus on the here and now.

Several members of his squad stood over him, and some grim-looking Hiveguard that he didn't recognize. He was in the hallway, lying among the rubble from the ceiling above.

"It's over," said one of the tougher looking Hiveguard. He extended a hand and helped Hung up. "Once the gun was shut down they were helpless. There were many, but we got them all."

"And what were they protecting so tenaciously?" asked Hung, shaking himself off. The big Hiveguard motioned him forward.

"Let's go find out."

They walked past the main choke point, where the Morganites had died in piles, next to their Q-cannon. Hung saw where the cannon was hooked into the base power supply by thick green cables.

They walked past the thick doorway that the Morganites had hid behind. Beyond lay a short hallway, lit with the bright lights again, and beyond that a tall, heavy-looking door.

A small Hive man was working there, fiddling with door circuits. After a time, the door hissed and swung open.

"Let's see what was so important to them," said the big Hiveguard, and they entered a dim room, several with guns drawn, although Hung's scanner showed no life forms present. But Hung could feel the space in this room, its vastness, and its peculiar mineral smell. Someone found a light switch and the room flooded with brightness.

It was a massive storage room, square and solid and utterly functional, with a ceiling that towered to fifty meters. Filling the room were stacks and stacks of huge mineral boxes, solidified blocks of raw material that could be transported easily from base to base. Two spindly yellow cranes on hover-bases waited in one corner.

"This is what they were defending?" asked the big Hiveguard. "There's a lot, but it's just a bunch of minerals." He started pointing and naming mineral boxes by the bands of colors wrapping their cool gray exteriors.

"Maybe that was just the place they chose to die," said another.

But Hung headed into the warehouse and toward the back, where an odd configuration of boxes had caught his attention. "These have been moved," he said, and tried to peer around them. "Let's move them back."

It took some time, with two of his squad activating one big yellow crane and moving the massive boxes out of the way. Behind the boxes was another cargo door, large and metal. And that opened to another room, a control room of some kind. Hung stepped in first, weapon drawn, and looked around in wonder.

It was a semicircular room, lit with a deep blue

incandescence, vast monitor banks along one wall. Above the monitor banks great windows opened into another chamber, as large as a small warehouse. In that room's center was a great metal ring, thirty meters in diameter, cut with grids like the gills of fish, and inside those gills a deep energy pulsed. Staring into the center of the ring, Hung saw a static field, pulling at his eyes. Stacked in front of the ring were five more mineral boxes, waiting like forgotten children.

"What is it?" asked the Hiveguard, coming up behind him.

"I don't know. But whatever it is, it belongs to us."

chapter ten

"WELL, WHAT DO YOU *THINK* IT IS?" THE ANNOYING young woman pushed a strand of black hair back behind her ears and turned her nose up, just a little, at Hung, who talked to her over his quicklink. As the ranking officer and hero of the assault on Morgan Minerals, he had taken it upon himself to report the strange ring back to command.

And now he talked to this woman who had somehow become Mia Yang's top advisor and confidant.

"I think it processes the minerals somehow, maybe makes them lighter or something. But I can't know. We should activate it."

"Not until the Talents get there. They'll arrive soon."

The Talents came, but they couldn't activate the ring. Trained engineers, they hovered over the consoles for a long time, and finally started pressing activation sequences. The ring started up, the energy pulses inside moving more and more quickly, like bright, living things struggling in a narrow prison.

A low hum filled the room and made the floor tremble.

"The display says Activate Matter Transmission," said one Talent, and Hung felt a chill wash through him. At this point the Talents ordered everyone out of the area, but he stayed. One of them activated a supplementary control. A thin, tensile hovercrane moved over one of the large mineral boxes and lifted it easily off the floor, then carried it steadily toward the ring.

Hung held his breath, and he was sure the Talents were doing the same.

The mineral box touched the ring, and there was a shrieking sound accompanied by a gout of fiery black light. Warning claxons started to sound, and the Talents worked the controls frantically.

The box fell back on the same side of the ring, its surface black and smoking.

"That's not it," said a Talent.

Mia stared at the vidfeeds of the Transmitter Ring, feeling a sense of wonder that was often lacking from her closed, dark world. Cassie looked over her shoulder.

"They can't get it to work," said Cassie. "The Talents have been at it for a day now, and nothing."

"They'll get it," said Mia.

"But if it really is a transmitter, the other side needs to be activated as well. Can they do it remotely?"

"They've tried, but they can't find a way. The sister to this ring is in another one of Morgan's bases, presumably, and if he knows we have this one, then I'm sure he's turned off that one."

"Think about this device as a tool of war," said Cassie, in wonder. "Do you think a living body can go through it as well?"

Mia looked at Cassie, and for one moment Cassie had the feeling that she was a moth pinned to a board, while calculating eyes examined her markings. Then the feeling passed as Mia turned away.

"I don't know. We have no data on it. Didn't know it existed!" She bit her lip, an odd habit that she had carried over a hundred years, and that made her look suddenly young. "Whatever the case, the world will be a better place without Director Morgan in it. And perhaps this device can help."

Pravin sat at a desk in his office, a large, high-ceilinged room with a sweeping view of the base. He leaned back in his plush chair, which gripped his body almost like a gentle hand, massaging him gently as he moved.

The reports that crossed his desk went from bad to worse. Miriam on the rampage, Morgan's central base fallen to the Believers, Zakharov assembling his deadly military to mete out justice.

And now his own Peacekeeper armies, suited up in their powered armor and pale blue helmets, assembling in formation at Haven City on the eastern edge of Peacekeeper territory. Preparing for the inevitable conflict ahead, he felt tension twisting at his shoulders.

Finally he stood up and stretched his back.

There were big decisions ahead, and although Zakharov laughed at the thought of Miriam entering University lands, Pravin's instinct was that he might be wrong.

He was old, and tired. What he really needed was someone to talk to.

He wandered the halls of UNHQ for a while, marking time until the meeting to decide final details on the attack against Miriam. He stepped out of the main UNHQ tower, and on impulse took a tram to a location on the far west side of the base, where green rolling hills had been seeded with a quiet blend of Earth and Chiron plants.

He walked to an area surrounded by a high metal fence, and passed through the tall iron gates. It felt as if he were outside, and the smell of the plants and the quiet sun soothed his spirit, although of course the tach field still arced high above his head.

Small white gravestones spread out in every direction. He walked on white gravel paths that wound through the cemetery, under massive willows, past benches where a few figures sat quietly. The gravel crunched under his feet and the heat in the air relaxed him, giving him the peace he had lacked in his office.

He was heading for a specific location, of course. Passing over a last low rise, he looked down the far slope and saw his destination, a set of grave markers underneath a large willow. There were four markers, arranged in a symmetrical pattern.

In front of them kneeled a figure with long, dark hair, head bowed as if in prayer.

Pravin hesitated, then walked down the slope, approaching slowly. At a respectable distance he cleared his throat, making his presence known. She looked up, her dark hair falling around her soft brown face.

Pravin stopped cold, and his heart began to hammer. The woman was Pria, and she stood in front of the four gravestones of his beloved family: Jahn, his son; Sophia, his son's wife; Noel, their son . . .

. . . and Pria, his original wife, who had died so long ago.

"Pria," he said softly, catching his breath. She looked up at him. "What brings you here?"

She shrugged, and turned away. It looked like she had been crying. Pulling a white handkerchief from a pouch in his belt, Pravin kneeled down next to her and handed it to her. She took it from him and touched her eyes.

He stood up and moved a few steps away, looking at the pale sky rather than at her. "I'm sorry," he said. As soon as he said it a wave of feelings cascaded through him, as he realized on how many levels just how sorry he was. It was like the two words held entire universes of meaning now opened to him. He felt a dampness at the corner of one eye, and his throat felt scratchy.

She swallowed. "Imagine being born for one single purpose, and no other," she said, dabbing her eyes. "Imagine having no identity of your own, no chance to know what it feels like to have an identity. To feel like you had been sold into servitude—"

"Let's walk," he said quickly. "Please."

He turned and walked away, and after a moment he heard cloth rustle as she got to her feet and followed him. He didn't look back at the gravestones as they walked away, down white gravel paths.

They continued for several minutes, not speaking. Pravin stared at the endless gravestones through eyes that prismed slightly through the beginnings of tears. Finally she spoke.

"I think it's best that I leave. You can't forget her, and I can't become entangled with you. There are too many issues between us."

"We can work it out."

"Now isn't the time." She stopped and looked at him, her brown eyes deep and fluid. "Pravin, I've been watching you, and monitoring the diplomatic reports. And I've read accounts of you and your wife. I understand why you loved her. You're an idealist, and I feel that this world needs you. I would only distract you from that."

He looked at her, filled with a rush of wonder. Her eyes turned suddenly bright and a flush came to her face as she fought back more tears. He reached out and took her hand.

"There's too much chaos now to hope for perfection. But I'll respect your wishes. I'm truly sorry to have brought you into this world, and yet I wouldn't have it any other way. You are not my wife, but you've become a touchstone for me, and for that I thank you.

"I'm sorry I brought you into this world. It was her sense of hope I most needed, and that I most wanted to find in you. But I was unfair. Please tell me what you need."

She grimaced, and looked at him. Tears streaked

her face. "You'd give me anything? A new identity, a new appearance?"

"I would."

"Then I want a transfer," she said. "I want to go far away, to a Gaian base on another continent. I think that will be best for all of us. I need time." She looked at him for a moment longer, her eyes flickering across his face. He didn't dare to move.

She turned and walked away, and he didn't follow her.

The Burning Sword was yet to come, but Miriam was sure Santiago would hold that, and Santiago's territory was beyond Zakharov's. The Tree of Knowledge was Zakharov's base, which would fall shortly. It was the Tree of Life that eluded her, and now she felt as if the long vision quest might be over.

They rode up in a tiny service elevator that still had power. At the top Pastor Prana led her through a dark, cluttered series of offices, and then down a long series of hallways that let skylight stream in. At the end she saw a mural that brought her up short.

Adam and Eve, the unholy serpent coiling around Eve's naked thigh, its eyes on a gleaming red fruit. Or were its eyes on her?

"The serpent," she said, and the pastor nodded in silence. He touched some secret combination and the mural slid up, swallowed into the ceiling.

Beyond lay a dark room, suffused with eerie light. Earlier, she had visions of rushing into a world of Holy brilliance, the Tree of Life blooming before her, but the glittering eyes of the serpent on the mural had shaken her.

Instead, this room was dim, and she could hear a

rhythmic rushing breath. She walked in slowly, seeking the bright center of her prayers, and somehow feeling that things had gone awry.

There were five platforms along the wall of the room. Two of them were vacant, their contents removed, but the other three held glass containers with complex equipment hooked up to them.

Miriam approached one of these platforms. Inside the glass case she saw the spinal column and the fleshy lump on top, and the eye floating against the glass. She stared at the display, half her mind wondering what she looked at, while in the other half a sick, secret voice already whispered the truth.

And then the eye, floating in its small plastic case, turned toward her, and she saw the pupil narrow.

"Abomination!" She recoiled, full of a sudden sickness. She retreated back to the door as if backing away from a pack of hungry dogs. The doubt she had banished quivered in her for one moment, like a plucked string. She could feel the sweat suddenly inside her thin white robe. "This is as far from the Almighty's will as we could want to be."

She turned and hurried back to the corridors outside, where the bright suns baked the tiles through reinforced synthglass. She looked out over the city, seeing the narrow streets and tall buildings even more clearly for what they were . . . atrocities, temples raised to an unnatural god.

She let out a few deep breaths. The ramifications of what she had seen cascaded through her mind, merging with prayers, sermons, different courses of action.

Pastor Prana finally walked up to her, an appropriately grim look on his face. She nodded to him.

"If that is the Tree of Life, that can't be what the Almighty intended for us."

"Truth, Sister."

Miriam glanced back toward the dark maw that led into the Clinical Immortality room. "Our purpose in life is to become one with the Almighty, to meet him face-to-face at last. That . . ." she pointed to the room with one long, pale finger. "That is Hell. That is the closest thing to Hell on this world I have yet seen."

Pastor Prana shifted from one foot to the other. "But what about your vision, Sister? The Almighty pointed you this way. We've taken three of Morgan's bases, and lost countless of the faithful, in pursuit of this goal. Why did the Almighty send us here?"

Miriam studied a spot on her white robe, wondering. "Perhaps to show us the path to avoid. Perhaps to show us how far the Morganites have strayed, and how righteous it is that they be destroyed."

But as she considered all of these reasons, none of them filled her with the Holy fire she had identified with the truth, the knowledge that God was whispering in her ear.

"I want you to destroy everything in that room," she said. "Do it now. Save nothing."

He nodded and turned back to the Immortality chamber, his long white robe sweeping out behind him. Miriam watched him walk off. At that moment, her quicklink beeped, and she answered. It was Kola.

"We found something, Sister. In the basement of the Morgan Bank building."

"I'm on the roof," she said. "What did you find?"

"A device unlike any we've ever seen. Perhaps you should come down and look at it. The techs are on the way also." Something rippled inside of her, and she felt her excitement build again.

If her vision of Hell existed at the top of this tower, then perhaps Heaven was underneath, in the basement where Kola waited.

Underneath the surface of Chiron, a line of commandeered Morganite blink displacers raced through the Magtube tunnels. Whenever a train approached they simply blinked, jumping ahead in space several hundred meters, and the trains went on unnoticing.

They moved quickly. Each one was packed with as many Believers as could fit, jammed into the tiniest spaces, uncomplaining. Their goal was University Base, in the heart of University territory.

Hung slumbered in a small plastic chair in the control room by the great ring. Two Talents were there, as always, poking around but accomplishing little.

Hung, for his part, had been in this room for days with little time off. The ring had become an obsession for him; while the Talents worked the banks of flashing touchpanels, he stared at the ring itself, at the energy that fluctuated quietly inside the gill-like slits. And when he fell asleep, such as now, he dreamed of its shape.

Even now he dreamed that he floated in space above the ring, watching dim faces, like ghosts, form and dissipate in the static field inside its center. And then he felt that he was falling, sliding down toward it, and he could feel his fall accelerating—

He woke up suddenly, sliding down in the chair. He caught himself, shaking himself awake.

Then he noticed the yellow lights flashing around the perimeter of the control room. The Talents bustled, calling information to each other, and the control panels had lit up in new streams of colored codes.

"What's happening?" He hurried over. There was a high-pitched hum in the air that hadn't been there before, and it made his heart vibrate.

"It's linked," said one Talent. "Wherever the brother to this one is, it's been turned on. They're communicating!"

And there, on one of the touchpanels, a vidfeed opened. Hung stared at the small rectangle as it opened into the world of this ring's counterpart, fingering his gun for no reason.

He could see in the background a room like this one, full of purple light and glass walls. He could even see part of another great ring, the twin of the one they controlled. And in the foreground was not the face of an angry Morganite soldier, but a fierce-looking man, tall and sunburned, with a silver cross gleaming on his chest.

"It's a Believer," said Hung, and one of the Talents glanced back at him. "The Believers control the other side of the transmitter!"

The Believer stared at Hung and the two Talents, his face grim. Then he smiled and lifted his hand in the old Earth peace sign. "Greetings, Hive," the man said in a deep, raspy voice. "The Almighty bless you. Do you know how to work this abomination?"

*   *   *

The Hive and the Believers stared at each other, an ocean and a continent apart, while two identical rings thrummed in harmony between them.

"We're here, in Director Morgan's Industry base," said the man on the Believer side, and then waited for an answer."

Hung stepped forward for the Hive, as ranking officer. "I'm Colonel Hung of the Human Hive. We've taken over Morgan's Minerals base here on Hive Continent. We've been trying to get this ring to work."

A woman stepped forward from the shadows. Hung stared at her; she was dressed in a pale white robe, now covered with a film of dirt. Her radiant green eyes had a hypnotic effect on him. "Are you Sister Miriam?" he asked.

"I am."

"I'll get Chairman Yang," he said, and bowed to her respectfully.

Chairman Yang arrived in the ring room soon after, dressed in a scarlet cheongsam that clung to her body from her throat down to her slippered feet. She went to the vidlink and greeted Miriam.

They spoke of the settlements, and of their position on each flank. They spoke of Yang's desire to live in peace below the ground, without the meddling of Santiago or Morgan or Skye, while building the spiritual foundation of her people. They spoke of Miriam's desire to sweep the corrupt settlements from the main continent, and bring the voice of the Almighty to every part of Chiron.

"Every part except these shores," said Yang, her face stern and her eyes clouded.

Miriam smiled, running her hand along her smooth white scalp. "The Almighty has brought us together. I would be content for the Word to be passed to everyone left *above* this earth."

"The settlement armies are gathering," said Mia. "You know that. We can send you some soldiers, but we have Santiago and Morgan still to worry about." Her mind went to her planet busters, four of them, waiting in silos not so far from this base. She knew Miriam would like one of those, but what did Miriam really have to offer her in return?

"Well, then," said Miriam. "You know my position."

"In truth, Sister, it's a pleasure to meet you at last. You lead mighty warriors and you scorn the materialism and decadence of the settlements. But, I fear your army will be wiped out."

Sister Miriam just nodded. "Let's try the transmitter," she said. "It's too fascinating to pass up."

Mia nodded. The Talents moved in, working with Miriam's techs on the other side. Hung hovered near the side of the room, watching the great ring hum with energy that seemed to suffuse the entire room.

One of the Hiveguard whispered something to Mia and she nodded, one tight, elegant gesture, and left the room. Hung felt riveted to his spot, watching the crane inside the Ring room lift one of the great mineral boxes.

The crane moved toward the ring. As the edge of the box hit the energy field inside the ring, the energy sparked and swirled, and the edge of the box vanished.

"Look!" said one of the Talents, and Hung looked at the vidfeed.

At the other end of the world, Miriam and Kola and her techs stared at the great ring through the windows. The field of color swirled within it, and Miriam could smell a rich smell, like ozone.

There was a flash of rich orange light, and from the ring the edge of a great black shape appeared, and then more of it and more of it.

"Almighty," whispered Kola, as the box pushed its way through from thin air, and then suddenly crashed to the ground. He turned to Miriam. "Sister, the uses of this device . . ."

She nodded. "The Almighty has brought us to this place. The Tree of Life was only a means to come upon this portal to the other side of Chiron. Let's see if a human being can go through. Bring me a Morganite, the most decadent you can find. Then there will be no risk of losing a soul."

Back on the Hive side, the Talents cheered, Hung right along with them. Mia reentered the room, a smile on her lips from the infectious excitement.

On the vidfeed, Miriam's face appeared again. "Success!" she said. "Morgan has quite a toy here. Now let us send you something back."

A hush fell over the room as the collected Hive citizens stared at the ring. Indicators lit up on the touchpanels, and inside the ring the energy field began to swirl, and then spark.

Hung had to blink. The rings were over thirty meters around, and what was coming through was a tiny speck in the center of the ring. He stared closer, trying to see what it was. It certainly wasn't a mineral block.

It was moving.

Everyone stared, shock mingled with stoicism settling together over the room. What had been a hand now became an arm, thrashing around, and then the beginnings of a head. The eyes came through, staring into this new world, and as the throat came through they heard a scream that echoed strangely.

Then there was another flash and the figure came through as if pushed, falling the fifteen meters and slamming into one of the large mineral blocks sitting there. He rolled around, groaning in pain.

Miriam came back on the vidfeed. "Did it work?"

"It worked," said Mia, stepping into the vidfeed. "If you had warned us we might have caught him."

"Ah. Unfortunate. That's a Morganite prisoner, by the way. Did he really pass through all right?"

"He did. He screamed, but it looks like everything is intact."

"Everything." Miriam formed the word into a smile. "I'm glad. If you do medical scans on him we'd like to see them."

"Good. What next? We both have troubles on our respective sides of the world."

"We'll meet again," said Miriam. "Perhaps in the NuSpace, where we can talk. And keep your eye on University Base. You may be able to reach me there."

"So that explains the empty cargo ships," said Cassie, from behind Mia. "Morgan has been sending equipment and soldiers back and forth through this contraption for months, I'd bet."

On the other side of the world, Sister Miriam waited for her blink troops to arrive at University Base.

Stanislav mounted the University Base perimeter turret, taking his shift on the wall. His belly ached and he felt horrible and he was sure that he had been "taken ill," which was the current University euphemism for "exposed to the deadly virus and will be dead in less than seven hours."

How typical, that a society that prided itself on logic and learning retreated behind a shield of words when faced with their own mortality.

No matter, the harried worker at the Genetic Clinic had scanned him and assured him that he was not infected. No doubt the ache was due to nerves, or the fact that he had been drinking all night until a cold sweat covered his skin, out of *fear* that he would be next. He hadn't left his small apartment in two days.

Until his Citizens' Guard captain had tracked him down and ordered him to the wall. And here he was, looking out over the rocky ground that sloped down from the north towers of University Base.

He stared at the scattering of rocks below, all white and gray and jagged. How he envied those rocks. You sat on the mountain, a little erosion, maybe someone kicks you downhill and you slide and come to rest and sit there for another decade or two. What a peaceful life . . .

Fifteen rovers materialized suddenly on the slopes in front of him, sunlight glinting off the jagged chaos of their outer shells, which had been fixed with more weapons than he had ever seen on

such a vehicle. Behind them a horde of dirty warriors clustered in a tight mass.

He saw them, they were there in a flash, and then
gone again as if they had been just a glint of sunlight. He blinked, and his head throbbed.

And then finally, finally, it got through.

"Blink displacers," he said. That had been a Morganite tech, but of course the Believers now possessed three Morganite bases.

And if they had blinked outside the perimeter,
and then blinked again . . .

He got on the link to command, that cold sweat
coating his skin again.

Pravin entered the NuSpace, nodding to the others there. It was a true burden of leadership that all
personal concerns, which rose up in his own life
just like anyone else's, must be set aside in times of
crisis.

And it was certainly a time of crisis. Despite the
glory of the Council NuSpace, and the perfect fa-
cade of their projections, they now resembled a
roomful of refugees after a bloody war.

Zakharov started the meeting, his voice as close
to panic as Pravin had ever heard him. "We have
reason to believe that the Believer army may be
heading for University lands. And she may have
something called blink technology, allowing her to
pass the tach fields."

"Ah," said Morgan. "Unfortunate."

"It's yours." Zakharov stared at Morgan, even his
projection flushing with anger.

"It's true I may have been less than forthcoming
about certain technologies cached in my base. But

it's only a few vehicles. Surely you can handle them, Prokhor."

"We're going to stop her," said Pravin. "Our response will be a coordinated attack, everything we've got, on both fronts, with Morgan and Skye on the Believers at Morgan Industries, and Zakharov and Santiago at University Base. I will send Peacekeeping forces to both locations."

"We have a problem," said Santiago in a cold, clear voice. "I have word that the Human Hive, which has already attacked Morgan, is gearing up for an attack on my bases on that continent. The new Chairman plans to use this time of turmoil to drive me off her lands. I can't let that happen. We know she has planet busters secreted away in her territory as well."

"What are you saying, then?" Morgan rumbled.

"I must cut my troop deployments in half."

"We have to end this Believer threat now, Colonel," said Pravin. "It's important that we all assist."

"I'll assist. But the Believers are almost played out. There isn't much more they can do, and if they try to enter my territories, I'll crush them completely."

"I will call some mindworms and locusts to help, but she's already proven she can survive that," said Deirdre quietly. "What other army do I have?"

"Wonderful," muttered Morgan. Zakharov sat in his chair, his face tightening. Morgan looked at him, then looked at Pravin. "If we will be facing these psychotics with lowered capacity, I say we hit them with everything, and I mean everything. I move that we lift the U.N. Charter against the use of chemical weapons and genetic warfare. Let's send Miriam to Hell, or Heaven, or wherever she wants to go, as quickly and efficiently as we can."

"But the Charter exists for a reason," said Pravin.

"She's used these methods on us. An eye for an eye," said Morgan. The scowl on his face was like a storm front rolling in.

"I agree," said Santiago.

"I can't support it," said Deirdre. "Never. It goes against the very fabric of nature."

"I'll support it," said Zakharov, his voice tense. "In fact, is there any provision against gassing mag-tube tunnels that are supposed to be empty?"

"That's three," said Morgan. "But you haven't cast your vote yet, Governor Lal. Are you going to make this difficult for us by vetoing, or are we going to eliminate this threat and stabilize the settlements once again?"

Pravin nodded. His thoughts had gone back to the early years, when he had a chance to end an attack on this very base with nerve gas and had refused. He believed, at that time, that Pria would have loved him for that decision, and supported him utterly.

But she was dead, so long dead he could barely reach back to her memory.

"Let's consider," he said slowly. "Our armies are strong. Is Miriam that much of a threat that we have to—"

At that moment Zakharov's projection flickered. He looked around, stunned, as if something had been done to him physically. The projection jolted again and he cried out as if in pain.

Deirdre was on her feet. "What's wrong? Academician?"

"They're here!" he said, and then the projection vanished.

chapter eleven

The settlements churned in war.

Believer troops, armed with weapons stolen from Morgan and Zakharov, surrounded University Base in its mountain stronghold and hammered it mercilessly. Blink hovertanks crossed the boundaries of the tach field and appeared in the streets, where robotic guns fired on them, sending synthmetal and fire rolling through the ravaged streets of the base, while University soldiers lay dead of the killer virus. Believers ran through the streets, wreaking havoc.

The hardened troops of Santiago and the noble troops of Pravin Lal hurried toward University Base, but the Believers were numerous and ferocious, and finally they reached the generator for the tachyon field and shut it down.

And so the Believers stormed into the streets of University Base, and the word came down through the Believers that Miriam herself, voice of the Almighty, was on her way to survey the streets of her most tenacious enemy.

* * *

"The field is down. We're wide open."

Zakharov felt as if ice water had been poured
through the fragile shell that was his body. He sat,
frozen, for a long moment, although the world outside kept tearing itself apart around him. The Believers poured through his streets, destroying his labs,
their stolen weapons blazing on pristine avenues.

He began scanning through video feeds, faster
and faster. He watched his citizens as their fragile
bubbles of intellect burst, confronting the raging
hordes that thundered down his streets.

He saw the finest minds of the settlements, sophisticated and richly rewarded for their brilliance,
falling to their knees as the Believers swung great
pieces of metal or fired bolts of energy into their
suddenly frail bodies.

And then he felt the very earth beneath him
move.

Daniel stepped in, his face cool and white. "Academician," he said through tight lips. "If you have a
plan, you must use it now. They're shelling the central towers."

"They can't," he said, his mind spinning. "They
wouldn't destroy all of the knowledge that's contained here. That would be utterly foolish!"

But at that moment a shock wave rocked the
building, knocking him off his feet. The room
shook and groaned around him, and he saw consoles crash to the floor. He felt weak as he tried to
stagger upright again.

And at that moment the first bolt of a truly deep
fear rocketed through him.

"Daniel," he said, staggering toward the assistant
who was always there, a stable part of his daily

world. But the young man lay beneath a fallen console, crushed, although his eyes still shifted back and forth, trying to make sense of the random patterns of light and shadow around him.

Alert sirens went off everywhere. But where were his guards? Why weren't they ready for this disaster?

He saw a small doorway, and remembered that it led to the escape pods. He pushed open the door and ran down a long, narrow hallway, lit by tiny white glowlamps. He could barely see, as his thin, bony feet skittered across the stone floor. He focused on the part of him that could analyze, that was above the animal fears that now drove him.

My base. It was all dying around him, as if it were a living being having its heart ripped out in front of him.

There was a loud noise, a boom so loud he could hear nothing, and a light so bright that his vision turned black. He was aware, in some tiny slice of consciousness, that he was thrown sideways hard, every bone rattling inside his frail bag of flesh.

And then darkness, for a long time.

Finally he came to, choking on the acrid smell of smoke and dust. He could see nothing; it was as if a sea of ink had swallowed him, and he had no bearings at all, although he could feel cold edges of stone all around him.

The hallway had collapsed. His legs ached. He tried to move, to feel around him, but he was like a child touching the world for the first time. Thoughts seemed to take forever to push their way from his fingers to the nerve centers in his brain.

He tried to turn around, but stone pushed at him

from each direction. He could feel a generalized sense of agony, and he tried not to acknowledge it, didn't want to know its source.

He lay there in the darkness, thinking about the end of his life.

He stayed that way for a long time. He could hear nothing but distant booming at intervals. He could feel nothing but cold on his skin, and hunger, although his stomach seemed eventually to shrink into itself and bother him no more. Chills wracked his body, and then those stopped, too.

There was only darkness around him; he closed his eyes and counted the seconds. Then he counted breaths, figuring as long as he breathed he still lived, although his brain could find no logical reason why continuing to breathe benefited him.

Hope. Do you remember?

The shaking and the distant concussions eventually stopped. He felt as if day flowed into night, slowly, although it was really darkness flowing into darkness.

And then, after a time that seemed like infinity, he felt his mind surrender. He craved death, wanted out of this dark pocket of hell, but his body would not relent. He knew he was trapped in a small, forgotten tunnel, he wanted to die, but even now he was aware of a thin stream of clean air still nourishing him from . . . somewhere.

His body would not let him die. His brain alone could not free him.

Long moments, segments of eternity, passed around him. He thought of Isaac.

* * *

And then he felt, as a slight tickling on his skin, a warmth.

Is that day? Is that the sun?

And then, after another eternity had passed, the subtle warmth left his skin, and there was a coolness.

Like the night.

And another eternity, and the subtle warmth came again. And when he had long ceased wondering if this was all a desperate illusion, his mind fending off madness, he felt the world shift around him.

He couldn't tell for a moment if the ground moved, or his own body, or the bones inside his body, each one separately. He blinked and a sudden, deep thirst overwhelmed him, and then he heard the grinding of rock, although it sounded like mountains shifting to his sensitive ears.

A single shaft of light, like a finger pointing, stabbed from the pitch blackness. He cried out as the light touched his eyes and seemed to burn him with its intensity.

Another rock moved, and another. He thought he felt his bones move, and he wanted to cry out, but had no strength to do so. A blaze of light like the sun itself came from the stones and engulfed him.

Hands reached out and grabbed his shoulders, which were like rocks in a sack of flesh. They dragged him out, into a world full of light, and he looked up.

There was someone standing above him, a woman, as thin as a pole, wearing a white robe, with snowy white hair. There were four men behind her, all in thick white and red armor, emblazoned with silver crosses, all holding weapons leveled. At him. His brain started to work again, putting together chains of cause and effect, presenting him with an answer.

"Miriam Godwinson," he croaked. She didn't answer. He thought of his base, all the collected knowledge, and the thought filled his consciousness. "You must spare this base."

"Why?"

"It's the mind of Chiron. The knowledge we've built and stored here is . . . invaluable."

"It hasn't helped you, Prokhor. Not really. And it won't help you now."

He swallowed, his throat so parched he felt as if he were swallowing hot iron. He shook his head. "I don't want to die."

"Why not?"

He blinked, his head spinning from thirst and pain. "Because I'm not finished yet. With my time on this world."

"Not finished yet?" His vision cleared somewhat, so that he could see her, standing over him in the control room. She seemed to smile, with that smug smile he had learned to hate so much. She kneeled down so that she was close to him, and there was a strange tenderness emanating from her. "You've lived two hundred and fifty years, Prokhor. If you're not finished now, then when?"

"Never."

She kneeled over him, and touched him. Her touch felt cold, as if there were no heat in her body at all. "No, Prokhor. You poor, pathetic soul. Whatever you need to do will never get done, because your mind can never do it. What you need doesn't exist in your head at all."

She stood up gracefully and studied him. "This base will fall, Prokhor. But I'm going to let you live. Another day, another year, perhaps. Because you won't find what you're looking for, not here and now, or ever. And I want you to think about that, for a long time."

She backed away, fading to a point of light, as he lost consciousness.

"You're looking in the wrong place, Prokhor. Remember that."

After a time, he awakened. The space around him was shattered and empty. He could smell fallen stone and burned circuits, and feel the broken stone underneath him. He saw cracked touchpanels, and Daniel still pinned, obviously dead, a faint odor coming from his body. From a passing glance it looked like the Believers had damaged the datalink consoles, tried to hijack them. He was sure they hadn't succeeded.

But why did she leave?

He got slowly to his feet, feeling as if someone had terraformed his spine. His quicklink was broken, and all the consoles were broken. He found himself in a fundamentally shattered space.

He went to Daniel first, slowly gaining a kind of second wind. But he knew he was badly hurt, and this adrenaline rush wouldn't carry him for long.

Daniel was dead, as a touch on the carotid told him, and the man's quicklink was dead, too. The entire room had been destroyed by the Believers.

Prokhor went out the main door, which was stuck half open. There were a few bodies in the hallway, and he could smell decay. Finally he found one with a quicklink that worked.

He didn't waste time, but dialed a priority diplomatic call in to Pravin Lal.

"Governor Lal, this is Academician Zakharov."

Pravin's face and voice came on almost immediately. Pravin's face was a battlefield of its own, with relief and fatigue and stress all warring there. "Academician! Where are you? We thought you were dead."

"I'm in the control room of University Base. I've been buried in stone. I need medical help, quickly."

Pravin seemed to consult with someone off-screen, in a staccato conversation, and then he returned. "We have agents there. I think we can help you."

"My base," said Zakharov. He felt a wave of sadness wash over him, unexpectedly. "Is it lost?"

"The Believers occupied it. They locked your people away, and laid waste to the entire place. Then they left, Prokhor. They've completely abandoned it."

He felt a glimmer of hope at that, and his ever restless mind kicked in again, starting up the relentless barrage of questions. *Why, why, why?*

Pravin continued. "She laid waste to everything. But we need you here, at UNHQ. Things have gotten very serious in the three days since she entered your base."

Three days?

"What's happened, Pravin? Tell me . . ."

"You're going to have to tell me everything you know." Pravin's face creased with sudden worry. "Prokhor, what is the Sin Gun?"

His heart started pumping faster, the fear of death closer than ever. "Why do you ask that?"

"Miriam has it. And I think she means to use it."

Pravin Lal sat in the conference room at the top of UNHQ Tower. He felt strangely exposed, more unkempt and less confident than usual, because this meeting was taking place in the real world, and not the NuSpace. There were no projections to protect his image here.

The Peacekeeping Forces had entered University Base after Miriam's retreat. She had apparently fallen back to her desert lands, back to New Jerusalem, but not before wreaking havoc on Zakharov's base and air power. Still, the combined armies of the four remaining settlement leaders now closed in on the Believer lands. Pravin didn't think any of the leaders would be too interested in showing mercy.

Mercy. His mind turned the word over. Seeing Pria had carried him back to far earlier days, when he really had burned with that idealism, when he believed that by acting with mercy and peace, he could build a world made of that fabric. But the years had proven him wrong.

Director Morgan entered the room, coming from his diplomatic suites at UNHQ. He was thin like all of them, but still with an impressive belly. He carried a large wineglass, and Pravin could see some of the liquid glistening at the corners of his mouth.

Zakharov was there as well, scars still on his face because the surgeons had no time yet to fix his wounds from the University Base attack. His eyes moved around the room constantly, and his face twisted into rage at odd intervals.

Deirdre Skye and Corazon Santiago had jacked in through regular holos, since the others weren't using the NuSpace. The elation of battle illuminated Santiago's face. Deirdre looked melancholy and small.

Pravin addressed Zakharov directly. "So what is this Sin Gun that we've just learned about?"

Pravin shook his head "It's a weapon. A new one, and quite powerful. But she'll never be able to use it."

"Why not?" Santiago's voice cut into the room like a hot knife.

"It has a security system on it, a complex one of my own design. She won't be able to activate the singularity without it."

"This is a matter of gravest concern," said Pravin. "We'll accelerate our attack on Godwinson. And I have more news. My spies tell me that she may be in league with Chairman Yang. I can't get the Hive diplomats to contradict this report."

"Leave the Hive to me," said Santiago. "If Yang's in league with Miriam she's just as dangerous; more so, because of her military strength. She took Morgan's base without a second thought."

Morgan snorted but didn't answer.

Santiago continued. "I'm going in with my best soldiers. It's time to trim the fat off the settlements, and deal with these outsiders for good."

Mia Yang met with Miriam Godwinson in the Nu-Space connector. It was odd to meet her in that environment; Mia hadn't used the connector much, but Jin had one he had acquired from Morgan.

The two faced each other in the Pagoda space that Jin had developed. The space was full of elaborately carved furniture, and tapestries in red and gold. The furnishings were meant to appeal to Morgan's taste, but Mia felt as if she were in a large import/export warehouse.

Miriam didn't seem to be bothered at all. The two sat on cushioned chairs and regarded each other across a low mahogany table. Looking at Miriam's open face and the simple white robe she wore, Mia felt as if they were on some kind of rendezvous in the rec commons, rather than deciding the fate of the world.

"Santiago is using nerve gas against my southern bases, despite the Council prohibitions," said Mia. "She's using the chaos to her advantage."

"Yes," said Miriam. "Between the two of us we've forced them into an attitude of cooperation."

Mia sighed and stared at the two jewel-encrusted glasses on the table. She thought for a moment before speaking, then looked directly into Miriam's fiery green eyes.

"The two of us have always been about ideology, and creating the best world for our people. By which I mean the best world for the human spirit, geared more to satisfaction and good work than materialism and decadence."

"Yes."

"But now it's become an issue of survival. We don't have much time. So let's put all our cards on the table."

Miriam rested her hands on her thighs and spread out her fingers, which were long and slender. "I have Zakharov's Sin Gun, the weapon he used to destroy Morgan Solarfex. But it won't be enough to destroy the approaching armies. It's not fully functional yet. Even if we had the gun, it couldn't destroy them all. It has limited range, and it can only fire a few times."

"Unfortunate. Why is it called the Sin Gun?"

"It's powered by singularity reactors."

Mia's eyes defocused as she considered the problem, even as a solution churned in her mind. "I have four planet busters, powered by quantum reactors. Each could eliminate a base or two of Santiago's, but after that the entire settlement army would turn against me."

Miriam watched her carefully. "The settlement army is approaching New Jerusalem. We don't have time to build more. But I've looked at the data on these singularity reactors. If attached to a planet buster, they would release all the power of the singularity in one instant. We could eliminate a fourth of the main continent with just one of these devices."

Mia nodded. "It's the most drastic step imaginable. I wonder why Zakharov never pursued it."

"He doesn't have planet busters. And he fears the environmental repercussions."

Mia looked at Miriam. "And you don't?"

"I fear nothing now."

"And my continent will be spared."

Miriam nodded. "There will be sin busters for each of us. Between us we can destroy the territories of Morgan, Zakharov, Skye, Lal, and Santiago. That leaves you and me, to divide the world between us."

Mia felt a kind of despair settle over her, though

what Miriam offered was everything she wished for. And it was the only way to guarantee her survival. She bit her lip, her thoughts drifting for a moment, searching the past, trying to penetrate the future. The image that hung above it all was that of her father, his calm, strict ways, and the way he had died in settlement captivity. She nodded, as if answering him.

"Agreed," she said.

In the hot lands of the Believers, a blink transport entered New Jerusalem and cruised down the narrow streets, finally stopping in front of the church. A small army of Believers climbed out and used a hovercrane to lift a series of objects into the church and to the main worship area there, which had been emptied of people.

"There it is."

Kola stood on one of the balconies overlooking the main floor, staring down. What rested on the empty tile floor below were a series of shapes that could have been children's building blocks, except that they were many times larger and far deadlier.

One shape was the squat barrel of what Zakharov's files had called the Sin Gun. And a series of five cylinders, each one a reactor that fed the gun for a series of shots, and then burned out.

"The singularity reactor," said Kola. He shook his head. "Zakharov has captured a black hole to do his bidding."

"The Tree of Knowledge," Miriam murmured. "This is the pinnacle of human knowledge on Chiron . . . a perfect killing machine."

"Still, we don't know how to use it," said Kola.

Miriam turned to him, her green eyes scanning him. "The Ideal worked in Zakharov's labs. He knows this gun."

"How do you know that?"

"He told us. I'll send for him."

Indeed, the man who came in, dragged by the Templars, was not the man who had challenged Miriam with his penetrating eyes. He was not the tall, powerful specimen that had awed Isaac. Now he was the husk of that being, his spirit broken when he lost his mind to the locusts and his flesh to the Penitence Square.

"Are you ready to be released from the worms?" Miriam asked him.

He nodded, his face covered with dusty ash.

"Then you have to do something for me."

His eyes had already strayed to the Sin Gun. He looked at it like a hungry man might look at a piece of fruit on a clean white table. She could see him trembling in the grasp of two Templars.

He wants to use his mind again, thought Miriam. *It's all he has.*

"I want these reactors transferred to the planet busters. Can you do that?"

He looked at her and nodded. One eye was green, one blue. His hair was matted to his skull, his face bruised. "Yes."

"Then do it."

Miriam was watching with Kola from the vestibule when the planet buster casings were finally closed, and they became their sleek, dark selves once again.

"Done," said Miriam. She took a deep breath, and let it out, feeling the power of the Almighty moving through her.

"That's enough firepower to wipe out the entire settlements," said Kola. He turned to face Miriam, and his eyes were swimming in complex emotions. "Are you ready to use them? Because the settlement army is on its way, and we've run out of tricks."

Miriam nodded. "Assemble the faithful. Send one sin buster to Yang, as we promised."

"I thought Yang was to get two busters."

"The other one we'll send back to Solarfex. After all, she wants Director Morgan eliminated more than we do. We're abandoning that base, and that territory, now. Any who straggle will be joining the Almighty."

"Then what?"

Miriam looked at him. "We'll detonate the planet buster, right there on Morganite land. There's no more time to waste."

The flash started in the heart of Morgan territory, in the great towers of Morgan Bank. It spread out in an instant, creating a great gap in the fabric of the world, a gap that was absolute darkness for a moment, and then absolute light, and then nothing.

Although Believers sometimes argued over how to save a soul, they never doubted that the human soul existed, and was immortal.

In one moment, in the heart of Morgan territory, ten million bodies vanished, ten million lives ended, and ten million souls were released from the world.

* * *

And as the planet buster flashed, Chiron screamed. The neural net of Planet, humming across tendril and fungus, locust and worm, twisted in agony as a vast piece of it was cauterized and destroyed, as if a hot iron had penetrated the skull of a human and seared off a tenth of its surface.

Millions of years of living memory were laid waste, and a thousand connections were lost in the blink of an eye. And into the injury fled a torrent of Planet's brood, trying to close the wound and recover what had been lost. Demon boils rose from the fungus, and hordes of teeming black locusts clouded the sky, and isles of the deep breasted the churning white waters and pounded onto the shore.

Alerts flashed at every base on Chiron as Planet's vengeance swept in from every side, turning the earth a flaming orange, the sky a buzzing dark cloud, the shore a white-frothed madness.

Pravin was awakened from a deep sleep as the aftershocks tore through the settlements. He felt his bed tremble, and then he was thrown sideways, his face hitting the cold floor. The room shuddered around him, as if a giant baby shook the world like a toy.

After a long moment the shaking stopped, and the alerts scrolled down his quicklink screen. He climbed to his feet, already hearing a terrifying silence in the world.

He looked out his window. The ground still seemed to tremble, and he had the odd feeling that he could taste ashes in his mind. Far to the northeast, he thought he saw a black cloud gathering, rolling across the world. He stopped all thought.

He hurried to the emergency Council room, which was set up in a secure area deep in the foundation of UNHQ. This room was almost purely utilitarian, with low white ceilings, lots of computer equipment, and no windows. The only sign of luxury were the large chairs, one of which Pravin quickly took. He had reviewed the reports, and knew something of the horror that had just occurred.

Zakharov showed up a moment later, and Santiago and Skye appeared on the holos. Everyone was white as a sheet, their eyes spinning with horror, and they looked at each other as if hoping this was all a dream.

Morgan was the last to enter. He looked weak and haggard, his back bowed. Pravin was shocked to see tears running down his face in thick, slow trails. He took his seat and shook his head.

"What happened?" Pravin's voice was hoarse. He felt despair saturate every cell of his body. When he looked at Deirdre, he saw tears running down her face as well.

"She did it," said Zakharov. "I don't know how."

"Did your gun do this?" hissed Santiago. She looked ready to jump through the holoscreen and throttle them all.

"No! This is not the gun. There is only one way—" He stopped and took a deep, shuddering breath. Pravin took the opportunity to do the same. "She's attached the singularity reactor to a planet buster. That is the only way."

"Look at it," said Deirdre. She had projected the satellite feeds into the room, and they all took a moment to stare. Where Morgan's territory had once been, with its mountains and mines and glowing cities, there was a wide, blackened swath of dead land, hundreds of thousands of kilometers in diameter. The center of the blast was now a deep, black pit of heat and bubbling rock at least the size of four bases.

"And Planet isn't discriminating," said Deirdre, her face pale. "Even our most harmonious gardens have been wiped out, the worms destroying everything. I've seen my best Empaths swept away by demon boils, found them thousands of kilometers away, tossed on the rocks with worms choking their song." She touched her hand to her lips, and Pravin could see that the hand was shaking. "I've never seen anything like this, Pravin. The locusts swarmed High Gardens, ripping the flesh from citizens in the streets . . ." She shook her head. "What Miriam did . . . this is the end."

"The end of what? Will Planet kill Miriam?"

She shook her head. "The end of everything."

"Can she do this again?" Santiago raised her voice again, and Pravin could see spittle on her lips. "Does she have more?"

Zakharov lifted his head. "She can do it again," he said. "She has up to four more reactors, and who knows how many planet busters. It's enough to destroy us all."

Then he looked at them, each and every one. "But I have a way out."

chapter twelve

"GOVERNOR LAL." THE VOICE FROM HIS QUICKLINK STARtled him as he continued to stare at Zakharov. He wasn't used to having these Council meetings in the "real world," with its attendant interruptions.

"Yes, Webster."

"Sister Miriam Godwinson has contacted you. Would you like to speak to her?"

Pravin looked around the room, at the other leaders. They were all silent, and looked somewhat appalled. Finally Deirdre nodded, followed by Santiago. Morgan and Zakharov averted their eyes.

"Patch her through," said Pravin.

Miriam's holo flickered to life in the conference room. She wore her simple white robe, and stood tall, with a silver cross gleaming on a silver thread around her neck. Pravin, staring at her blank face and green eyes, had the distinct feeling that the Miriam he knew was no longer on this world.

Finally Morgan spoke, looking at her from under a dark brow. "What do you want?"

She nodded. "I want to tell you that there is still time for your redemption, you and all of your citizens, if you embrace the word of the Almighty."

"Will you spare the other territories, so that no more lives are lost?" Pravin asked, and he couldn't keep the anger from his voice.

"Only you can save yourselves," said Miriam, her eyes vacant, as if she listened to a voice just out of their range of hearing. Pravin noticed a tremble in her face, and her hands. "I've come to tell you that the Almighty has shown us the way to Heaven, and there we go willingly. We have faced you all, and we have not feared the fire, nor the thunder of your weapons, nor pain nor death nor the world beyond. And the Almighty has shown you that our way is superior."

"Your way is luck and fanaticism," said Santiago, and Pravin motioned to her for silence.

But Miriam only turned to her, her green eyes otherworldly even in the holo. "We've proven our superiority, Colonel Santiago. Now go and tell your citizens the truth, which is this:

"The way of the Almighty is the only way. I'm giving you seven days to consider my words, and to surrender to me. From then on I will decide the future of humanity on Chiron, and I will direct all planetary policy.

"If you refuse, we will destroy you all, and sweep this world clean of the unbelievers. Everyone in this room will die, and every citizen under you will die, and you will all go face the judgment of the Almighty. So if you care for your people, you will tell them that their final hope lies in forgiveness, and surrender.

"But be warned, that if you try to find us, or lift your hand to us in any way, we will destroy the territory of the aggressor, immediately, and then we will destroy the others, one by one. Prokhor," here she looked at Zakharov, who stared back at her with a boiling hate. "As promised, I'll save you for last."

And with that she vanished in a flash of light.

Pravin looked around at the others, letting them absorb Miriam's words before speaking.

"She's already dead," said Deirdre. "Chiron will never survive what she's done. The world will turn on her, and kill her, and us, and everything. There's nothing we can do."

"I won't surrender," said Santiago. "She's left Morganite territory, or she would have been destroyed with the sin buster there. She must be somewhere in the outskirts. If we can find her, we can launch an attack, and destroy the other planet busters, then try and save Chiron."

"Yang may have some, too," said Morgan.

"Then we attack Yang as well. It's better than nothing! We can't do as she says, go home and pray and wait for our deaths."

Pravin turned to Zakharov. "Prokhor, you said something before Miriam appeared. You said there was a way out. What did you mean?"

He looked at them from under craggy brows. "It isn't a way to stop Miriam. It's a way to save ourselves." He looked around as a silence settled over the room. Even Santiago stared at him. "It's a project I've developed. I used the technology underlying the NuSpace projectors, and combined it with some of Morgan's research into Clinical Immortality. What I have is crude, but it will work for us.

"It's a cryocell, rather like the ones that held us on our trip from Earth. I use a scaled down Clinical Immortality that doesn't require the spine-and-brain extraction. It will keep our minds alive for around two hundred years, even though our bodies can never emerge. Our minds," and here his eyes seemed to flare, "our minds will be held in a modified NuSpace, a communal projection of virtual space. We'll be able to talk, to touch, to live in a world of our own making. Anything we want we can create with our minds."

"But it won't be real," said Santiago. "Our bodies will be lying there like the dead. Is that what you're saying?"

Zakharov shrugged. "You won't know that. You won't feel your real body, any more than you do in the NuSpace. You are what your mind perceives. And this projection will be so much richer and more powerful than any reality we could hope to inhabit. There will truly be no sickness, no death. We can live in any world we choose."

"And when our bodies die, what then?" asked Deirdre.

"We die with them," said Zakharov, with one short nod. "We can't reproduce or raise real children, of course. But for two hundred years, we'll live in a true Utopia. And more importantly, in this mountain room, which I've named the Journey Room, we'll be safe from Miriam."

"Why don't we just live there, then?" asked Pravin, his mind trying to grasp what Zakharov suggested. "Why go into the NuSpace?"

"It's too small, a tiny secure lab deep in the mountain. It can hold us in stasis, but there's no food or space. We would go mad from boredom." He let out a deep breath. "This is one of my finest creations. It's a way out of Miriam's grasp. Let her have this world . . . we'll exist in a better place, hidden away from her."

"How many?" Pravin asked quietly.

"Two thousand," said Zakharov. "That's all the cells I can finish and set up in the mountain lab in such a short time."

Pravin nodded again, and then lapsed into thought. "I want to see this lab." He looked at Deirdre and Morgan. "Will you come?"

Morgan nodded after a moment. Deirdre seemed to be weighing something in her mind, and then her shoulders relaxed and she nodded, too. Santiago stared at them, her eyes black with fury. "I won't succumb to this ridiculous plan. We can't give up now!"

"Of course we'll try to find another way," said Pravin. "But if this is our last hope . . ." He looked around. "Each of us must select who will join us in this new world. But let's all hope Miriam comes to her senses."

Emerging from the NuSpace, Santiago left the small room and walked the hallways of her Sparta Command. Her base had been built into a masterpiece of survivalism, vast halls where warriors trained, and the most cutting edge technologies for shaping a human being into a disciplined fighting machine.

She thought of Earth, and of the powerlessness

she had felt on the violent city streets. She had spent every moment of her life since then to escape death, and powerlessness, and despair.

She, and only she, was the master of her life.

She activated her quicklink, and issued a command.

Moments later, the Spartan needlejet screamed low over the burned wasteland that used to be Morgan territory. Its target was a small cluster of buildings surrounding a dark hole, a crude silo driven into the earth in the Believer lands.

The Spartan pilot linked back to command. "Avenger One to base. I've sighted the targets. Looks like four buildings and one silo. Do I have permission to fire?"

"Fire at will," came the reply.

The needlejet sailed through the air at high speeds, far above satellite range. Two missiles broke off from the underbelly of the jet and their boosters fired, sending them toward the targets below. The needlejet was long gone by the time the missiles rocketed straight into the earth and detonated, engulfing the buildings in a ring of fire.

The needlejet turned and roared back, doing a ground scan again. The pilot shook his head, puzzled.

"Avenger One to command. Target still there. Repeat, no damage to target."

"Say again, Avenger One? Repeat . . ."

But the pilot slowed and looked at the scorched earth where his missile had hit. All four buildings stood, and the silo still yawned from the earth.

Then, as he watched, the whole group winked out.

The pilot felt a lump rise in his throat. "Blink technology! Command, it blinked out, the whole thing, buildings and silo! We need an immediate scan . . ."

From a hundred kilometers away, where the ruins of New Jerusalem still waited under the sky, a long, dark shape rocketed into the sky and headed for the territory of Corazon Santiago.

Pravin stared at the holomap, which rippled and pulsed as the information from sensors and satellites updated the terrain each moment. The chill had long since passed, leaving a dull emptiness. There was no way that anyone could comprehend the magnitude of what was happening on this world.

Santiago's territory, laid to waste. The finest soldiers on Chiron, all of their collected hours of training, numbering in the millions and millions, all destroyed in one instant.

He shook his head, and then noticed a contact from Deirdre Skye, which he opened. She looked haggard, her natural beauty marred by pain.

"The Santiago blast took out two of my bases as well, Pravin. I was too close. I fear that I'm next."

"We don't have much time, Deirdre. Come to UNHQ with your best and brightest. We're going to see Zakharov's mountain room."

"I'm coming," she said.

After she broke the link, Pravin thought of her beautiful Gaian bases, lush gardens set against a wilderness of flowering plants, the true Eden that Miriam missed, right underneath her nose.

And then he remembered Pria, and her request to transfer to the Gaian territories.

* * *

Feeling rushed back into his body, an odd mix of panic and hope. He went to the nearest touchpanel and clicked through the personnel files until he found her.

Mahadevan, Pria. The false last name to protect her genetic identity.

As he read the file a prickling started at his spine, like a tiny finger of hope. He could feel his heartbeat pounding in his chest.

She hadn't transferred. She had requested the transfer, but had never followed through. He used his locator and found her current location, right back in her chambers. He ran, trying not to think too hard, just wanting to feel the first spark of hope he had felt in a long time.

He arrived at her chambers, which were located in a tall, hotel-like complex near the UNHQ main tower. He took the elevator up to the top floor and hurried to the pale gold door to her apartment.

He rang the door chime and waited, his heart still pounding, staring at the tiny glass eye that monitored the door. After a long moment the door slid open.

He straightened his uniform and walked through.

The apartment was spacious, decorated in pale colors. Low, comfortable furniture filled the main living room area; through arches he could see back into other rooms as the apartment stretched back. The place was a mess, with clothes and other items strewn everywhere. Some large silver suitcases were open on the floor, but he couldn't tell if they were half packed or half unpacked, or a mix of both.

Pria sat on a long white couch, wearing a pale blue dress that showed her smooth brown shoulders to good effect. Both hands were pressed between her knees, twisting a white handkerchief, and he wondered briefly if it were the same one he had given her in the cemetery. She looked down at the floor, which was covered in a plush white rug, and then she looked up at him.

He stopped and watched her for a long moment, then he walked slowly through the room and sat down next to her. He could hear the slight sniffling noises she made. Slowly, awkwardly, he reached out and put his arm around her, felt her stiffen and then slowly relax. He felt her give her weight to him.

"I'm frightened," she said quietly. "I'm scared we're all going to die here."

"It's all right," he finally said. She turned her face to him, but he kept looking ahead, studying a juncture where the white wall curved into an arch by the door. There were so many things to say about the two of them, about the way he had used her, about how she still had nothing else and would never know anything else.

But he also felt the first tenuous string of affection between them. After so much time spent together, he felt as if he did know her, and did love her, and as his memories of the original Pria faded, it was as if this woman was an extension of Pria, but also her own being. She was all he knew.

"I don't want to die," she said.

"I don't either. You can come with me." He explained the Journey Room to her, and the escape it promised. He saw that her lip was trembling, and he put his arm around her, pulled her in close to him. *We're just two warm bodies now, floating in an unexplained void.*

He felt her lips brush his ear, she had moved so close to him. "You mean this is really the end of the world?"

He nodded. "If we stay here, Miriam will destroy us, or Chiron. I lived on Earth, in its final years. The wounds that it left go deep. I would never want anyone to experience that again."

"But inside this Journey Room . . ." She shook her head and leaned back to look at him. "I've lived my whole life as someone else, as if I occupied the body of another. I don't want to do that anymore."

"But surely you don't want to die?"

She looked off into space, her hand stroking her belly. Then she turned to him. "I've come to believe in you. I've come to believe that you're a good man who sometimes makes mistakes. If you'll take me, I'll go with you. But if there's another way, please, let's take it."

"All right."

She blinked. "I heard of a place. A Gaian base, hidden deep in the fungus."

He felt her trembling, and he squeezed her arm. "I'll ask Deirdre Skye. If such a place exists, she would know of it."

The settlement leaders traveled to University Base by secure copter, outfitted with photon armor and every kind of stealth mechanism available. They rocketed over Pravin's sun-speckled bases, with noble spires reaching for the sky. They flew near the smoking wasteland that had once been Morgan's territory. And they flew into Zakharov's lands, and to University Base, where signs of damage were evident everywhere.

They continued past University Base, up higher into the gray rock mountains, and finally to a small outcropping, so high up that snow blew at a steady, bone-chilling pace across the face of the mountain.

They all deplaned, Pravin and Deirdre and Morgan and Zakharov. Two tough-looking guards in thick white camo met them and escorted them to a thick shield door set back in the rock. Pravin looked around; it would be almost impossible to see this door from any angle, land or sky.

The door hissed open. It was as thick as Zakharov was tall. They continued down a narrow metal hallway, and from there to a series of stairs and lifts that took them, slowly, deep into the mountain. By the time the trip ended Pravin could feel the tons of earth above them, pressing down and dampening his spirits.

But that earth, as Armageddon rolled on above them, was their new best friend.

Prokhor motioned them down a wide hallway. He seemed anxious and subdued, the sense of defeat palpable around him.

"The Journey Room," he said.

They found themselves in a long wide room with gray rock walls. Half of the room was completely empty and bare. The other half contained hundreds of metal coffinlike tubes, lined in perfect rows. Beyond those a variety of consoles blinked and flashed. There was little lighting in the room, and the walls were utterly bare and smelled of cold metal and stone.

Pravin, Deirdre, and Nwabudike walked forward,

moving among the cells. Each cell had a complex
life support monitor unit at the head, connected to
the cell itself. Pravin was startled to see names engraved at the head of each cell.

"Why the names?" he asked, looking at Prokhor.

Prokhor shrugged. "For posterity, I suppose. If
some alien race comes down from the sky to re-
claim this world, they will know who passed here."

"Or if Miriam finds us, she'll know which plug to
pull," said Morgan.

"I've brought a tree with my supplies," said Deirdre.
"One tree, picked from my garden, with some soil
and sunlamps to nourish it. I'm going to put it here,
in this corner of the room, so that we'll have something to remind us of the lives we're leaving."

Pravin nodded, but Prokhor snapped at her.
"What good will that do? We'll be in these cells,
dead to the world."

"It's as you said, Prokhor. Something for the universe to remember us by. You built the Journey
Room, and Morgan's power and his immortality research keep it running. Why not give me a last
chance to leave something beautiful behind? Besides, it will ease our minds as we wait our time to
go under."

Prokhor shrugged. "Do it, then. But tomorrow,
we're shutting the vault and putting everyone
down." He walked away.

"Thank you," said Deirdre. Her eyes were alight as
she stared into the corner, already creating the
scene in her mind.

Miriam stood in a private room in the ruins of the
great church back at New Jerusalem. Half of the

church had crumbled, and the streets outside were blackened by the shadows of the Believers who had remained at the base, and who had suffered death by the Sin Gun.

So the ground is doubly sanctified . . . once by the priests, and once by the blood of the faithful.

She sat on a low plastic crate and stared at a small mirror that she held. As she looked at herself, she marveled at all the Almighty had given her: skin and eyes and hair, and a mind to think and limbs to move and a world to unite.

She slid her hand across the soft skin of her scalp. She had a headache, a splitting headache that had grown worse with time. She found it very difficult to concentrate, and an odd halo flared around light sources.

There was a knock at the door and it opened. Kola stood there, though he stopped when he saw her.

"Is everything all right, Sister?"

"Of course." She set the mirror aside and looked at him. He walked to her slowly.

"Do you really mean to go through with this?"

"Yes. There is no other conclusion to be reached. Even if we don't launch the others, the damage is done."

"What do you mean?" His hand strayed to his belt, where a Q-gun was clipped. But he didn't draw it.

"The damage is done," she repeated. An odd light had began to suffuse her vision at random times, as if angels had come down to touch the objects around her. "I may have made a terrible mistake."

"Or not," said Kola. He set his jaw and stared at her. She nodded.

"Thank you. The Almighty will welcome us all. Are the other planet busters ready?"

He nodded. "They are. Just give us the word."

"The word is all I have ever given you," she said, and smiled up at him. "I'm going to the NuSpace, for one last time."

Miriam waited by a small river in the Nu Space, winding its way through a green land that seemed suffused with light. Graceful white birds sailed overhead, angling into warm breezes. There was a flickering and Zakharov appeared.

"What's all this?" He looked around the river, and at the grass below his feet as if it might be toxic waste.

"Something for a change, Prokhor. You spend all your time up in the mountains. I thought you might enjoy this."

He stared for a moment, his eyes pulled to the horizon, where the silver band of river vanished into a haze of light. Then he shrugged and sat down in the grass. Miriam smoothed her white robe, though in her projection the robe was never wrinkled. She looked at him.

"Why did you call me here?" he asked.

"To gloat. Thank you for giving me the chance."

His face twisted in bitterness. "This is no time to joke. What you have done is beyond redemption. You have killed this world."

"Perhaps." She looked away from him. "Not so long ago, I was like you, Prokhor. I lost my faith. My mind rose up, assuaged by doubts, seeking hypotheses, taking refuge in reason. But I can't live that way."

"So you kill everyone else?"

"What can I do? I had a vision, bright and burning, as real as anything I've ever felt. To refuse it would have been to die, and to die going against the beliefs that I've built my entire life around. And now I think it's all coming to an end, which is fitting."

She rubbed her head, which was smooth and white. She looked back at Zakharov. "I don't know how this all happened. Looking back, it seems incredible. But it's the will of the Almighty."

"Don't start that again," said Zakharov. "You know nothing. You've ruined everything that humanity has fought for."

"And everything humanity has fought against." She gestured to the pale sky above. "Could you live here, Prokhor? In a world that exists in your senses only, that you know to be false, where even the laws of science are what you choose them to be? It would seem the ultimate hypocrisy. In a way it's closer to the way I live, in a world built only on the faith that it exists, and that I can shape to my own making."

She stood up. Zakharov stared at her, his eyes dark underneath his brows. "I hope someday you'll realize what you've done here."

"Perhaps. Good-bye, Prokhor. I would like to have traded places with you, even for a moment."

"So you could see the world as I do, based on reason? I'm surprised."

She smiled again. "No. So you could see the world as I do."

She vanished. Zakharov looked around the world of the NuSpace, at trees and water that existed only in his mind. After a moment, he vanished, and that world existed for no one.

It was late at night, but in the heart of the mountain, who could tell? Deirdre wore a skirt and a tank top that left her thin arms bare, and right now she ran her hands through the soil into which she would move the medium-size apple tree she had transported from her gardens.

She wiped her forehead and stepped back. Two Empaths assisted her, both of them destined for a journey cell tomorrow, and all three of them thankful for the hard work to take their minds off the inevitable. The apple tree pushed its delicate green branches toward the sunlamps they had positioned in the corner of the Journey Room, bathing the tree in rich golden sunlight. Deirdre was adding a few small flowers in the soil bed, just for effect, and their perfumes teased her nose. A dewy mist glimmered on the plants, the smell of rich soil underlying everything.

She only left her work once, when one Empath had taken the lone University guard behind a thick tree and made love to him in a quiet corner. While they dallied, Deirdre quietly crossed over to the cells, staring at the names as she went down row after row. Finally she found her own, and stared at it.

It's time. The world no longer holds the beauty it once did for me.

After a long moment she turned away, and was shocked to see Prokhor Zakharov, a harsh figure in the uneven light of the Journey Room, standing over another cell. He remained utterly still, staring down at it. Quietly, she walked toward him, until he looked up, though it was as if he looked through her.

"Lady Skye," he said. "Deirdre."

"Hello, Prokhor. What brings you here?"

"Just looking . . ." He waved his hands at the cells around him. Then he shook his head. "Did you know the first time I chose a NuSpace environment for myself, it turned out to be a gray cube?"

She chuckled. "Mine was a garden, of course."

He walked over to meet her and they turned back toward the tree. He gestured to it. "That's nice. It will ease our entry, I think. You have great imagination, Deirdre. It's truly your strong point."

"Thank you. It won't last long, but it doesn't have to."

"Neither will we."

And there was the reminder again, that their bodies would eventually die. "But we'll have a good time in there, right? We can live like gods in those virtual worlds."

Zakharov nodded, clasped his hands behind his back, and walked back toward the main door. "I'll see you then, Skye," he said, without looking back. Deirdre nodded and continued back to her one tree, and the golden light around it.

Deirdre awoke to sunlight on her face, and she stretched and blinked, feeling, for one moment, as if she were a child, sleeping next to a sunny window back on Earth.

Then the muted sounds of voices and the undercurrent of fear, like a smell that assaulted her nostrils, brought her wide awake. She sat up to see hundreds of people, people from all factions, milling around in the Journey Room. They all wore somber gray jumpsuits and clustered in small groups. Many came to her one tree, smelling the blossoms, touching the soil, thanking her. She smiled and realized that she had teared up, and all around her others had teared up, and most of these people let the tears roll down their cheeks, with no shame.

Over an intercom she could hear names being called. She watched as one man hugged several friends good-bye, crying openly, and then he crossed to a cell where two of Prokhor's tech scientists waited. The man took off his jumpsuit and the scientists wiped him down with some kind of chemically treated cloth. Naked, he climbed into the cryocell and lay down. This man chose to give a last little wave, his hand poking up above the rim of the cell, and Deirdre heard some quiet laughter. She realized that she was laughing, too.

The scientists bent over him and attached some tubes and monitors to the body in the cell. Then the cell closed and sealed, and the life support monitor lit up. On a great touchscreen on the wall, another light switched from red to yellow, and another mind entered the NuSpace.

Name after name was called, and the room began to empty. There were fewer to say good-bye to, and Deirdre now noticed several individuals remaining in the room.

She saw Zakharov, staring at the process absently. She saw Morgan, pacing back and forth, perhaps thinking of ways to exploit his position even in the virtual Utopia they entered. She saw a woman with sleek black hair that reminded her for a moment of Santiago, and her proud ways.

And she saw Pravin, standing with an Indian woman with long dark hair, and Deirdre's heart suddenly jumped for no reason. The woman looked familiar to her, but in the darkness she was difficult to see. It warmed her, though, that Pravin seemed happy, and held this woman's hand.

She walked over to him. He was talking to Prokhor, who stared at him with a quiet expression. "We won't be going," said Pravin. "We'll take our chances out there. And there are some others above who will go with us."

"You won't last long," said Prokhor. "It will be just like Earth again, the chaos and violence. And no genetic treatments, Pravin. You'll live eight years at most."

"But a good eight years it will be. Enough to start again."

Deirdre watched the exchange. She had confirmed the tiny Gaian base, lost in the sea of fungus on the Eastern Continent. She sent a last good wish, to him and the woman who stood so close by his side.

For herself, she couldn't watch the world be torn apart again.

Behind her she watched as one of the Empaths approached a cell, helped by the tech. He took his white cloth and used it on the Empath, wiping each part of her body with a quiet, loving care. They kissed briefly, and he squeezed her hand for a long moment and looked into her eyes, and then he helped her down into her cell. After a few more preparations, the tech watched as the cell closed forever.

It was just the five of them now, and the two scientists. Without being told they all came together in a small group, their shoulders touching. Deirdre smiled at Pravin and took his hand, and he squeezed her hand and reached out for Morgan. Morgan nodded slowly and took Zakharov's hand. Zakharov stared at them all, and then Deirdre saw that a small tear traced its way down his craggy face, and then he took Deirdre's hand, completing the circle.

"Thank you all," said Pravin. He looked at each one of them, thinking back on a triple lifetime of memories. They all nodded back, and there was nothing more to say.

Deirdre went to her cell, looking one last time at the tree, which seemed a long way away now, a green and gold jewel at the far end of this dark room of sleeping bodies. She slipped off her jumpsuit, feeling the chill of the air on her skin, and then one of the scientists started wiping her with the cloth, which was even colder. She looked down and noticed that the young man had sandy blond hair and a strong, solid face.

"Will I see you in there?" she asked, suddenly wondering what would happen to the two techs.

He nodded and managed a smile. "We'll be there. I'll put him in, and then I'll do myself. For us it's automated." He motioned her into her cell.

"Good," she said. She lay down in her cell, which was full of a thick, clear liquid that chilled her to the bone. He reached down and cradled her head, so she wouldn't go under yet, and then the other one started putting needles and tubes on various places on her body. She lay there quietly and thought about her garden. Could she make a better one in the next world? Even more beautiful than anything on Chiron?

"Okay," whispered the blond tech. He slipped a long, thin tube down her throat. She gagged for a moment, and imagined it kind of poking down inside of her. Suddenly she felt a great fatigue wash over her body, and the lights of the world seemed to dim. He released her head, and she was sinking slowly back into the liquid.

It took a long time. The cold liquid seeped up around her head, to her ears and her face, and then over her nose and mouth and eyes, and she felt the back of her head come to rest on the cold bottom of the cell. At that moment she felt her face go slack, and she stared up at the young tech through the waters, at his blond hair, and she thought of the golden light falling down through her garden, and the people she would see on the other side.

Then her eyes closed, the cryocell closed, and the machine launched her into her final dream, away from the troubles of the world.